First Carroll & Graf edition 1997

Carroll & Graf Publishers, Inc.
260 Fifth Avenue
New York, NY 10001

Library of Congress Cataloging-in-Publication Data
Gilbert, Michael Francis, 1912–
Into battle / by Michael Gilbert. — 1st Carroll & Graf ed.
p. cm.
ISBN 0-7867-0398-9 (cloth)
I. Title.
PR6013.I333515 1997
823'.914—dc20 *96-30928*
CIP

Manufactured in the United States of America

INTO BATTLE

Michael Gilbert

Carroll & Graf Publishers, Inc.
New York

Contents

Part I	*Portsmouth*	1
Part II	*London*	83
Part III	*Le Touquet*	171

Contents

Part I	*Portsmouth*	1
Part II	*London*	83
Part III	*Le Touquet*	171

PART ONE

Portsmouth

1

Korvetten Kapitan Willem von Holstern, being the senior of the twelve German naval officers in the private dining room at the back of the Royal Duke Hotel in Portsmouth, was, naturally, allowed the floor whenever he wished to speak.

"I observed," he said—and the babble of competing voices quietened deferentially—"the hulk of Lord Nelson's old battleship *Victory* rotting in the harbor. This seemed to me to be symptomatic of the so-famous British Navy. Imposing in reputation but rotten at the core."

A burst of applause and laughter greeted this sentiment.

"Might I add, sir," said Oberleutnant Zimmer, "that a determined attack, delivered from below *and* above, should be sufficient to demonstrate most amply what you have said."

"*Über and unter*" came the chorus. It was like the baying of a pack of hounds.

In the passage outside, the young waiter, Andrew, had his chair tilted against the wall. This was not only comfortable but also enabled him to hear most of what was being said. "Indeed," he thought, "if they say it much louder it will be heard in the street. Oh, oh. Here comes trouble."

This bit of trouble was Leutnant Felix Sauervein, a foxy-faced character who had been out of the room on some business of his own and now appeared at the far end of the passage.

Andrew, hastily tilting his chair forward, overdid the movement and landed on his hands and knees on the floor. The German officer stood for a moment looking down at him dispassionately, then kicked him to his feet.

"You are here," he said, "to take our orders. Not to lounge outside the door or to crawl on the floor. Come, stand upright when a German officer speaks to you."

This was in German, and the waiter seemed to understand the meaning of the last words, or, perhaps, of the gesture that accompanied them and pulled himself up into a sloppy parody of attention.

There came a bellowing from the dining room.

"Allow me to translate," said Sauervein. "They require a replenishment of the beer. To be brought without delay. You understand that?"

Andrew bobbed his head.

"Then fetch it. *Schnell, schnell.*"

As Andrew, who seemed incapable of moving quickly, was starting to shamble toward the door at the end of the passage, it was thrown open and a man appeared, blocking his way. Andrew knew him as a Major Richards, a regular patron of the Royal Duke, whom he had disliked at first sight, with his coarse red hair and his hooked nose.

"You are having trouble, Lieutenant?"

"Nothing that I cannot handle, Herr Major."

"I observe that you have the right technique for dealing with these peasants. They understand only a direct order and its ruthless enforcement. Tell me, am I to understand that your visit terminates in two days' time?"

"That is so. We have orders to be ready to depart at an early hour on the day after tomorrow."

By this time Andrew had managed to extract himself. The major looked after him thoughtfully. Then he said, "On behalf of the people of Portsmouth, allow me to say that we shall be sorry that the goodwill visit of such a splendid unit of the Imperial German Navy as the Panzer Schlact Kreuzer Kobold should terminate so abruptly. We had been told that you would be with us for another week at least."

"Orders," said Sauervein. "Orders that brook no delay. I'm sure you understand."

"Yes. I understand the importance of orders. Ah, here is the faithful peasant."

Andrew had staggered in, carrying, with some difficulty, a

small keg of beer. The tap on it appeared to be badly fitted, or only partly closed, as a thin line of beer followed him as he tacked toward the dining room door and pushed it open with his foot. His arrival was greeted with a volley of orders, some of them in German, some in what the speakers imagined to be English. Gathering the general import of what was wanted, the waiter dumped the new keg on the table, picked up the empty one, and turned to go.

He was stopped by a shout from the captain. Then he saw that twelve used mugs had been arranged on a tray and that there were twelve unused glasses beside it. He gathered that he was to remove the dirty mugs, and himself, in preparation for some ceremony that was to follow.

To carry a keg, even an empty keg, and a tray was clearly impossible. His lips moved as he tried to work out the answer to this problem.

The captain gestured to one of the young sublieutenants, who, after considering rapidly whether it would be more demeaning for an officer of the Imperial Navy to be seen carrying a keg or a tray of beer mugs, seized the keg, while the waiter picked up the tray and followed him out. As soon as the sublieutenant was back in the room and the door was shut, the twelve empty glasses were charged.

"In truth, gentlemen, it should be wine," said the captain. "But since the toast that I will propose is, in a sense, directed toward our hosts, it is appropriate that we should honor it in their own national beverage. And might I ask you to moderate, if not your zeal, at least your voices. Very well, then, gentlemen. *Der Tag.*"

The waiter, who was by this time back at his post outside the door with a trayful of fresh mugs, thought that *"Der Tag,"* repeated in a sibilant whisper, sounded more menacing than if it had been shouted. However, this was not his principal concern. What he was wondering was how many times the mugs were going to be filled and emptied before the party was over. A great many times, he feared.

And feared truly, as the draining of bumpers was followed by singing, and the singing by further drinking. Andrew, with one eye on the clock, began to wonder whether there was any chance of his getting home to his own supper, which would already be in the oven.

When he came to Portsmouth he had found lodgings with a retired petty officer, a Mr. Stokes, and his wife, who was an excellent cook. Their charges were moderate, which was as well, since the rewards of casual labor, in the hotels around the docks, would not be considered large, even if occasionally increased by tips from satisfied customers. He did not anticipate any generosity from the German naval officers. Indeed, he would be lucky if he avoided a complaint about his sloppiness and inefficiency.

When the party finally broke up and the Germans started out, in varying degrees of steadiness, for the picket boat that would take them back to the cruiser, it was with scant hopes of a pat on the back that Andrew received a summons to present himself in the manager's office.

Here he found the manager talking to Captain von Holstern. He was relieved to note that both men were laughing. They had been conversing in excellent and idiomatic English. No doubt, thought Andrew, one of the reasons for selecting this particular officer to head a goodwill mission would have been his command of their language.

The manager extracted a crumpled ten-shilling note from his wallet and handed it to the waiter. He said, "Your fee, as agreed. Very well. Be here tomorrow, promptly at nine o'clock. We shall have further work for you."

It seemed, then, that the captain's report had not been adverse. A surprise, but a pleasant one.

"Since, Captain, you are honoring us with your presence for tonight, I must see that your room is made ready for you. So, if you will excuse me."

A second surprise. The captain of a warship deserting his command and doing so when departure was imminent. There must have been any number of last-minute arrangements to make.

Or was all that sort of thing left to his first lieutenant, allowing the captain a last night of relaxation onshore?

As the manager bustled out, von Holstern signaled to Andrew to stay. He said, "You are surprised, perhaps, that I made no complaint of your conduct. Your lounging outside, when you should have been standing behind my chair to attend to my wants. Your clumsy handling of the beer, so that much of the last cask was wasted. Well?"

"Yes, sir. I was surprised. But pleased."

"And you have no idea why I was so friendly to you?"

"None at all, sir."

"Or why I have bespoken a bed here for tonight?"

"No, sir."

"The reason should have come to your mind every time you faced a looking glass. Come and stand by me."

Andrew shuffled forward.

"No. Closer. Much closer. That is better. Has no one ever told you that you were a very attractive boy?"

"No, sir."

"Now you are being modest. And I imagine you are not so well off that a small gratuity—shall we say five pounds?—would be unwelcome."

"That would depend, sir, on what I had to do to earn it." The tone was still respectful, but there was a hard edge to it that the captain either failed to notice or chose to ignore.

"The answer is very simple. No, stand still. All you have to do is to come back, in about two hours' time, when the last of the customers is leaving. I will let you know which is my bedroom. I shall expect you there."

This was put more in the tone of a command than a request. When Andrew said nothing, the captain added, more sharply, "You understand me?"

"Yes. I understand you. And I find the idea entirely unattractive."

"The money is not sufficient, perhaps?"

"It is not a question of money. The suggestion you have just made is a filthy one and unworthy of an officer in the navy. In any navy. Even a German one."

Before von Holstern had time to say anything Andrew had gone out, shutting the door firmly behind him.

Had the captain not been so angry he might have noticed that, for the first time, the waiter was speaking like an educated man. But he was too shaken with rage to think of anything except the incredible fact that he, an officer of the German Navy, had been insulted by a waiter. "Even a German one!" And this from a common, vulgar boy trained to fetch and carry, like a house dog, who should have been honored to have his head patted.

He was unaware that he had been speaking aloud and that the door behind him had been opened until Major Richards said, "Your pardon. I heard you talking and hesitated to intrude if you had someone with you. But since I am on the point of departing and may not see you again—"

Feeling that he was, at least, dealing with a man of his own class, who would sympathize with him, von Holstern said, "I was talking to myself. I apologize for such eccentricity. To tell you the truth, I was doing it in an effort to calm myself."

"Has something occurred—?"

"What has occurred is that I have been insulted."

"By the young man whom I observed scuttling down the passage?"

"Yes. By him."

The major said, "I ought to be surprised. But really I am not. I have noticed, recently, a tendency in the lower classes to speak with less than proper respect to their superiors. It is not something, I imagine, that would be tolerated in your homeland."

"In my homeland, which is Prussia, it would not have occurred. But I can assure you that if, inconceivably, it had occurred, it would have been punished by a public whipping. I only regret that such a measure of redress cannot be exacted here."

"Perhaps something of the sort might be arranged. Unofficially."

The captain looked at him for a long moment, then whispered, "If only it could be. But I do not see how."

The major had settled himself on the edge of the table and was swinging one of his neatly shod feet. He seemed to be weighing up the advantages and disadvantages that might accrue from this unexpected development. He said, "You sail at an early hour on Thursday. That is, the day after tomorrow."

"Yes."

"Then if the ceremony that I have in mind took place tomorrow evening, you would be away before any possible repercussions could occur. If, in fact, there were any repercussions, which I doubt. No great power is likely to upset its relationship with another great power over the sore backside of a potboy. More particularly, at a delicate moment like the present. The days are past when England was prepared to go to war because a merchant skipper forfeited one of his ears."

As the major spoke, he was, without appearing to do so, watching von Holstern very closely. He could see the desire for revenge battling with the prudence his position demanded. He thought it might be interesting to prod him a little further.

He said, "Of course you would not, yourself, appear in the matter. You will be returning to your ship tomorrow and will be staying aboard until you depart."

"Correct."

"But you have reliable subordinates."

"Very reliable."

"Men who would be as enraged as you were to think that the German Navy had been insulted."

"Their pride is no less than mine."

"And I have one or two equally reliable friends in the town. One of them happens to be a butcher. He has a useful van in which steaks and chops and offal of all sorts are transported.

"Offal," said the captain. He was beginning to smile. "Yes, offal indeed."

"What easier than to pick up this youth when he returns home tomorrow evening and transport him to some suitable location. I had in mind the strip of Southsea Common that runs down there to the edge of the sea. It is usually deserted in the evening. There, what has to be done could be done. Your ship is lying off the South Parade now. With a good glass you might even be able to witness the punishment. Or, at least, to hear the screams that the prisoner will utter when the whip is applied."

"Yes," said von Holstern, his thin lips coming together. "I think that would be appropriate. Most appropriate."

* * *

When Andrew got back to his lodging, which was in Eastry behind the Royal Marine barracks, he found that Mr. and Mrs. Stokes were out at some naval function that included womenfolk. They would not, he guessed, hurry home. It would be such an excellent opportunity for them to discuss and dissect the rumors that were circulating—rumors of mobilization, rumors of war. Upon Portsmouth, the head and the heart of the navy, such rumors would flock like starlings coming home to roost.

He found that a cold meal of pie and salad had been left out for him. He set out his place at one end of the kitchen table. The other end was occupied by the Stokes's only child, Dorothy, known to all as Doll. Doll was twelve years old and had been so deeply in love with Andrew from the moment of his arrival that she spent most of her day thinking about him and most of her nights dreaming about him. At the moment she was preoccupied. Andrew moved up to see what she was doing.

She said, "We have been told to write a story, in French, about an animal. Any animal we like. I'm afraid I've made lots of mistakes."

Andrew read what she had written, while Doll looked at him anxiously.

"It's very good," he said. "My only criticism would be that you seem undecided about the sex of your leading character. Since you have described the tiger as *méchante,* one would suppose it to be feminine. In which case, surely it should be *tigresse.*"

"Oh, dear. I do find these genders so muddling. Why should everything have to be male or female? And how is anyone supposed to know which is which?"

"It is difficult. I suppose French children come to know it instinctively."

"Do you speak French?"

"A little," said Andrew. "And here's your father and mother."

Realizing that any chance of concentration had gone, Doll took her work away to her bedroom to finish her story, and Andrew sat down to eat his supper and listen to the latest news. He gathered that the so-called courtesy visit of the Panzer Schlact Kreuzer *Kobold* had not been an unqualified success.

"Bad mixers, the Germans," said Mr. Stokes. "Diddun really lay themselves out to be pleasant. If you ask me they only came to find out what they could about us, in case they had to fight us."

"I do hope not," said Mrs. Stokes. "And, oh, dear, did you see those two Zeppelins that went over this afternoon?"

"Spying," said her husband bitterly.

* * *

When Andrew showed up at the Royal Duke next morning his arm was grabbed by Bob and he was pulled into the pantry where the waiters congregated when not on duty. Bob was a cheerful Devonshire boy, with a face like a russet apple and an impertinent outlook on life. Andrew enjoyed his comments about the guests and the senior members of the staff.

He said, "Better watch out. The old man's a bit raw this morning. I think the Germans may have pushed off without paying for all the beer they drank."

"They've gone, then?"

"Pissed off first thing this morning. Speaking for myself, I'm glad to see the last of them."

"Me, too," said Andrew. "That Captain von Holstern, he was a real sod. Do you know, he actually made a pass at me."

Bob said, "No. Did he really? I'd heard that Germans were like that. Naval types particularly. And I can tell you something else about him. Only keep it to yourself." Bob dropped his voice and sounded as solemn as he was capable of sounding. "Just after you left yesterday I ran into that Major Richards, coming down the passage, heading for the manager's office. I wondered if perhaps he was going in to make a complaint. Something about the service. So I thought I'd listen for a moment. Only it wasn't the manager in the office, it was that German captain. The one you didn't fancy. And here's the odd thing. Did you know that the major spoke German? And I mean, really spoke it, not just *ja* and *nein* and *ein Bier bitte,* but rattling away like as if it was his native tongue."

"No," said Andrew slowly. "I didn't know that. What did you make of it?"

"I did just wonder if he might be a spy."

"Do you—?"

"Don't say it. I know. I know. It's just my imagination. My mother always used to say to me, you let your imagination run away with you, Bob, and one of these days you'll find yourself in trouble."

"I wasn't going to say I disbelieved you. What I was going to ask you was if you happened to know where the major lives."

"I can tell you that. He's rented Fairford Manor. The old house on Gilkicker Point."

"The one on the cliffs, beyond the Naval Hospital?"

"That's the one. It belongs to the Fairford family, but when the admiral died old Lady F. couldn't run it on her own and started to let it. The first man who took it was a professor who collected butterflies. He was chasing one when he fell over the cliff. I expect you know the story."

Andrew nodded. Everyone in Portsmouth knew the story.

"Major Richards took over from the professor's widow. I don't fancy he'll go falling over the cliff. I'd say he's a man who sleeps with both eyes open."

"And you think he's a German spy."

"And now *you're* laughing at me."

"Certainly not. Don't you see that if he *was* a spy, the old admiral's house would be just the place for him? It's right over the harbor entrance, and what with the dockyard, the gunnery school on Whale Island, and the signal training station on Tipner, in the course of a year half the British Navy comes through there, right under his nose."

"Then you're saying I might be right."

"When you add the fact that he speaks fluent German, yes, I do think there might be something in it."

"Then oughtn't we tell someone?"

What Andrew might have said was interrupted by the arrival of the manager. He said, "I'll need both of you this evening. I can promise you it won't be such a late party as yesterday. It's a group of Americans—lawyers, politicians, and such. They'll be having a drink here around six o'clock, then going on to a special performance at the Opera House. The drinks will be chiefly shorts, gin and whiskey—bourbon whiskey—I imagine. They'll be in the big saloon. You do a shuttle service between the bar and the guests. Get on now with cleaning out the room. And give the glasses a good polish. Americans like clean service."

"And cheerful service," said Bob with a grin. Americans always tipped well. The prospect seemed to have driven all thoughts about spies out of his head.

The guests who assembled that evening were certainly more agreeable to serve than the Germans. They were a mixed bunch of lawyers, politicians, and businessmen, middle-aged and clearly well heeled. Andrew guessed that one of the objects of their visit might have been to report back to their government on exactly what was happening across the Atlantic and on the mood of the British when faced with the possibility of war.

A number of local notabilities had been summoned to meet them: the port admiral, Admiral Manfred, who was acting as host; Sir John Smedley, chairman of the Portsmouth Bench; and Superintendent Marcher, head of the Portsmouth Police, with his wife—known, inevitably, as the marchioness. Also a number of locals who seemed to have come along for the drinks.

Andrew organized his round so that he could hear as much as possible of the exchanges between the admiral and a clean-shaven, formidable-looking hunk who was addressed by his friends as "Sam" and by his juniors as "Judge." Though he held the floor at his end of the room he was clearly being careful to say nothing that might embarrass his hosts, and the smooth flow of his platitudes was only once interrupted.

This occurred when his attention was caught by the arrival

of Major Richards, who had come in alone and was scattering apologies around for his lateness. His apologies, Andrew thought, should more properly have been offered to his host and, once supplied with a drink, he did indeed drift toward the admiral, but when he became aware that the judge was looking at him, he seemed to change his direction and slid away into the far end of the room. It was a perfectly natural movement, noticed by Andrew only because he had not taken his eyes off of him from the moment he came in.

At half past seven the party dispersed, but there was an hour of clearing up to do before Andrew could get away. He did not resent this. He was well pleased with the evening's work. Not only had he earned a further ten shillings, but also the manager had agreed that the twenty-five-dollar note slipped to him by one of the Americans should, when changed into British money, be divided equally among Andrew, Bob, and the two barmen. This would put more than a pound in his pocket.

The Royal Duke stood at the far end of the South Parade, opposite the pier head. His shortest way home took him along the promenade. There were still a few hardy visitors occupying deck chairs on the sand, but the water, in the fourth week of June, was still too cold to tempt bathers.

The promenade ended just short of the Marine barracks, and Andrew turned left into an area of small houses on small streets.

Petty Officer Stokes, seeking peace and quiet after forty years of cramped quarters, noise, and movement, had chosen a cottage at the far end of a quiet cul-de-sac, bounded on one side by an ironworks store and on the other by the wall of the naval cemetery. Andrew had never before seen any vehicle in it and was therefore surprised to find a horse-drawn van standing there, apparently unattended.

He looked up as he passed it, to see where it came from, but the name on the side had been painted out. He had not much time to think about this since, as he reached the front of the van, the door opened and two men jumped out. Three more appeared from the far side. All of them were grinning as they grabbed him, picked him up, and tossed him into the back of the van.

Since odds of five to one made any offer of resistance futile, Andrew suffered this indignity in silence. Two of the men went back to the driving seat and the other three climbed into the back of the van. In that cramped space the four bodies were so tightly pressed that the main danger seemed to be suffocation—a thought that worried Andrew, who was flat on the floor, more than the three men who were on top of him.

When he had got some part of his breath back, helped by the fact that his nose was inches from a crack in the floor of the van, Andrew started to think.

His captors were Germans—sailors or stokers he thought, certainly not officers. Presumably, therefore, off the cruiser *Kobold.* Where were they taking him? And, a more uncomfortable thought, what were they planning to do with him when they got him there?

He had the impression that they were running westward, back through the center of the town, and this was confirmed when he heard the deep bell of the old Portsmouth Cathedral ahead of them, telling out the last quarter before nine.

Could they be planning to take him across in the ferry? If so, surely he could shout for help. No. The van had slowed and was now heading south. It seemed to have come out of the area of streets, onto a rougher surface. This would be Southsea Common, on which he had sometimes walked—sand hills, stunted grass, and a few scattered trees. They must be heading down toward the water's edge, an unattractive stretch of shingle and rock pools, very little visited except by mussel fishers.

The van stopped, the door was opened, and he was dragged out. Two of the men grabbed an arm each, one walked behind him with a hand on his collar, and two went ahead, to a point where a post had been set up in the shingle. All of them seemed to be in the highest spirits, as though they were setting out for an unexpected treat. The one who seemed to be the leader said, "Muster hands to punishment. Lash his wrists to the post. And we'll have his coat and shirt off."

This involved two men trying to do two different things at the same time and resulted in a moment of confusion. Seeing his chance, Andrew hooked his feet from under one of the two men, toppling him into the other; tore himself free from the third, leaving him holding the coat; raced down the sloping shingle; and threw himself in a long, shallow dive into the sea.

When he surfaced and looked back, he realized a number of things—some pleasant, some unpleasant. He saw that none of his captors had any intention of coming into the water after him. He noted that the current of the Hamble River, pouring into the Solent and helped by the ebb tide, was carrying him away from the shore so fast that there was no need for him to swim; also that the water was cold. He could see his attackers lined up on the edge of the shingle. Although deprived of the final treat they had been promised, they seemed happy at what they had accomplished. As he drifted farther and farther from the shore he heard them shouting and laughing and began to wish that he could be as happy as they were.

He was a good swimmer, but he saw no prospect of reaching dry land until the ebb had run and the tide started to make. It would be a long swim, and by that time the cold combined with the effort to keep afloat would have weakened him significantly. The prospect was not a pleasant one.

When a black shape loomed ahead of him, stationary and too solid for a ship, he guessed what it was. There were two or three rocks in Spithead that were dignified with the name of forts. In Napoleonic times each of them had been equipped with a gun, to help the navy deal with the fleet of flat-bottomed boats that the Corsican had collected as his invasion armada.

When the supremacy of the British Navy had ensured that there was no danger from that source, the guns had been removed, and the only people who visited them now were occasional fishing parties. The one he was approaching must be Spitbank Fort. He directed himself toward it and hauled himself out onto a patch of sand between two fangs of rock.

How long would it be before he could start back? And would it be wiser to wait for morning light? The truth was that he was afraid to start in case his strength failed halfway.

He was shivering now in deep, uncontrollable spasms.

2

"What's wrong with the girl?" said Mr. Stokes irritably. He had come home after an agreeable session at the Warrant Officers' Club and was not best pleased to find his daughter in hysterics and his wife at her wits' end.

"I don't know what's wrong with her. Perhaps she'll tell you."

"Haven't you got *any* idea?"

"What she said—when she left off sobbing for a minute—it sounded so much nonsense to me—was that she was up in her bedroom doing her homework and she happened to look out of the window and saw something."

"Saw what?"

"Saw something that upset her."

Mastering his impatience with an effort, Mr. Stokes said, "Didn't she describe it? Was it a dragon, or a lion, or a horse with two heads?"

"It was something to do with a van and a lot of men and Andrew."

"Our boarder?"

"Who else? You know she's been crazy about him ever since he arrived. My guess is she'd been thinking about him so much she's started imagining things."

"You could be right."

"She's up in her room now. Why don't you have a word with her. Maybe you can make some sense out of it."

In his capacity as petty officer, Mr. Stokes had often had to deal with young sailors—some of them homesick, some defiant, and one or two actually insane. He had developed a bluff and reassuring manner that was usually effective. It worked evenutally with the tear-stained Doll, whom he found lying face downward on the bed. He did, at least, get a coherent story out of her, which was more than his wife had done.

"They came in a van. They looked like sailors."

"German sailors?"

"Foreign sailors."

"So what did they do?"

"Andrew was coming home. As he walked past the van, they grabbed him and threw him in. It was horrible the way they treated him. Like they didn't mind whether they hurt him."

There was one thing that supported the story of the van. The horse had left indisputable evidence of its presence, which Mr. Stokes had nearly trodden in on his way home. And in any event, since the road served only the back entrance to the factory and a side gate into the cemetery, vans were a rarity in it.

But the sailors. Surely that part was a fantasy. Why should anyone wish to kidnap a waiter? The whole idea was crazy. Yet now that his daughter was speaking more rationally, her words had a ring of conviction.

Finally Mrs. Stokes, who had joined the conference, made a suggestion. She said, "Do you think, if we could have a word with—who is it?—the other waiter. The one Andrew was friendly with."

Her husband said, "You mean Bob. We might talk to him, if we knew where he lived."

"I can tell you that," said Doll. "It's only two streets away. Let's all go and see him. Let's go quickly. Now."

Her father tried to veto this suggestion. He thought it was something he could handle better on his own. But his daughter, as usual, was too much for him, and he let her have her way. Bob had finished his supper and was very willing to devote his attention to discussing the mystery.

He said, "There may be something in it. Andrew told me that the German cruiser captain had made a pass at him. Andrew turned him down flat. And told him just what he thought of him. I reckon that captain's a vicious type. He might—it's possible—have gotten some of his men to pick up Andrew and carry him off. I don't mean kill him. Rough him up. If you see what I mean."

Mr. Stokes said he saw exactly what Bob meant and that the matter must be reported to the police. He said, "We'll leave you out of this bit, Doll. You've had enough excitement for one night. Bob'll take you home."

Doll agreed to this. The fickle young lady was beginning to cast Bob as a possible substitute for Andrew.

Inspector Tillotson, who was on night duty at Milton Road Police Station, listened with unexpected patience to what Petty Officer Stokes had to tell him. He said, "I've got a daughter of my own. About the same age as yours. A few months ago, on account of something she'd picked up at school, she got the idea that our dog turned into a wolf once a month. When the moon was full." He chuckled. "Actually he was a friendly old spaniel who wouldn't hurt a bunny rabbit, whatever the moon was doing. But could we persuade her? Not on your life. Luckily the old dog died of distemper. However"—he sat up straight in his chair to indicate that the informal part of the interview was over—"that doesn't deal with your complaint. And I'll confess to you that it puts me in a difficulty. Suppose everything you've been thinking is true. Suppose the German captain arranged the whole thing as a piece of private vengeance. Tell me this: *What are we going to do about it?"*

After an uncomfortable pause Mr. Stokes said, "Well, I suppose you could . . ." and then stopped, because, as a naval man, he saw the hideous difficulties looming.

"The *Kobold* is booked out at 3 A.M. this morning. If we wanted to stop her, we should have to take official action, through the navy and the port authorities. And they wouldn't agree to take any step unless we could produce positive proof that they'd kidnapped this young man and were carrying him off. But just suppose that they did hold this ship—a unit in the Imperial German Navy—and the whole thing turned out to be an illusion brought about by something your twelve-year-old daughter thought she'd seen. What do you imagine the result would be?"

"I hadn't exactly thought it through," agreed Mr. Stokes slowly, "but now that you put it to me, I do see the consequences might be unfortunate."

"Unfortunate! It'd be an international incident. It would play into the hands of the politicians on both sides and would be a meal for the press."

It was clear that Mr. Stokes had no wish to provoke an international incident or to be a meal for the press.

Seeing that he had made his point, the inspector said, "So let's be practical. If those unknown characters have got hold of your boarder they might intend to rob him, or to beat him up. When they finish whatever they're planning to do, they'll dump him somewhere. Right?"

"I suppose that's right."

"Well, we've got night patrols covering all parts of the town." He looked at the charge room clock. "The reliefs will be going out in half an hour. I'll give them special instructions to keep their eyes open. If there's anyone needing help, they'll help him."

This did seem to be the only practical solution. It had a modest element of hope in it. Mr. Stokes departed to relay this hope to his wife and daughter.

A few minutes after he left the police station, Superintendent Marcher, on his way home, looked into the charge room. He made a habit of calling in on the night duty officer in this way to create the illusion that his unsleeping eye was on all police matters during the watches of the night. In fact, the powerful series of drinks, prepared for him by the marchioness, rendered him incapable of any constructive action except early retirement to bed.

Inspector Tillotson told him, in a fairly lighthearted way, about Mr. Stokes, his daughter, and her illusions. Also of the steps he had promised to take. The superintendent expressed his approval.

"It won't do any good, but it covers us. That's the main point. As a matter of fact, I was having a word earlier this evening with Sir John. He asked me to impress on all ranks the necessity for keeping a cool head. If this threat of war with Germany comes to anything—myself, I'm sure it will fade away as it did three years ago over Agadir—but *if* it should, one thing's certain: There'll be a lot of public hysteria. People will see German agents everywhere."

"Spy mania," suggested Tillotson.

"Exactly. And our job will be to cool it down. Treat every case on its merits. In strict accordance with the evidence. Pass that on to your men. Sir John is going to speak to his fellow magistrates. Between us"—the superintendent drew himself up and squared his shoulders—"we should be able to keep the ship on a straight course."

* * *

Thinking about it afterward, Andrew was never certain whether, despite the cold and the discomfort, he might have dozed off for a few minutes or even longer; but he was quite clear about what had called him back to full awareness. "Navy stroke," he said between chattering teeth. "Must be."

Somewhere in the darkness a six-oared or eight-oared boat was being rowed and was approaching. It was not heading directly for the rock, but its present course would bring it close. For a moment he wondered if his attackers might have gotten hold of a boat and be coming after him, but he dismissed the idea. They had been a crowd of louts. This boat was proceeding under discipline.

He shouted. Then again. And again, desperately.

A voice called out an order, and the next moment a ship's cutter, skillfully handled, ran head onto the sand and grounded.

Two sailors jumped ashore.

The voice said, "See who it is. If it's some boozer sleeping it off, he can stop there."

Andrew, speaking as best he could, said, "Not drunk. Very cold."

One of the sailors said, "Looks as if he's been in the water, sir. He's not in a good way at all."

"All right. Bring him along," said the voice.

When Andrew tried to stand up, his legs gave way under

him and he was half carried, half dragged down and lifted into the boat, which was expertly kedged off the sand, backed, and swung around.

The journey was not a long one. Their destination, as Andrew had begun to suspect it might be, was the battle cruiser *Queen Mary,* which had been lying at anchor for the past week off Calshot Buoy. Its commanding officer was a man who was already being talked about, sometimes with admiration, sometimes with horror. Andrew had heard about him even before he came to Portsmouth, and a friend of Andrew's landlord, dropping in for a drink, had filled out the portrait. " 'Blinker,' they calls him. 'Blinker' Hall, on account of he's got a twitch in one eye. But it don't stop him looking at you like he was drilling a hole in your head."

"Would that be the man," Stokes had asked, "who had a chapel built on board?"

"A chapel, a rest room, and a bookstall, too. And that's not all." He had paused to give full effect to his final bombshell. "He put in a *cinema.*"

His audience had gaped at him.

"Spoiling the men, some people call it. Encouraging indiscipline. But I don't know. The ones I met seemed a happy enough crowd, and as for indiscipline, I don't fancy any of them tried any tricks on him. No, sir. He'd have had their guts for garters."

As they approached the *Queen Mary* Andrew found himself debating two matters. The first was a practical question: How on earth was he expected to get onto the battle cruiser, whose steep side was now looming over them? He was still shaking with cold and his legs and arms felt unequal to any strenuous effort. The second was a more theoretical question but just as important: Was his rescuer in fact the remarkable character he had been told about? If he was, explanations could be made to him that could not properly be made to anyone else.

The first problem was soon settled. After an exchange of shouts, a sling was lowered and passed under his arms, and he was hauled aboard bodily and dumped on the deck. The second matter was settled when his rescuer was saluted and welcomed by a man with a commander's rings on his sleeve.

This, then, must be the redoubtable "Blinker" Hall. He started to scatter orders, directed mostly at the chief petty officer who had lined up with the commander.

"The first thing this scarecrow needs is a shower bath, a thorough toweling, and dry clothes. Get 'em from the dunnage and put 'em down to me. Next, a strong drink. Then he may be able to tell us his story."

An hour later, feeling a lot better, Andrew was able to make his way unaided to the captain's cabin. Hall was behind his desk, signing the last of a batch of papers and hurling them at his clerk with an order to get going on them, which the clerk appeared to understand, removing himself and the papers without comment.

As soon as they were alone, Hall swung around and said, "Sit down. Tell me about yourself."

A pair of cold, gray eyes discouraged dissimulation or delay.

Andrew said, "In Portsmouth I go under the name of Andrew Shuter. My real name is Luke Pagan. I was in the Metropolitan Police and reached the rank of sergeant in the CID before I joined MO5. I've been working, for the past year, for Vernon Kell."

"Yes. Vernon asked me to keep an eye open for you, in case you needed help. But I didn't expect to find you perched on a rock, like a storm-blown seagull. How did that happen?"

"It's an odd story, sir. I don't understand all of it myself. I've got a job as potboy at the Royal Duke . . ."

Hall was a good listener. He let Luke's story flow without interruption until he came to the scene in the manager's office. Then he said, looking as though he could hardly believe what he was being told, "Say that again. He offered you five pounds. What for?"

"To go to bed with him," said Luke.

He thought he had never seen such a look of revulsion and disgust on a human face. Hall's upper lip was drawn away from his teeth, and his eyes were half closed, as though he were shutting out a sight that nauseated him.

During the uncomfortable pause that followed, Luke remembered having been told that both of Hall's parents had been deeply moral people. A lot of it seemed to have washed off on their son.

Shying away from this distasteful topic, Hall said, "I can guess the rest of the story. No need to tell me. It was an act of revenge by von Holstern. Typically Prussian. You were able to listen to these people?"

"Some of the time, yes."

"Do you speak German?"

"My real languages are Russian and French. I learned both of them when I was young."

"Best time to learn a foreign language. Any others?"

"When I joined MO5. Kell put me through a crash course in German. I've reached the stage when I can read it—print and written—and speak it, but not really fluently. I would never pass as a German, but I understand it well enough."

"So," said Hall. "Two and a half languages. Not bad, but not as good as your chief."

"Not by a mile," agreed Luke.

It was common knowledge that Kell had spoken German, Italian, French, and Polish, all fluently, before he went to Sandhurst and since joining the army had added Russian and three of the Chinese dialects.

"So what did you pick up?"

"A lot of it was braggart talk. *Der Tag.* The day was fast approaching when they would crush all their opponents. More particularly the British Navy."

"And did they specify," asked Hall dryly, "exactly how they were going to carry out that part of their program?"

"Not in detail. What they did say—it was a sort of battle cry—*'über and unter.'* "

"Interesting," said Hall. "*Unter* would refer, no doubt, to their growing fleet of submarines. We have been warned about them. *Über* must mean Zeppelins. We'll be able to deal with them when our warplanes can get above them. Was there anything else?"

Had there been anything else? Luke remembered the look on the American judge's face when he spotted Major Richards. It was no more than a vague impression. He could have imagined the whole thing. Hall, he felt certain, was interested in facts, not theories. He said, "There was a lot of boasting and shouting and singing. That's all."

"Very well. The next thing we shall have to think about is what we're going to do with you. We could, of course, put you up here for the night, but by the time you got back tomorrow someone would have raised storm signals."

"I agree, sir. I must get back as soon as possible."

"Who are you lodging with?"

"A retired petty officer. William Stokes."

"Bill Stokes. A first-class man. He was with me on the *Natal.* He'll back up any story you choose to tell."

"I was often out late. If I'm back by midnight he won't have started to worry."

"And when you do get back, say as little as possible."

"If you think that's best."

"If you tried to make a fuss the captain would say that it was you who made an improper advance to him, which he rejected indignantly. And to give you a lesson had his sailors treat you to a ducking."

"I've no doubt you're right," said Luke. "If you could arrange to have me put ashore, I'll think up a story about a drinking spree with friends that got out of hand."

"In any event," said Hall, "the *Kobold* will have cleared Portsmouth by dawn, so I think we can regard this episode as closed. Just as well to clear the decks. I've got a feeling there's going to be a lot of work for your people to do very soon."

"Then you're sure that war's coming?"

"Of course, you won't have heard the news yet. We only got it ourselves this afternoon. It seems that yesterday a Serbian student assassinated the Austrian archduke Ferdinand and his wife at a place called Sarajevo, where they were on a visit of ceremony and friendship."

"And you think this will lead to trouble?"

To Luke it seemed comfortably remote. Trouble in the Balkans. Nothing unusual about that.

Hall said, "When you light one end of a carefully laid fuse and the other end is resting in a powder barrel, no great intelligence is needed to anticipate an explosion. This is how I see it. Austria will send Serbia a note of protest in the strongest possible terms. Serbia will apologize, but not profusely enough to satisfy Austria. So a further note will demand a more abject apology, coupled with the giving of undertakings that Serbia cannot possibly comply with. To reinforce the menace of this note, Austria will mobilize, forcing Serbia to follow suit. Germany supports Austria. Russia backs Serbia. France comes in behind Russia. General mobilization. Ultimatums with short time limits for compliance. Now the fuse is near the powder."

"Too near for anyone to stop it?"

"I fear so," said Hall. He shook his head as though to shake off the visions he was seeing. "Anytime now we shall be ordered north to our battle stations. Which means we shall be unlikely to meet again. A pity. There are things I'd have liked to discuss with you."

He got up. Luke, seeing him clearly for the first time, realized that he was quite a small man.

"I told the cutter to stand by. Your clothes are still too damp to be worn with comfort, so I've had them parceled up for you. Please regard the clothes you are wearing as a gift from the Royal Navy. I'll wish you *bon voyage.*"

When Luke reached his lodging there was a light on in his landlord's room, and he found Mr. Stokes smoking what was evidently the last of a series of pipes. He jumped up when Luke came in, started to say something, and broke off to stare in astonishment at his lodger.

To make up a story accounting plausibly for his arrival home at midnight, patently sober and wearing the off-duty garb of a naval rating, was altogether beyond his power of invention. So he had decided to fall back on a modified version of the truth.

When he had finished, Mr. Stokes said, "The trouble is that Doll saw you being kidnapped and what with one thing and another we had to tell the police. They had patrols out searching every hole and corner in Portsmouth for your battered body."

"Awkward," said Luke. "I'm afraid you'll just have to tell them that I was at a party and have just gotten home."

"They won't be best pleased."

"I realize it's put you in a hole and I'm more than sorry, but that's the way it's got to be."

"Did Captain Hall say so?"

"It was his suggestion."

"Then it must be done. No one on the *Natal* argued with him. Not twice." He knocked out his pipe and stomped off to propitiate the police.

Luke went up to his bedroom and lay down. He was deathly tired, but he knew he was not ready for sleep. He heard Mr. Stokes come back and go up to his room, and ten minutes later he was snoring. It seemed that his encounter with the police had not disturbed him unduly.

Luke rolled off his bed and plodded across to the window. From it there was a good prospect southward over the cemetery wall—an expanse of blue-black sky, spangled with stars, in the light of a near full moon.

As he watched, the intruders came. Two cigarlike shapes drifting in from the southeast, throwing their shadows on the sleeping town. Their course, he calculated, would take them directly over the harbor.

What eyes were peering down at them? Shortsighted, bespectacled German eyes. Were white, pudgy hands even now fingering the bomb release?

Craning out of the window, he watched the obscene intruders until they were out of sight. In a way their presence had helped to clarify his thoughts. He was out on a limb in Portsmouth. He needed help—help that could only be found in London, specifically from his old friend Hubert Daines, who had extracted him, by force, from the ranks of the Metropolitan Police and had sponsored his attachment to MO5.

Having reached this sensible conclusion he went back to bed and, at last, to sleep.

* * *

The next day, as his train trundled toward London, his thoughts were running in two directions. Backward over what he had already achieved that morning, and forward over his plans for the future.

After breakfast he had informed Mr. Stokes that an urgent matter had cropped up that called for his attendance in London and might keep him there for a few days. Mr. Stokes, whose house did not boast a telephone and who was aware that his lodger had received no letter, was beginning to wonder whether there was something odd about him.

He said, "Will you be keeping your room here?"

"Certainly," said Luke. "That is, if you can put up with me after my behavior yesterday."

"I did get my ears chewed off by that inspector," Mr. Stokes agreed. "He accused me of being a scaremonger."

Luke said how sorry he was, adding that now that those Germans had taken themselves off, there probably wouldn't be any more trouble.

His next step had been to present himself at the Royal Duke and explain to the manager that his mother was seriously ill, that he would have to go to London at once, and that he would be there indefinitely. The manager had proved sympathetic. Though not strictly obliged to do so, he had paid him for a broken week's work and had moreover given him the pound fifty that represented his share of the twenty-five-dollar tip from the Americans.

This had given him the opening he was looking for.

"Nice people, those Yankees," he said. "And I'd guess that some of them were pretty important—you know, higher-ups, that sort of thing."

The manager agreed with him. They had all been men of note in their own country. He only wished it hadn't been such a hurried visit.

"One in particular. The one they called 'Judge.' He'd have been a well-known lawyer?"

"Indeed he was. None other than Justice Samuel Rosenberg of the Supreme Court."

Luke had noted the name carefully.

Before he left to catch his train he had had a word with Bob, who said, resentfully, "It must have been a bloody good party last night. You might have let me in on it."

"It was an unexpected party," Luke said. "The sort of thing that gets sprung on you. If I'd had time to think, I'd certainly have suggested that you come along. In fact, there were moments when I'd have been very glad to have you with me."

"It'd have been a last chance."

"How so?"

"You know I've been looking for a permanent billet. Well, I've landed one. At the Mariners' Rest Guest House in Southampton."

"So the Royal Duke loses two of its best and brightest servants."

"If trouble's coming," Captain Hall had said, "clear the decks." His efforts that morning had gone a certain way in that direction. Now he had to think about the future, particularly about Major Richards. Ex-major, presumably, but of what unit in the army? Maybe the War Office would be able to help.

Looking back out of the window as the line climbed toward Hilsea, he could just see the yards of Nelson's *Victory*, which Captain von Holstern, God rot him, had insulted, and beyond that the cliffs of Gilkicker Point, looking down into the entrance of Portsmouth Harbor.

Was there something there that warranted looking into, or was his imagination playing tricks?

He must think about it—logically, clearly, dispassionately.

A few minutes later, in spite of the discomfort of a train, which was third class in every way, he was sleeping the sleep of exhaustion, waking only when it was running through the outer suburbs of London.

3

"I am well aware," said Luke, "that the traditional female spy is willing to be seduced by enemy officers in order to wheedle vital secrets from them. But I'll be everlastingly damned if I was going to let myself be buggered by a German cruiser captain."

"Oh, I don't know," said Hubert Daines. "A really keen intelligence man—"

Luke looked around for something to throw, but finding nothing suitable, contented himself with grunting.

"In any case," he said, "I doubt if von Holstern could have told me anything useful. He was a typical Prussian, solid brass from the neck up. I passed on to Captain Hall the only snippets I'd gathered while listening to him and his junior officers."

"What did you make of Hall?"

"Astonishing personality. I did wonder if he was 100 percent fit."

"Ah, you spotted that, did you? The doctors say that it's asthma that makes him so breathless. It may mean him losing an active command. But it won't mean the navy losing him. No, sir. He'll be put into the place where he's really wanted—in charge of naval intelligence. They're waiting for him in the Admiralty with open arms. Tell me: Did you get onto anything really useful?"

"I'm not sure," said Luke slowly. "Maybe I did catch the tail end of something that might be important. There's a man who calls himself Major Richards; I say, 'calls himself.' For all

I know it may be his real name. The main thing against him is that he's got a house that is ideally situated to watch all that goes on in Portsmouth Harbor."

"Nothing suspicious in that."

"Not by itself. But there were three other little things. His friendship with von Holstern and his fluency in German. And last but not least, the flicker of interest that Judge Rosenberg showed in him."

"Rosenberg being one of the Americans you were telling me about?"

"A leading member of the party and high up, now, in their judicial system, but he may have been a criminal lawyer once. A lot of their judges come up through the district attorney's office."

For the first time Luke seemed to have captured Hubert's whole attention and interest. He said, "You call them three little things. It's just possible that they might add up to a big thing." He thought for a moment, then said, "So I'm going to tell you something that is known, at the moment, to only a handful of people. It's a curious story—really almost unbelievable—and I need hardly say that it stays under your hat."

He stared at the traffic that a policeman was holding up at the point where Cromwell Road crossed Queen's Gate. Then he said, "Think back to 1907. No doubt you remember the fuss there was in London—"

"Please bear in mind that in 1907 I was fifteen years old and my time was spent in helping my father look after Sir George Spencer-Well's pheasants."

"I expect that you sometimes had a moment to read the papers."

"Occasionally."

"Then it cannot have escaped you, even in your rural seclusion, that in the autumn of that year our good King Edward—lover of peace, we called him—invited the Kaiser to pay us a state visit."

"Yes. I remember reading about the state visit."

"Good. Well, the Kaiser arrived, accompanied by a pantomime troupe of aides, secretaries, courtiers, and camp followers, all duly observed by Superintendent Patrick Quinn. Have you met him?"

"Once. Short, pointed beard and looks like an archdeacon."

"He's a very shrewd operator, who's been in charge of the Special Branch at Scotland Yard for ten years or more and knows all there is to know about guarding notable visitors. He soon concluded that one or two of the Kaiser's gang were almost certainly involved in intelligence operations."

"Were spies."

"Not in the accepted sense of the word. No. But one of them, Captain von Rebeur-Paschwitz, might have been described as a spymaster. He was known to hold a top post in German intelligence, and so Quinn kept an extra-sharp eye on the gallant captain. He soon discovered a curious fact about him: It seemed he had no duties to perform. Not even ceremonial duties. He spent his days in hearty eating and drinking and his evenings in visiting music hall performances and entertaining the performers to supper."

"The female performers?"

"Oh, yes. His tastes seem to have been entirely normal. And so it went on until the official visit ended on November 18. After which the Kaiser, who must also have been enjoying himself, stayed here for several weeks in a private capacity as a guest of Colonel Stuart-Wortley, in Highcliffe Castle, near Bournemouth. Rebeur-Paschwitz stayed on, too, but he seemed to prefer the attractions of London."

"But surely," said Luke, "if he was *in attendance* on the Kaiser—"

"The point did not escape Quinn, who was now sure that he was on to something. Being chronically shorthanded, he had roped in helpers from MO5. I was one of them. In the end there were four of us on the job. One evening, toward the end of his visit, the captain dined at the Army and Navy Club—he'd been made an honorary member—and set out after dinner apparently to do some sightseeing, in the Oxford Street area. And if there had been any doubt in anyone's mind about what he was up to, the captain's subsequent movements would have set it at rest."

Luke had stopped interrupting. He could see that Hubert was reliving the wild November evening when four sweating investigators had clung desperately to the coattails of one German officer.

"He took three different cabs, in succession, with a short walk between each. I can see, now, that if we'd attempted to do the same thing we would have been spotted at once. However, we didn't. We used our legs. A man who is in good shape can keep up with an unhurrying cab. Luckily the streets were fairly crowded, and in the end we clung on to him long enough to find out where he was going with such elaborate precautions. It was, on the face of it, a simple answer. He wanted to get his hair cut."

Luke was provoked into saying, "I don't believe it." To which Hubert said, "Nor did we. But there he was, in a barber shop, still open at ten o'clock at night. And in no very fashionable quarter of town. It was on Caledonian Road, number 402A, opposite Pentonville Prison. He wasn't there long—hardly enough for a short back and sides. Then he came out, looking like a man who had done a good evening's work. Quinn let him go. He had gotten the information he wanted."

"We soon found out all about that barber, Karl Ernst. A very solid citizen. Half of his customers were guards or officials from Pentonville Prison, and the other half were local residents, mostly Germans. Nothing to raise any suspicions. Nothing at all, except for that one, curious, unexplained visit, which had aroused the highly developed suspicions of Patrick Quinn, who needed and happily possessed the patience to take the next step, which was to twist the wrist of the home secretary."

"Winston Churchill," said Luke with a smile. "Not an easy wrist to twist."

"On this occasion he proved unexpectedly cooperative. He was persuaded to give the post office a blanket instruction to open all mail coming into and going out of that barber shop. Quite an operation. It meant employing a special section at Mount Pleasant to open and remail every letter that passed, and one of Quinn's own men had the job of translating them.

Before long they'd given us the whole framework of the German spy system in this country."

"Totally fascinating," said Luke and meant it. "But how does it fit in with something that I may—or may not—have stumbled on in Portsmouth?"

"The intercepted letters gave us the names and addresses of 95 percent of the German spies in this country. As soon as war's declared, they'll be taken in."

"And shot."

"No. They've been operating in peacetime. That's not a capital offense. In fact, as our daft laws stand at the moment, I doubt whether they've been committing any offense at all."

"So . . . ?"

"So they'll be interned—put somewhere where they'll be of no further use to Gustav Steinhauer, their hardworking and not overly intelligent boss in Berlin. But—and it's a big but—that still leaves the missing 5 percent. Two or three really dangerous men. We know they exist, just as a fever sufferer knows there are bugs in his blood even though he can't see them. He deduces their presence from the results they produce. An indication of the importance of these men is the precautions our correspondents took. They must have been taught the old army rule 'No names, no pack drill.' One man who is mentioned regularly seems to have been of importance in the London circle—possibly in charge of it. He is referred to only as *der Vetter*—the cousin. When Steinhauer had a message for him, it was sent to one of the other correspondents, who was told to pass it on to him personally. Another man was operating somewhere on the south coast. On the rare occasions that he is mentioned he is called *der Richt Kannonier*—the gun layer. They praise the important work he is doing, but are careful to say no more."

"And you think that Richards might be *der Richt Kannonier?*"

"If he is and if you can prove it, that'll be a long step forward. Meanwhile, I can be doing two things at this end. I can ask the War Office to see whether they can identify Major Richards. And I can ask our New York contact to put through a very tactful inquiry to Judge Rosenberg. Meanwhile, you go back to Portsmouth and keep an eye on Richards."

"He's got an assistant—chauffeur, bodyguard, handyman—what you will. A bearded tough of unknown nationality—central European, anyway—who does the shopping and helps around the house. The locals call him the bosun. If an eye has to be kept on both of them, it'll be a two-man job."

"I agree. But in the limited state of our manpower, I'm afraid I can only offer you one assistant. He's newly enrolled and somewhat wild and irresponsible. Nevertheless, I think you'll find him helpful." With a short pause for effect Daines added, "His name's Narrabone."

"For God's sake! You don't mean—is it really Joe?"

"Yes. Joseph Narrabone. You seem pleased."

"Joe!" Luke was almost speechless with delight and gratitude. "How did you work it?"

"It seemed to work itself," said Daines modestly. He was pleased with the effect of his carefully nursed bombshell. "Losing a leg in that Leman Street explosion ended his career in the police, but it was no bar to his enrollment in MO5."

"Joe!" said Luke. Joe, who had been to the same village school where Luke had been a shiningly virtuous head boy and Joe had been, without any near competitor, the worst boy in the school. Joe, who had joined the Metropolitan Police a few weeks after him and had been his prop and stay against the slings of bad men and the arrows of superior officers.

"Major Richards," he said, "look out for your bloody self. Here comes the old firm."

4

The first of July, in the year in which Europe plunged, like the Gadarene swine, over the cliff with the apparent object of destroying itself at the bottom, fell on a Wednesday. It was late in the afternoon when Luke and Joe arrived in Portsmouth and presented themselves at the house of Petty Officer Stokes. Joe had insisted on walking the half mile from the station to demonstrate his mastery of his artificial leg.

Mrs. Stokes welcomed them and offered Joe the empty room next to Luke's. Her husband, she explained, was up in London bullying the Admiralty about his pension, and Doll had gone to stay with a school friend. That meant that she was alone in the house and only too glad to have their company.

She said to Luke, "For I can't abide them creatures."

"Creatures?"

"The ones that come over at night."

"Zeppelins?"

"Is that what they call them? I call them slugs."

"Orter be a law against it," said Joe.

Luke said, "I'm afraid we shall be in and out at all hours. If you could trust me with a front-door key, you wouldn't have to sit up for us."

Mrs. Stokes thought she could trust him. Discussing him with her husband, they had both come to the conclusion that he must be in Portsmouth on some undercover government work. Mr. Stokes was influenced by his connection with Commander Hall. Mrs. Stokes, more simply, thought that no one could really be as naive and guileless as he looked. It must, therefore, be camouflage of some sort.

"Supper at seven," she said. "Unless you're thinking of eating out."

"Certainly not," said Luke. "Best grub in Portsmouth."

After supper they sat on Luke's bed with the map spread out in front of them.

It was clear that, if they wished to keep an effective watch on Major Richards's house on Gilkicker Point, they would have to close up on it. There was no spot on their side of the harbor entrance that would give them the sort of observation they wanted. They would have to cross by the ferry and make their way up through the Alverstoke suburb of Gosport. After that the map showed nothing between the last line of houses and the point. It could be anything from open country to closely cultivated farmland.

"Whatever it is," said Joe, "there's bound to be cover. We can get close up to the house and set up an observation post. Might have to dig ourselves in."

"Reconnaissance first," said Luke. "Action tomorrow as soon as it's dark."

It turned out to be an evening of surprises.

The first was that the stretch of land above and beyond the Alverstoke houses was neither open country nor farmland. Since their map had been printed, the land had been acquired by the Gosport and District Golf Club and now comprised the last three holes of their course—intervals of smooth turf and carefully cultivated rough. Also, a clubhouse had been built, and although it was eleven o'clock when they passed it, there still were lights in the downstairs windows and the sounds of loud voices from the bar.

"Lazy slobs," said Joe. "How I hate 'em. Too much money in their pockets and no thoughts in their upper-class nuts except bloating themselves by eating too much and muddying their so-called brains by drinking too much."

"You're just envious," said Luke, who knew Joe too well to take his diatribes seriously. "All the same, we shall have to keep our eyes open when we tackle the next obstacle."

This was the second surprise: an efficient-looking fence of diamond wire.

Fairford Manor was a substantial Jacobean building, with outhouses and stabling and a garden that descended in terraces from the northwest frontage of the house. It had, originally, been surrounded by a simple brick wall, which was now supplemented by this formidable fence. Luke guessed that it might have been erected by Admiral Fairford's widow, left alone in the house and apprehensive of intruders.

Whoever had put it up, it was a factor to be considered.

"Damn," said Joe. He kicked the fence, which twanged back at him resentfully.

"Doesn't help," agreed Luke.

"You remember when we were put on to watch that East London soap factory—the one that turned out to be manufacturing dynamite—we were at it for nearly a week, I dug myself a snug little hide, diddun I? Well, we're not going to be able to do anything like that here, are we."

"That's right," said Luke.

"If we lifted a single piece of turf out here, we'd have the golfers around our necks. And if we got into the garden, it'd be even worse. The gardener would spot it and raise hell."

"Right," said Luke.

"And instead of agreeing with me like a bloody gramophone record, suppose you produce one of your bright ideas."

"I'm thinking," said Luke.

While they were talking they had been moving, clockwise, around the outside of the fence and had reached a small knoll that overlooked the edge of the cliff on one side and the garden on the other. The original wall stopped here, but the wire fence turned the corner and continued along, flush with the edge of the cliff. Below them they could see the lights of the ships at anchor in the harbor. The house was black and silent. From where they were standing they had for the first time a view of the rear of the building.

"Strange sort of affair," said Luke. He was looking at the squat, one-story annex sticking out at the back. It was clearly of recent construction. The more they looked at it the odder it seemed. It was a small, square, battlemented addition, totally out of keeping with the rest of the building.

"What it might be," said Joe, "Diddun Mrs. Stokes tell us the admiral had been an astro—something?"

"An astronomer."

"Just the word I was thinking of. He liked looking at the stars and the moon. So he builds that new bit, takes his telescope up onto the roof, and does a bit of astronomizing."

"Could be," said Luke. It seemed an expensive way of building a mounting for his telescope, but the old boy had money and could indulge his hobby. He said, "It'd be a useless little room, wouldn't it? There's just the one small window on this side—heavily shuttered. Could be one on the other side, but nothing at all on the end overlooking the cliff."

Joe, who had better eyes than Luke, said, "It may be short of windows, but there's a big overhead light in the roof. You can just see it, between the battlements."

Now that Joe pointed it out he could see it, and it did offer a possible explanation of the whole setup. The admiral could have his telescope mounted inside the room and do his viewing through the overhead light, which would be openable.

"I think that's right," he said. "No doubt it suited the major, too. Up there on the roof, with his own telescope, he'd have a grand view of the harbor. So here's where we split our forces. You stay put and keep your eyes open. If the major comes up onto the roof, you'll be able to see him. I'm going to have a look around the garden."

"What'll you be looking for?" asked Joe gloomily. He didn't like being reminded of the old days when he had been the more active of the two. Give him back his leg and he'd have been over that fence in no time.

"What we really need," said Luke, "is a spot that will give us a view of the front of the house, so that we can see what visitors the major has. Preferably high enough for us to be able to look down into the house. And a bit on one side, so that we could keep the roof of this annex under observation."

"Easy. All we've got to do is anchor a balloon about forty feet above the bottom left-hand corner of the garden."

"An invisible balloon, of course."

"Of course," said Joe. He seemed to have recovered his spirits.

"I'll be having a quick look at the garden. I don't imagine I shall find anything, but you never know."

"Bear in mind that if that bosun comes rushing out at you, you won't be able to get back over that fence in a hurry, without me to give you a leg up."

Luke had this thought very much in his mind as he scrambled awkwardly over the wire fence and dropped down on the other side. He remained on hands and knees for a bit, to see what lay ahead. He was in the northeast corner of the garden, which was laid out in flower beds, weed-free and neatly edged. Either the bosun had been busy with hoe and spade or, more likely, the original gardener had been retained.

Picking his way among the beds, he came out onto the front drive and went forward cautiously. The left-hand side of the drive was one continuous bed, containing thorny-looking shrubs. The other side was a strip of turf. Clearly anyone approaching the house and not wanting to make a noise crunching up the drive would step off onto the turf and advance along it. That was quite clear.

The caution that had been bred into Luke when he acted as assistant to his gamekeeper father alerted him to the possibilities of the situation. About fifty yards from the house he found the trip wire he had expected. It was cunningly set, six inches from the ground, between forked sticks.

Luke looked at it with distaste. He wondered what other traps there were. He was beginning to dislike and distrust the garden. Neatly shaved and cultivated, it offered no sort of cover, no possible lying-up place.

"Get out of it," he told himself, "before you do anything stupid."

Five minutes later he was back on the safe side of the fence. Joe was where he had left him, perched on the knoll, clasping his knees.

"You look happy," said Luke. He said it resentfully. The futility of their excursion was weighing on him.

"I *am* happy."

"I'm glad someone is."

"And why am I happy? Because I've found my balloon."

"You've done *what?*"

"I've been thinking. About what you said. How unfortunate it was this golf course had appeared. All the *dis*advantages of it. Remember?"

"Of course I remember."

"Right. Now try thinking about the *ad*vantages. What we've got to do is start thinking"—Joe brought out the next word with justifiable pride—"constructively."

"Meaning?"

"Take a look at the southwest side of the garden. And what do you see? You see a line of well-matured beech trees, just outside the fence. Planted, I'd guess, to give the house some protection from the land breeze that blows most evenings. Look at the one at the right-hand end of the row. The tallest, as it happens. If we were roosting on top of that, we'd be in our balloon, wooden we?"

"Yes," said Luke. "We would. But how do we get there?"

"If we come tomorrow night with a few nails and pegs we can make a way up that tree that even I could manage. And that's the advantage of it being on a golf course. If you treated a tree like that anywhere in open country, you'd soon have a pack of nosy kids climbing the tree. Not here. The only boys who come here are caddies, carrying golf clubs. And the golfers are keeping their eye on the ball. Not looking for nests in the trees. Right?"

"Joe," said Luke, "you're wonderful."

After some deliberation they abandoned the idea of nails as being too noisy to fix, and prepared a number of wooden pegs, sharpened and painted black. They also bought a brace and bit. They found that the pegs, judiciously placed, provided an easy way up the tree. From the top of it they had a bird's-eye view down into Fairford Manor. The tree being offset to one side, they could keep the roof and skylight of what they had begun to call the Telescope Room under observation. For the rest, they were able to watch the inhabitants of Fairford Manor going to bed.

It was an orderly progress.

First the female contingent, a middle-aged housekeeper and her daughter, went up to their bedrooms on the top story and drew the curtains, thus sparing the observers the embarrassment of watching them undress.

A full hour later they saw the major get up from the table in the ground-floor room that was evidently his study and ring the bell. This produced the bosun. The two men stood for a few minutes, talking. Then the bosun disappeared and they heard the sound of the top and bottom bolts in the front door being shot. The lights in the study and the front hall went out, and in the silence that followed they heard footsteps going upstairs.

"One of them or both?" said Luke.

"Difficult to tell," said Joe.

"The major may be going to bed, or he may be going up onto the roof of the Telescope Room for a look at the boats in the harbor."

"So how does he get there?"

"Either there's a ladder on the far side that we can't see, or maybe there's a way out from one of the rooms at the back."

They had borrowed a pair of night glasses from their landlord and took it in turns to keep them focused on the roof of the annex. They kept this up for more than an hour, but no one appeared. The only sound to break the deep silence was the humming of the generator that supplied the house with electricity.

"All gone to bed," said Joe. "What say we do, too?"

"Motion carried," said Luke. He added, "From now on we'll take it in turns. I'll do tomorrow night."

"Then bring a bit of plank with you. Fix it between these two boughs. Give you something to sit on. Squatting here has given me a numb bum."

This seemed to Luke to be sensible. He was beginning to feel the onset of cramps himself. He wondered how Joe, with his peg leg, had put up with it.

They were back in bed by two o'clock and rose late on the

following morning. Luke decided to stay indoors and write the long report he was preparing for Hubert, to be handed on, if he saw fit, to Vernon Kell. He was careful not to be too optimistic about possible results of their efforts. Joe had disappeared on some mysterious business of his own and had not reappeared when Luke set out. It was a much colder night, and he was glad to put on an overcoat, which helped to conceal the two-foot length of board he was carrying.

By ten o'clock he was comfortably established on his treetop seat. He noted that the study was in darkness, but the hall light was on and the front door had been left ajar. When the bosun appeared, smoking a cigar and strolled a few paces up and down the drive, Luke deduced that the major was out and that his factotum was waiting up for him.

The bosun went indoors again. One hour had crept past and the better part of a second one when Luke heard the sound of wheels on the approach road and saw the lights of a car. The gate must have been left open, since the car drove straight through and stopped in front of the hall door. The bosun appeared and switched on the porch light.

It was an impressive car, one of the latest Lanchester tourers, painted battleship gray. The uniformed chauffeur jumped out and held the car door open while the occupants sat for a few minutes, finishing their conversation.

Then the major emerged and as the other man leaned out to say something, Luke had no difficulty recognizing him. It was Sir John Smedley, chairman of the Portsmouth Bench, whom he had last seen at the party given to the American visitors.

As the conversation continued, Luke was now able to pick up snatches of it. There was a reference to "Friday" and to "the Guildhall." This was followed by something deprecating that John had to say about rumormongers.

Rumors of what? Luke wondered. The coming of war?

The car drove off, leaving the question unanswered. The major went in, the front door was shut, and the porch light and hall light were turned off. No light in the study, no movement on the roof of the Telescope Room. Presumably the major had gone straight up to bed. Since no light appeared at any of the windows on his side, Luke deduced that the major's bedroom must be in the far side of the house. This was a logical supposition, since it meant that it would overlook the harbor.

After waiting for a further hour, Luke climbed down. He skirted the clubhouse, where a noisy Saturday night party was going on, crossed by the ferry, and made his way home to bed.

The next morning, at breakfast, Luke could see that Joe was pleased with himself. He knew that he liked to hunt his own line and produce the results when he was ready. So all he said was, "I hope you had a good day."

"Smashing," said Joe. "By my calculation me and Mr. Hobhouse between us we put away ten pints of wallop and near half a bottle of Scotch. What about you?"

Luke knew that Mr. Hobhouse would be explained in due course, so he contented himself with recording what he had heard and said, "Can we find out what's happening at the Guildhall on Friday?"

"Our host will know," said Joe, and departed to consult Mr. Stokes, who had returned, empty-handed and resentful, from London.

When he came back he said, "Seems it's a Masonry party. All the nobs around here are Freemasons."

Luke digested this information in silence. If it was true, he could see rocks ahead.

Joe was on watch that night; Luke on Monday; Joe again on Tuesday. The results were uniformly disappointing.

They became acquainted with every move of every member of the household, and none of them gave any grounds for suspicion. Neither the major nor the bosun had been sighted on the roof of the Telescope Room. The major, like his watchers, seemed to find time hanging heavily on his hands and had taken to playing patience. Joe, who had an excellent view of the cards, maintained that, more than once, he had caught him cheating.

By day Joe continued to cultivate Mr. Hobhouse, while Luke concentrated on his study of the German language. It was when he was getting ready to set out on Wednesday night that Joe said, "Do you think it's possible that we're chasing a red herring?"

"It's possible," said Luke, "but don't forget what the great Fred Wensley taught us when we were recruits: 'In all watching, the secret of success is persistence.' "

Joe said, "Might suit some people. I prefer action. And action's what I've been taking."

"With Mr. Hobhouse."

"Right. So let me tell you something about him. He's a great drinker. What you might call an alcoholic champion."

"And what does he do when he isn't drinking?"

"He takes photographs. Sometimes on the beach or the pier. Sometimes on High Street. Snapping people he thinks are promising subjects."

"Meaning people who will pay him for the photographs?"

"Right. Tourists mostly. They pay him the money and give him the name of the hotel or boardinghouse they're staying at, so he can let them have the photograph when it's developed."

"Seems to involve a good deal of trust."

"You mean he might walk off with the money and not produce the photograph? He couldn't do it. He's licensed by the Council. Any complaints and he'd lose his license. No, he plays fair. Very well thought of is Mr. Hobhouse. That's why he took a lot of persuading before he'd do what I wanted."

"Which was . . .?"

"To hang about outside the Royal Duke. It's still the major's regular watering place. And get a full-face snap of him as he came out."

"Did you explain why you wanted it?"

"Sure. I told him I was a private detective, looking for evidence in a divorce case. He didn't like it. I offered him a fiver for the photo. He said it might cost him his license. I went up to ten pounds. He weakened. Then to fifteen. He fell."

Luke drew a deep breath and said, "Where are we going to find fifteen pounds?"

"Telephone the boss. He'll authorize the payment. When you explain what you want the photograph for."

"If you'd explain it to me," said Luke patiently, "then perhaps I could explain it to him."

"To send it out to America, of course. If Judge Rosenberg recognizes it we might be getting something on the major. Which we won't do by sitting watching him play cards."

"Yes," said Luke. "I suppose we might." He didn't say it with any confidence.

The afternoon mail brought a letter from Hubert Daines. He said that inquiries at the War Office had produced a negative result. They had accounted for all the Major Richards on their books, and it was clear that none of them could be the man at Portsmouth. However, as they pointed out, this was not conclusive. He might have been on some other force—in America, Canada, Australia, or New Zealand. They promised to extend their inquiries but warned that it was going to take time.

And time, thought Luke, was a precious commodity. The Continental news had been so muted lately that anyone who could read between the lines could see that trouble was coming—was indeed very close. Week by week the days were running off the reel.

Wednesday was a windless, moonlit night, with a ground mist that had come up at dusk. As Luke climbed into his observation spot he was thinking that they had reached a low point in their inquiries.

Could Joe be right? Were they barking up the wrong tree? Had all their thinking been muddled nonsense? This gave rise to another and even more disturbing speculation. They had assumed, when they first saw it, that the annex at the back of the house had been built by the old admiral as a place from which to pursue his astronomical studies. Very possibly it had been. The large skylight in the roof certainly supported the idea. He could have had his telescope mounted inside the room and by opening one or another of the shutters in the skylight he could have kept any required portion of the heavens under review. That was all totally feasible.

But—and as the fallacy which had followed from this line of reasoning struck him—Luke felt inclined to kick himself.

Even if all that was true, *why should Major Richards wish to go onto the roof of the annex with his own telescope?*

What he was thought to be doing was spying on the ships in the harbor. No doubt this was correct. *But why should he make his observations from the roof of the annex?* He had the whole house at his disposal. Why not take his observations, far more easily and far more safely, from one of the bedroom or attic windows at the back of the house?

It was at this moment of extreme doubt and gloom that he saw them, dimly visible in the moonlight.

Two Zeppelins, coming directly toward him.

5

It was difficult to judge distances at night, but he thought that the Zeppelins were about half a mile away when he first saw them. They had covered most of that distance when the light appeared.

It was a thin thread of illumination, shining upwards from the skylight of the annex. And he could now see that it was not appearing steadily, but in groups of longs and shorts. Clearly a message. Equally clearly a message intended for the Zeppelins, as no one else could see it unless they were, like him, more or less directly above the skylight.

—/UUU/UUU/UU/UU/UU/UU/U/U/U/U/U/U/U/U

He fumbled for his notebook, managed to find the pencil in the one pocket he had not put it in, and scribbled desperately. He was conscious of a feeling of triumph. Their suspicions of the major were justified. He was a German spy. All that they had been wrong about was his method of working.

He had no need to go onto the roof of that convenient annex. All he had to do was to sit *inside it* and turn the light on and off.

Simple and safe.

By this time the Zeppelins had swung away inland.

It was a pity that he had been so intent on watching their arrival that he had missed the beginning of the message, which might contain the key to the whole. Next time he would get the full message and, God willing, would understand it.

He was in such a hurry to discuss this development with Joe that he climbed down at once and set out for home. The unwisdom of going so early was brought home to him when he ran into a group of golfers coming out of the clubhouse and had to dive for cover.

Fortunately they were so busy discussing something that had happened that afternoon that they had no eyes for him. ("Moved the ball with his toe." "Are you sure?" "Dead sure. He thought I wasn't looking." "Always knew he was a bloody cheat.")

Luke waited until the voices had died away in the distance, then followed discreetly.

He found Joe sitting up. Luke poured out his news and produced the crumpled page from his notebook.

"Morse code," said Joe at once. "Longs and shorts. Must be."

"If they're all shorts it's a pretty odd message."

S/S/IIII/EEEEEEE

"Not crystal clear," agreed Joe. "Needs thought. This message—whatever it turns out to be—the Zepps would be the only people who would pick it up."

"I think that must be right," said Joe. "If you look at that annex with its side windows shuttered and no window on the end—which was natural enough when the admiral had used it as an observatory—"

"Point taken," said Joe. "And you only saw it because you were up in my balloon."

"All credit to you," said Luke handsomely.

"Then the next thing is to find out when the Zepps are likely to show up next."

"If they're following a timetable."

"The Huns are a regular sort of bastards. When it comes to dropping bombs it'll be just the same, you'll see."

"Then we must have a word with Mr. Stokes. He may be able to help us."

Mr. Stokes, brought into conference, said that the Zeppelins hadn't been absolutely regular in their visits, but

Wednesdays and Saturdays seemed to be their normal days. Why did they want to know?

Luke looked at Joe, and Joe gave a nod, which meant that he considered the ex-petty officer reliable and discreet.

Luke said, "We've had our eyes on a Major Richards for some time now."

"The one who has the house up on Gilkicker Point and hangs around the Royal Duke?"

"That's the man. Well, we've found him tonight apparently flashing a message to the Zepps, through the skylight in an annex. For all we know he may have been doing it for months. Tonight's the first time we've been able to pick it up. I've got the end part of it here."

He pushed the paper across.

Mr. Stokes translated it automatically into Morse. When he had done so he stared blankly at the result.

"Must mean something, I suppose," he said. "I mean, he wouldn't just sit there turning the light on and off for no reason at all. But I can tell you one thing: I'm not really surprised. I've run into the major a couple of times and he seemed to me to be a slippery sort of character. Might he be a German?"

"Yes. That's possible."

"Perhaps the Germans have a Morse code of their own."

Luke and Joe looked at each other. The idea had not occurred to them.

Luke said, "I've always understood that the Morse code was universal."

"Must be," said Joe. "SOS is the same in every language, 'ent it?"

"Well, I'll give my mind to it," said Mr. Stokes. He had scribbled the letters down on a piece of paper. "I'll sleep on it. That's the way I've found to get the answer to a tough problem."

This seemed so sensible to Luke and Joe that they made for their own beds.

Next morning Joe said, "It's my night for the crow's nest. Not much chance of Zepps, not if the major is going to this piss-up at the Guildhall. I've got a lot of social drinking to do, so I may make straight for Gilkicker without coming back here."

"Mr. Hobhouse, is it?"

"No. It's Sergeant Twomey."

Luke knew better than to ask questions. The name rang a faint bell. After some thought he tentatively placed Twomey as a member of the Docks Police who dropped in occasionally to the Royal Duke when coming off duty. He could not conceive what use he was going to be to Joe, who could not have known him for much more than a week. But where the cultivation of friends was concerned, Joe was a fast worker.

Deciding that exercise might clear his brain, he set out on a twenty-mile circular walk. Up Portsea Island to Wymering, across the top of the harbor to Fareham, then south through Gosport and home by the ferry. He arrived pleasantly tired and hungry but without any flash of inspiration. He decided that he ought to wait up for Joe, and scrambled back into wakefulness when he heard the front door opening and closing.

Joe had had the blank evening he had expected. The major had come back surprisingly early, by taxi, from the Guildhall and had gone straight to bed.

"What I thought," said Joe, "was that the Docks people must have a proper record of the visits of the Zepps—particularly as they seemed to cross right over them. Well, Sergeant Twomey—a good chap, I met him through Hobhouse—says that a friend of his—of Twomey's, I mean—in the Docks office, can probably give him the dope and not ask too many questions. O.K.?"

"Very O.K.," said Luke, "and better than anything I can report." He told Joe about the walk he had taken.

"I'm not sure that exercise is the answer," said Joe. "I get my best ideas when I'm sitting still."

After breakfast on Friday morning Mr. Hobhouse arrived with the promised photograph. It was a good, clear, front-view picture of the major coming down the steps of the Royal Duke. Luke paid the fifteen pounds he had been authorized to draw from his imprest account and thanked the photographer, who seemed to have something on his mind.

He said, "I was talking to the wife about that photograph and I can't conceal from you that it worried her. What she said didn't worry me as much as it worried her, but I said I'd raise it with you."

"Raise it, then," said Luke.

"It's just that she wants to know, when this picture's produced in court, will you have to say who took it?"

Luke, fortunately remembering Joe's cover story, said, "That will depend on the barrister."

"The barrister?"

"The attorney who's appearing for the lady in the case. You won't expect me to mention names."

"No names," agreed Mr. Hobhouse. "That's just it. I wouldn't want *my* name to appear at all."

"We'll do what we can to keep you out of it," said Luke.

When Mr. Hobhouse, faintly comforted by this assurance, had departed, Joe said, "Anyway, we've got the picture. He can't take that back. What's the next step?"

"I've been thinking about that," said Luke. "It should be sent to America and shown to Judge Rosenberg as soon as possible. Best if I take it personally to Daines. He'll have some way of getting it across."

"Send a destroyer," said Joe.

"If he thinks it's important, he might even do that. If I'm late back, could you stand in for me tonight? I'll do your stint on Saturday."

"Fair enough," said Joe.

* * *

Captain Vernon Kell had been running MO5 since its formation in 1909. In five years it had grown from tiny beginnings into a competent professional outfit in close liaison with Scotland Yard and the Special Branch. On that day in July 1914 Kell was one of the busiest men in England, and it was late on that Friday evening before he could spare the time to listen to Luke.

Luke had been interviewed by him when he joined MO5 and had been fascinated by the contrast between his heavy military mustache and the pince-nez glasses insecurely attached to the bridge of his formidable nose. On the present occasion he confined himself to the shortest possible recital of facts. He had the impression that every word he spoke was being recorded, analyzed, and locked into place in the memory of the man behind the telephone-cluttered desk.

When he had finished, Kell asked, "In short, you think that Major Richards is *der Richt Kannonier?*"

"I think he might be."

"Would you undertake to prove it in a court of law?"

"No, sir."

Kell thought about it. The boy could have said, "In all the circumstances it might not be easy . . ." Instead he had said, "No, sir." Kell approved of that. He said, "I can give you one piece of information: We've had reports—secondhand, but reliable, I think—that the man you call the bosun has been talking to sailors in the port. Any scraps of information he picked up would, no doubt, be passed on to the major. What we have to find out, and be able to prove convincingly, is just how he passes this information on to the Germans."

It occurred to Luke that he knew the means that were used without being able to unscramble the method.

Caution warned him not to talk about it. Wait until he had the whole thing in his hands.

Kell said, "An investigation into dock procedures is almost certain to involve you in discussion with the authorities. In which case you may find this chit useful." He had been scribbling as he spoke. "I take it you're not going back to Portsmouth tonight?"

"No, sir," said Hubert. "He'll be staying at my place."

"Right." He looked at what he had written, which seemed to amuse him. "I'll have this typed out and signed by someone more important than me. You can pick it up tomorrow morning."

Taking this as a dismissal, Luke and Hubert removed themselves. Before they were out of the room one of the telephones on the desk had started to ring.

Luke got back to Portsmouth soon after midday and found Joe finishing his lunch. He reported a negative watch.

"Not that I expected anything. Wednesday and Saturday.

Those are visiting days, aren't they? You'll get something tonight."

"Hopefully, yes," said Luke. How are you getting on with Sergeant Twomey?"

"I've got a heavy date with him and some of his mates this evening. While you're snoozing on the top of that tree I shall be drinking for England against some of the top performers in Portsmouth."

"Would you see if you can get the sergeant around here sometime tomorrow? Lay it on a bit. Say it's important. Be mysterious."

"No problem, being a Sunday. Shouldn't have any duty. Probably be glad to come."

As Luke settled into the treetop perch that evening—Joe had added another piece of board as a backing, and it was comfortable enough to relax on—he was thinking about Major Richards. If he was a German spy he was formidably equipped, with his mastery of English, his uncheckable military background and his easy social manner, which had assured him of entry into the upper levels of the Portsmouth hierarchy, while the bosun insinuated himself at a lower level. Between them they must be completely knowledgeable about what ships were in port, valuable information indeed in the event of war.

Moreover, it was information that the Zeppelin would be unable to obtain by merely overflying the port, which was sometimes covered by mist, while some of the ships—the submarines in particular—would be out of sight.

What followed from this was so clear that Luke was surprised he had not spotted it at once.

"Hold it. Here they come. Dead on time, the bastards."

The light in the annex started to flicker and Luke started to write, noting the difference between longs and shorts:

—/—/—/UUU/UUU/UUU/UU/UU/U/U/U/U/U/U/ U/U

Not unlike last time, but with small differences. And if he had cracked the code, small differences were to be expected.

A light went on in the major's study. The major, who seemed pleased with himself, poured himself a stiff whiskey and water, took out two packs of cards, and laid out a complicated game of patience.

Luke watched for an hour. The patience didn't seem to be coming out. Finally the major swept the cards off the table, got up, turned out the lights in the study and the hall, and disappeared from view.

On previous occasions Luke would have felt obliged to continue his watch in case the major appeared on the annex roof. Not now. Now he knew better.

When he got home, Joe was still out. Drinking for England. Luke grinned at the thought. It was a duty that Joe would not find irksome. Luke took himself off to bed and slept dreamlessly.

Next morning Joe reported success. Sergeant Twomey had, somewhat reluctantly, accepted the invitation. He would be with them around midday for the promised drink.

"Make it a good one," said Joe. "These dockies absorb drink like a camel getting ready to cross the Sahara."

But Sergeant Twomey was a surprise. Luke had expected a cheerful, rum-budded boozer. In fact he turned out to be a leather-faced Cornishman on whom drink had no apparent effect. When Luke casually introduced Kell's name into the conversation, Twomey said, dryly, "Aye, I've heard of him. A lot of people claim to know him. Mostly I've found they were lying."

"Since I work for him," said Luke coldly, "I don't have to *claim* acquaintance with him."

This produced a long pause. Then Twomey asked, "You mean you work for one of those secret service outfits up in London?"

"Yes."

"And does the other bloke—the one called Joe—who's always filling us up with drink—?"

"Yes."

"He might have saved himself time and trouble. Everyone knows there's some dirty business going on around the docks. What with those Zepps flying over twice a week and that mid-European turd who can't talk proper English crawling around asking us questions, which we've now given up answering. Well, if there's anything I can tell you that's going to help, fire ahead. What is it you want to know?"

"It's very simple: There must be someone in the port organization whose duty it is to keep a daily record of what ships are there."

"An attendance state, you mean."

"That sort of thing."

"It's not part of my job, but I have to see it from time to time."

"Fine. Now, this is important. In this document, *just how are the ships classified?"*

Twomey thought about this. Then he said, "As long as I've been there they've always been dealt with in the same way. Under six heads, 'A' to 'F.' 'A' is battleships, all types, dreadnoughts, *Queen Elizabeths,* the lot."

"Right," said Luke. "I've got that. That's class 'A.' "

" 'B' is battle cruisers. 'C' is armored cruisers. 'D' is destroyers. 'E' is submarines. 'F' is what you might call the tail. Corvettes, minelayers, sub chasers. Is that the sort of information you're after?"

"That," said Luke gratefully, "is exactly what I wanted and hardly dared hope I'd get. Just one final point before we get down to serious drinking: Could you forget, totally, that we've had this conversation?"

"I've forgotten it already," said Sergeant Twomey, smiling for the first time.

Luke had thought it wiser to deal with the sergeant on his own, but as soon as he had absorbed the promised drinks and taken himself off, he called Joe in and they sat down with paper and pencil to put the final pieces together.

Luke said, "If we're going to make six groups out of the longs and shorts, the only way would be to have three groups of each."

"One long, two longs, three longs. One short, two shorts, three shorts."

"Something like that. Now look at the second message. It starts with three longs. Maybe the first message did, too, but I wasn't quick enough to get it. Since we've got to begin somewhere, let's assume that three longs stand for a group 'A' ship."

"That'd fit all right," said Joe, who was beginning to sound excited. "They've had a dreadnought in dock for some time. The brain boxes on Whale Island are calibrating its guns."

"So, if we follow the classification Twomey gave us, the next group, two longs, would be battle cruisers, and one long would be armored cruisers. Then, I think, three shorts for destroyers, two shorts for submarines, and one short for the smaller craft. The snag is that the shorts could just as easily be the other way around."

"Couldn't be," said Joe. "Are you telling me they've got *eight* destroyers in port? Where've they hidden 'em? No, I think we've got it right now."

"I think we have, and the really important thing is to examine the *changes* in the second message. If we're reading the code correctly, it means that since Wednesday one destroyer has come in and two subs have gone out, and if we find that that's what's actually happened, it'll be a real clincher."

Joe was grinning. He said, "What was it they used to put when you wrapped up one of them problems in geometry? Not that I ever did, but I expect you did."

Luke cast his mind back to the sun-bedabbled classroom in a Norfolk village school.

Joe said, "What it meant in plain English was, 'Bob's your uncle.' But they wouldn't put anything common like that. It was something in Latin."

"What they put," said Luke slowly, "was *'Quod erat demonstrandum.'* "

It had the sound of a great Amen.

6

Luke had not had a lot of experience contacting important people on the telephone, but he knew that it needed patience and persistence. That Monday, when he telephoned the dock office and asked to speak to Admiral Manfred, he expected to encounter, successively, a telephonist, a secretary, a junior aide, a more senior officer, and maybe, if he got that far, the port captain.

What happened was quite different.

The operator asked his name and put him through to a female, who spoke crisply. She repeated his name, to make sure she had it right, and asked him to hold the line. After not more than two minutes, she was back. She said, "If you will come at once, the admiral will see you."

When he reached the port headquarters building the sentry had evidently been told to expect him and handed him straight over to a messenger, who led him through a series of highly polished corridors and entered, without knocking, past a door marked "Private."

This gave onto an anteroom where two naval officers were sitting: one a middle-aged commander, the other a very young sublieutenant. Their desks were so placed that no one could enter through the door beyond without squeezing past them.

The messenger looked at the older man, who nodded without speaking. Then the messenger knocked at the inner door, opened it without waiting for an answer, and held it for Luke.

Feeling by this time slightly dazed, Luke went in. He had

seen Admiral Manfred once before and recognized his smooth helmet of white hair and his red, salt-cured face. He remained seated behind his desk, but motioned to Luke to take the chair opposite him and said, speaking fairly brusquely, "If, Mr. Pagan, you've been wondering why you've been accorded a red-carpet reception, I should explain that I've had a letter about you from Commander Hall." A pause; then, "It seems he found you on a rock."

This made Luke laugh, and the atmosphere seemed a little easier.

"He told me that you were attached to a security outfit he knew all about and that, in certain circumstances, we might find you useful. In short, that if you had anything to tell me, I was to listen to you. I'm listening."

Luke compressed his activities of the last ten days into as short and comprehensible a form as he could manage. When he had finished, he added, "Of course, I've been keeping my own people in the picture."

"Who do you report to?"

"Directly, to a man called Daines. Through him to Captain Kell."

"Vernon Kell?"

"Yes."

"Which means MO5."

"Right, sir."

The admiral thought about this for a long moment while he chivvied a bronze monkey around the desk with the blunt end of a pencil. Then he said, "Since you've asked to see me urgently, do I gather that something has happened since your last report went in?"

"Yes, sir, it has. On Saturday night, for the first time, I got a full message. I've written them both down. The incomplete one I told you about and the full one, so you can see the differences."

The admiral pinned the papers down with the brass monkey and inspected them one after the other. Then he said, "Yes. I see. By the code—as you've explained it—this would mean that a destroyer has come in since Wednesday and two submarines have gone out."

"That's as I read it, sir."

The admiral pressed his bell twice and said to the sublieutenant who came in, "Go down to the dock office, Philip, and get me copies of the daily state for the past seven days."

The sublieutenant looked as though he was going to salute, thought better of it, and departed.

"You can't imagine," said the admiral, "how long it took me to convince that young man that he was in an office and not on a ship. I had to threaten to fine him half a crown every time he said 'Aye aye, sir.' Now, to business. Do you know anything about Zeppelins?"

"Not a lot, sir."

"Nor do I. But I do know that you don't steer them like a motorcar. They don't jink about. You set them on a certain course and it takes them time and effort to change onto another one. For the past two months those Zeppelins have been appearing, twice a week and directly overhead. How do you suppose they got there?"

"Set a compass course," said Luke, hoping to sound intelligent.

"Unlikely. Being the size and shape they are, they're very responsive to wind forces. If they come from the Holstein peninsula, where most of them are built and launched, they could steer southwest by keeping the northern coast of Europe in sight, but sooner or later they'd have to launch out across the Channel. That's where they could easily be diverted by wind pressure from a set course. Coming at night, what they'd really need is a light to aim at. So, next question. Where is the major's bedroom?"

"I've never been able to see his light go on when he goes to bed, so I assume it's at the back of the house."

"Quite. Then his bedroom window, or perhaps the attic above it, would be an ideal place to set a guiding light, which will be even more necessary to them after this evening, since I intend to enforce a blackout in the port. A practice measure, you understand. Should war be declared, it will, of course, become permanent."

"Won't the government impose a general blackout?"

"Interference with the liberty of the subject. Tricky matter.

Maybe in a few months' time, when they've had a few bombs dropped on them. Until then Major Richards is free to turn on any lights he chooses."

"I think," said Luke, "that if that's the truth, the sooner he's behind bars the better."

"I agree," said the admiral. "But there are difficulties."

Before he could say what they were, he was interrupted by the return of the sublieutenant with a small clip of papers. The admiral said, "Thank you, Philip," and he departed, as slowly as he dared. Clearly he longed to find out what was going on.

When the door was shut the admiral, flicking through the papers, said, "Thursday, one destroyer came in. It and the other two will be going out as soon as repairs are finished. They're all wanted for the grand fleet review next Saturday. Two submarines left on Friday, for the Mediterranean. Very well. I agree. That appears to confirm your reading. But we've still got to be careful. Major Richards has got a lot of good friends in Portsmouth. Also he's a Freemason. And the chairman of the Portsmouth Magistrates, Sir John Smedley, is not only a Mason but also a leading one, a provincial grand master, or something of the sort, so you see—"

"Yes," said Luke sadly. "I see very well."

"It doesn't mean that we do nothing. It means that we go carefully. Step at a time. You've convinced me, but if I'm going to convince other people—people who matter—I shall need a little more. At the moment we've got one broken message and one complete one. Give me a second complete one—which you ought to get on Wednesday night—and if it tallies with actual ship movements, I reckon we shall have enough to convince anyone who isn't so shortsighted that he can't see the end of his own nose."

"Right," said Luke.

"One other thing: I take it you realize that if you're going to take any actual steps against Major Richards you'll need to have the police on your side."

"I do realize that, sir. MO5 has no powers of arrest. In London we use the Special Branch. Here it will mean the Portsmouth Police."

"Which means Superintendent Marcher."

Luke guessed from the tone of the admiral's voice that he had some doubts about the reaction of the superintendent.

"He's not a bad chap," said the admiral. "His wife's a holy terror. A broadside from her and you'll be swimming for the shore. It's a pity the chief constable's away, in Canada on some official jaunt. He's a good chap. As it is, we'll have to deal with Marcher, and he'll be inclined to follow Sir John Smedley's lead."

Luke said, "Maybe a chit I got from Captain Kell would help." He showed it to the admiral, who read it and said, "Might help. Might just put his back up." Seeing the look on Luke's face, he added, "Don't think I'm just making difficulties. I'm trying to be realistic. If I followed my own inclinations I'd report our suspicions to the police at once, and ask them to pull Richards in. You know what Nelson said to his captains: 'Lose not an hour.' "

As the admiral said this, he was looking out the window. His office was so placed that he had a view across the dockyard, out to the port entrance dominated by the bulk of the cathedral and beyond it to where the ruffled waters of Spithead glinted under the warm July sun.

Luke wondered what else he was seeing.

A German fleet, storming in, directed by Zeppelins, guarded by submarines. *Über and unter.* Was this to be Germany's unheralded stroke that would win the war when it had hardly begun?

The admiral turned away abruptly from the window and said, "Let me see your Wednesday night results as soon as possible. Meanwhile, I suggest that you and your friend keep out of the public eye."

When he passed on this advice to Joe at breakfast next morning, Joe said, "Lie low for two days? No objections here. Doing nothing is something I'm good at."

This was the cue for the arrival of a flustered Mrs. Stokes. She said, "I didn't want to let him in, but I couldn't stop him."

"Who?"

"It's the police."

"Mustn't keep the law waiting," said Luke.

It was a red-haired man, with the stripes of a sergeant on his arm, who advanced on Luke and Joe as they finished their breakfast coffee. They put down their cups and looked at him. He drew a deep breath and said, "I am Sergeant Beatty, of the Portsmouth Borough Police. Is one of you Joseph Narrabone?"

"Yes," said Luke. "One of us is. Might we see your warrant card?"

The sergeant said, "A policeman, on duty, in uniform, does not carry a warrant card."

"All right," said Luke cheerfully. "We'll take you on trust."

"Then you are—"

"No. This is Joe Narrabone. And now that we know one another, perhaps you'll tell us what it's all about."

"My instructions are to request Joseph Narrabone to accompany me to the police station. A complaint has been made concerning him that Inspector Tillotson considers serious enough to justify further inquiries being made."

"A complaint about *what?*" said Luke.

The sergeant looked upset. He had his brief and was unwilling to go outside it. In the end, he said, "About a photograph."

Luke and Joe looked at each other with dawning comprehension.

Luke said, "Would it be a Mr. Hobhouse who made the complaint? Mrs. Hobhouse, for a dollar."

The sergeant, on firmer ground now, said, "I am not entitled to reveal—"

"All right," said Luke. "We understand all that. But if the matter is what I think it is, we are both implicated and will be delighted to give the inspector any information he wishes. But we are *not* going to be marched off as though we were already under arrest. Is that clear?"

"I'm not sure—"

"If the inspector wishes to question us, he can have us. On our terms. You go ahead. We'll come along in ten minutes, when we've finished our coffee."

The sergeant seemed unhappy. Luke, who had once been a policeman himself, was certain that he had no authority to take them into custody. Finally, realizing that refusal would get him nowhere, the sergeant took himself off.

"Wanted to march us there in chains, diddun he?" said Joe. "What a turn-up."

"Just the sort of turn-up we didn't want," said Luke.

Inspector Tillotson looked like an intelligent dog—a cross-breed, perhaps, thought Joe, who had owned one once who had been too intelligent and had been shot by a keeper.

He looked up as the two of them were shown into his office and barked out, "The complaint I'm investigating only concerns one of you. I don't need the other."

Luke, who had determined to be as conciliatory as possible, said, "I understand, sir, that the complaint is about the taking of a photograph. Since the only photograph with which we have been concerned is one we jointly induced Mr. Hobhouse to take, it seemed to me that we should both be in a position to help you."

The inspector, who was ostentatiously making notes on the pad in front of him, said, "Repeat that, please. You induced Mr. Hobhouse to take this photograph." He seemed pleased by the admission.

"Quite correct," said Luke.

When he had made a further careful note the inspector leaned back, paused to give weight to his words, and said, "Under the bylaws of this borough a person is only authorized to take photographs of members of the public and offer the print for sale to the person photographed if he is licensed to do so. On the present occasion Mr. Hobhouse was not doing this. He was taking a surreptitious photograph on your instructions for the purpose of a lawsuit. In other words, you were procuring and abetting a breach of the bylaws. Have you anything to say?"

Said his piece nicely, thought Joe.

Luke said, "Yes, sir. First, the photograph was not taken for use in legal process."

This was so unexpected that the inspector forgot to make a

note. Instead he said, "Then you were lying to Mr. Hobhouse?"

"Yes, sir."

"That makes the offense more deliberate and less excusable."

"Yes, sir."

This repeated agreement seemed to baffle the inspector, who was driven to asking the question he had hoped to keep in reserve. He said, "Then perhaps you would explain why you needed the photograph and why you obtained it in such an irresponsible and unauthorized manner."

"That's not quite correct, sir. I did have authority to act in the matter." He took out the envelope that contained the letter Kell had given him. "But under the conditions on which that authority was given me, I am only permitted to show it to a chief officer of police. In the case of Portsmouth that would be your chief constable, but I understand he's abroad. It will therefore have to be shown—if I am forced to produce it—to Superintendent Marcher and to no one else."

That's thrown him, thought Joe. He was a student of human nature, and the expression on Tillotson's face delighted him. It was a mixture of curiosity, hesitation, and disbelief.

Before Tillotson had time to say anything Luke added, "I am, at least, entitled to tell you one thing, on the understanding that it goes no further. I am acting in this matter with the concurrence of the head of the port, Admiral Manfred."

By this time most of the disbelief had evaporated, but the curiosity had redoubled. Tillotson was eyeing the envelope hungrily. He said, "If I undertook to say nothing about it—"

"The fact that you had seen it might put you in a very awkward position in the future."

Knockout, thought Joe.

"Very well. The superintendent is free at the moment. I'll ask him to see you."

Luke wondered, afterward, exactly what he did say to Marcher, who received him with cold politeness. Luke watched him read the letter, which he himself had read so many times that he knew it by heart.

To whom it may concern:
The bearer of this letter, Mr. Pagan, is engaged on security work of national importance. He is authorized to show the letter only to chief officers of police in any place in which he may be operating. Such chief officer is requested to afford him any assistance that may be in his power and to refer any questions he may have, under confidential cover, to Captain Vernon Kell, at the Home Office, Whitehall.
From the commissioner of the Metropolitan Police.
[Signed with a bold slash in black ink] Basil Thomson.

Marcher pushed the letter back to Luke as though glad to get rid of it and looked at him for a long moment. His thoughts could be spelled out from the expression on his face. Could he really be expected to cooperate with a boy half his age? A boy who, at first encounter, had looked guileless to the point of naïveté? Could he possibly be a member of one of those recently formed and secretive outfits he had managed so far, thank goodness, to steer clear of?

Despairing of reading the riddle, he confined himself to saying, "Are you allowed to explain to me what you're up to? For instance, what's this story Inspector Tillotson has been telling me about a photograph?"

"I'm afraid we had to break the local rules there, sir. We needed a good photograph of this man to send to America. It should have arrived there by now."

Before Marcher could ask the question that was on his lips, Luke added, "I wonder if you recall one of the guests at that drinks party at the Royal Duke."

"A party," said Marcher with the suspicion of a smile, "at which you were handing around drinks."

"I was indeed, sir. Do you recollect one of the Americans his friends called 'Sam'?"

"Certainly. It was Supreme Court Justice Samuel Rosenberg."

"Well, he's one of the people in America whom the photograph will be shown to. I have a feeling he will recognize it."

Marcher could not be headed off. The question had to be asked.

He said, "And who, exactly, is the subject of this photograph?"

"He is the present tenant of Fairford Manor House on Gilkicker Point."

"Then you are talking about Major Richards?"

"A man who passes under that name, yes, sir."

"When Tillotson told me, I could hardly credit it. Surely no suspicion of—of, well, anything discreditable can possibly attach to him. What is he being suspected of?"

"There is a supposition, but no absolutely conclusive proof, that he may be signaling information to the two Zeppelins that have been overflying the port so regularly. I don't want to say any more than this at the moment."

"Quite so," said Marcher. "But—"

"Conclusive proof of our suspicions may be available within the next few days. At the moment, we cannot call on you for assistance. When—and if—we do, you may have to move very quickly. Meanwhile, I'm sure I needn't impress on you that what I have told you is to go no farther."

"Quite so," said Marcher unhappily.

* * *

On Tuesday night Luke was in the crow's nest. As he anticipated, he saw neither Zeppelins nor lights.

On Wednesday night, before climbing into observation, Joe had moved around to a point from which he could see the back of the house. Sure enough, a beacon light was shining from a top-story window. Zeppelins ahoy, he thought, and had hardly reached his perch before they were overhead.

He had pencil and paper ready, but hours of practice had made him so skilled in reading the code that he was able to note the changes on sight.

In preparation for the grand review that weekend, the port was emptying steadily. The capital ship had gone, along with both of the battle cruisers and two of the three destroyers. The only new arrival was an armored cruiser. The submarine and the small craft were unchanged.

Joe saw no point in hanging around, and was back with his report before eleven o'clock. The admiral had given them his home telephone number, and Luke was resolved that he should have the results at once. Unfortunately, there was no telephone in the house and the nearest phone booth he knew of was in the main line station, which was half a mile away.

"Five minutes if I run," he thought. "Lose not an hour."

He caught the admiral at the point of going to bed and poured out the news. Every time he paused, the admiral grunted. The grunts became increasingly menacing as he went along. At the end he said, "I'll check up your results first thing tomorrow. If I find that they're right—as I've little doubt I shall—I will have a word with the superintendent."

7

It was clear to the admiral, as soon as he was shown in, that Superintendent Marcher was nervous. This was not necessarily a good thing. Sometimes it was easier to deal with a man who was full of self-confidence. The sparks might fly, but results could be obtained. A nervous man was apt to roll himself up in a ball, like a hedgehog.

Considering this, the admiral decided to start with a plain statement of his case.

He said, "You will have noted the regular visits we have been having lately from Zeppelins L3 and L4."

Marcher admitted, cautiously, that he had noted them.

"Then you will have seen that they came in on a bearing of roughly 315 degrees, in all types of weather, and arrived directly over the port. Our Zeppelin experts have assured me that this was a remarkable feat. So remarkable as to be incredible, unless they had some help at this end."

"I must take your word for it," said Marcher politely.

"Once we appreciated this, we started looking for possible helpers. There was one obvious candidate. A mid-European, name thought to be Schneider. Known to all as 'the bosun.' He has been hanging around the port for the past two or three months. Lately the port employees have gotten so tired of having drinks pressed on them and being asked questions that they've decided to send him to Coventry. He's no longer allowed into the port, and the more responsible men say no to his drinks. I doubt whether he can get much useful information now."

The superintendent had been listening to this with interest

and, it seemed to the admiral, with a measure of relief. He said, "Splendid. So you're no longer worried by him."

"Not directly, no. But we still had to locate the light the Zeppelins were steering on. We considered a number of possibilities. For instance, the ships in the port were often careless about lights. Not last night. The blackout I imposed was, I assure you, complete. But still they arrived. Dead on target, as though drawn there by a string, so we had to consider other possibilities."

"The golf club, do you think?" said Marcher. He had a map open. "They are probably careless about lights."

"We considered the possibility. But the clubhouse is what gunners call 'hull down' to the sea. Meaning that the slope of the land conceals it. Once the Zepps were over it they could see the lights, but they wouldn't serve as guides from a distance. No. Once we thought it out we saw that there was just the one obvious place: the house on Gilkicker Point. For some time now"—he was choosing his words carefully—"our people have had the house under observation. On three occasions, when the Zeppelins arrived, they were able to read a message that was being sent to them by turning the light on and off in the old observatory room at the back."

He explained the code to an increasingly worried Marcher, who said, "Are you telling me that this man Schneider not only guided the Zeppelins to the port but also told them what ships were in it?"

The admiral said, "I think it's highly unlikely that he did any such thing without the full concurrence and help of his employer."

Marcher had seen this coming. Before dealing with it, he moved to safer ground. He said, "You mentioned your 'people.' Might I know who they are?"

"Yes. They are two agents of MO5."

"Pagan and Narrabone?"

"You know them?"

"I have had dealings with Pagan on two occasions. On the first—about two weeks ago—my men were sent out on a wild-goose chase looking for him, when he was, in fact, at a drunken party. On the second occasion he was, as he admitted, in breach of our bylaws."

"Over securing a photograph."

"Yes."

"And you think these two facts—I can give you the true story behind the first one if you wish—justify you in ignoring the evidence that the man who calls himself Richards is, in fact, a German agent."

Marcher hesitated. Then, "All I can say, Admiral, is that I would regard evidence from such a source with some hesitation."

The admiral drew a deep breath and let it out again slowly. He said, "I am responsible for the port and everything in it. If their Zeppelin fleet, guided to it, succeeded in destroying the port they would have struck a deadly blow at our navy. It's not only the ships in it, though we should be sorry to lose them, but in addition the dock contains the most fully equipped and up-to-date workshops in the country. They are geared to repair, reequip, and turn around a ship damaged in action—even badly damaged—within forty-eight hours. If war started with a naval clash in the Channel or the North Sea, the loss of this facility could tip the balance. It might mean the loss of the war at sea, which, in my book, means the loss of the war itself."

The admiral had spoken with such evident sincerity that Marcher's defenses were beginning to crumble. He started to say, "I'd like to . . ." and then held back, with an almost physical effort, the words that would have completed the sentence.

Finally he said, "On the evidence so far, I should need the backing of the chief constable or the chairman of the bench before taking action against Major Richards. Sir John's in London at the moment. I'll have a word with him tomorrow morning."

"And the chief constable?"

"Colonel McCann will be back in the second week of August."

"We must hope," said the admiral, "that the Germans will be considerate enough to wait that long."

* * *

"I left it at that," he told Luke on the following morning, "because I could see that I wasn't going to get any farther unless I could produce some new evidence. I'm not at all hopeful that Smedley will come down on our side, though he might sanction some preliminary inquiries, or a watch being kept on Richards. That would be better than nothing."

It was as well for his peace of mind that he was not in the superintendent's office at that moment.

Sir John had returned from London a happy man. On the previous evening, at his club, the dinner table conversation had turned to the question of German spies. Although it was not a services club, its members being mostly lawyers and businessmen, their views seemed to Sir John to be sound. This may have been because they coincided with his own.

"It's up to people like us," he had pronounced, looking around the table, "to see that the man in the street doesn't lose his head. There are a lot of alarmists about—most of them should be behind bars—but as long as this misbegotten government leaves them at liberty, we can at least do everything in our power to see that they aren't listened to."

This sentiment had met with vociferous approval.

When, therefore, he heard the superintendent's suggestion that some preliminary steps—he refrained from saying exactly what steps—should be taken against Major Richards, his first reaction was indignation. His next was to laugh.

"My dear Marcher," he said, "I'm surprised at you. You've been listening to fairy stories. Soon you'll be saying that you believe in Father Christmas. Two idiotic young men tell you they have been seeing lights, and you propose to rush off and make a fool of yourself."

"I wasn't going to suggest anything drastic—"

"If that young man—what's his name?—Pagan was as drunk as he was when your men wasted their time searching the gutters for him, the lights he saw were probably inside his own head."

"Admiral Manfred seemed to think—"

"Yes. I always thought him a sound man, and I'm sorry that

he's been deluded by these two charlatans. Tell me again about this 'chit' that he showed you."

"You can see it for yourself. He left me a copy."

When Sir John had read it, he laughed even more heartily. "If you think," he said, "that the head of the Metropolitan Police has the right to issue orders—framed as requests—to the head of a borough force, a totally independent body, then he needs a few lessons in police organization. But I'm sure you weren't impressed by this piece of impudence."

Marcher, who had been impressed, said, "I read it only as a request for assistance from one branch of the force to another."

"Then let me tell you this." Sir John leaned forward. "If you were so misguided as to order the detention of Major Richards, the result would be an action in the High Court for false imprisonment, coupled with an action for damages for libel, or slander, or both. And if I was called on to give evidence I would be forced to tell the court what I've told you—that Major Richards is a man of unimpeachable character. He showed me—in confidence, of course—letters from highly placed friends in America, one of whom described him as 'the best type of thinking patriot.' No, no. My advice to you is to await the return of Colonel McCann. He will view the matter rationally, I'm sure."

"And in any event," thought the unhappy superintendent, "the responsibility will be his, not mine."

* * *

Since he had promised the admiral that he would speak to Sir John, the superintendent felt bound to telephone him and tell him what had transpired. It was a carefully edited version of the truth.

"In short," said the admiral, "he won't play."

"I'm afraid that's so."

"The fact that he's chairman of the bench doesn't give him any authority over you."

"No direct authority, no, but—"

"But you would find it difficult to go against his advice.

Even though you were convinced that delay might be dangerous."

Marcher, who was at heart an honest man, said, "I suppose that's right. And I'm trying not to let myself be influenced by the fact that Major Richards is a personal friend of Smedley's."

"I'm glad about that. It means that you are keeping an open mind. If proof was forthcoming that the major had committed a criminal offense, that would, I imagine, change your views."

"It would be a different situation and I would be prepared to view the matter differently."

"I hope so," said the admiral. But he said it to himself after hanging up.

Luke, also, was on the telephone.

If a climax was coming, it seemed to him that communications would be important and he had approached an old lady who ran a candy store on the next street. Succumbing to his youth and charm, she had surrendered to him the telephone newly installed at the back of her shop, and had unwillingly accepted payment in advance.

"Use it when you like," she said. "I'm getting so deaf I can't understand more than half of what people say on it. You're young, I expect you'll manage." Luke had thanked her warmly.

He had just concluded a long call to Hubert Daines, bringing him up to date. Daines said, "We're none of us happy about the position. So much so, that Kell is sending me down to lend a hand. Not that he mistrusts you; in fact, he was unusually complimentary about what you've been doing. But the sky looks uncommonly black, and if the storm breaks over Portsmouth, two heads may be better than one. Can you fix me with a room somewhere?"

"No problem. Plenty of rooms at the Royal Duke. When are you coming?"

"I can't get away before the weekend, but should be with you on Monday. Meanwhile, Kell's view is that we've got to wait for an answer from America."

When Joe heard this he said, "If we've got a couple of days to kill, why don't we go out and get good and properly stinking. That'll take up one day, and the hangover will fill up the other."

* * *

That same evening Sir John Smedley gave his wife a modified version of what he had said to the superintendent. His wife was embroidering the cover for a fire stool. She did not always listen patiently to her husband, but on this occasion she allowed him to hold the floor. When he had finished, she threaded her needle with wool and said, "Well, I hope you know what you're doing."

Sir John, who went his own way in most matters, had, nonetheless, a considerable respect for his wife. He found the comment disturbing. He said, "What do you mean?"

"I mean what I say. I hope you've thought carefully about your own position in the matter."

"Yes. I may say I've thought very carefully."

"That's all right, then," said his wife and dug her needle firmly into the canvas. "Why do they choose three different green wools that are almost indistinguishable?"

Sir John was unable to help her on this point.

* * *

It had been a long day. And when Luke, expecting neither Zeppelins nor lights, had climbed into observation, he found it difficult to keep his eyes open. He was sitting so still that an owl alighted on the bough beside him, looked at him gravely for nearly a minute, and said what sounded like "You, too."

"Me, too," agreed Luke. "Sitting here waiting for something to happen, and if it does happen, without a blind idea what to do about it."

As sometimes happened when he was sleepy, his mind started out on a track of its own. It started from the blackout in the port. From where he sat he could see that it was totally effective. Trust naval discipline for that. But there were plenty of lights in the houses around the port. Might it have been possible to impose a blackout on them, too? He thought not. It would have raised immediate protests. Liberty of the subject. The parrot cry of democracy.

From which stemmed further uncomfortable thoughts.

How could a country that was organized like England—tier upon tier of interlocking authorities, often at enmity with each other, parliamentary bodies, county councils, local councils, intelligence organizations, police authorities—hope to defeat a monolithic and despotic authority? As part of his education when he joined MO5, Kell had given him a number of books about Germany to study and think about. If a national blackout had been considered necessary there, the order would have come from the army and would have been obeyed. And anyone found behaving like Major Richards would have been put up against a wall and shot.

Luke felt so depressed that he abandoned his watch and went straight home. Joe was out. He went to bed, but slept so badly that he was awake, well after midnight, when he heard him come in.

On Saturday, surprisingly, the Zeppelins did not appear. Sunday night was blank, too. A quiet weekend in Portsmouth. Not so elsewhere.

The terms of the Austrian ultimatum were so arrogant and threatening that the British ministers had to forgo their normal weekend leave, and the Cabinet was in session all day. It was on that Saturday evening that Churchill wrote to his wife, "The Austrian note to Serbia is the most insolent document of its kind ever dispatched. Europe is trembling on the verge of a general war."

He was the only Cabinet minister whom the prospect of war seemed to exhilarate rather than alarm.

On Monday morning Hubert Daines, arriving in Portsmouth, brought with him a letter from Kell.

"He doesn't often write letters to his subordinates," said Daines. "I fancy he had two reasons for doing it on this occasion: to sort out the legal position in his own mind, and to have it on record in case he has to defend his department."

The letter began:

I have spoken to the attorney general. He said that to proceed against Major Richards we must have a definite, provable criminal offense.

Showing a light from his attic and playing with the lights in his annex doesn't amount to such. In default of a criminal charge we have to rely on the Official Secrets Acts. The earlier one, of 1889, is a broken reed, since you have to prove intention. A man is caught taking photographs of warships. So what? His granddaughter back home wants them for her album. The Act of 1911 is an improvement. Under it, if a man is behaving suspiciously, going into places he ought not to, it's up to him to prove that he wasn't *doing it to help a potential enemy. Much better. But there's a snag: No prosecution can take place without the fiat of the attorney general, and he told me quite flatly that in this particular case he was not prepared to issue it. Not without proof of a criminal act.*

"Back where we bloody started," said Luke.

"Might he be provoked into assaulting one of the golfers?" asked Joe.

"Too clever for that," said Hubert.

What maddened Luke was the feeling that time was running out.

He turned over in his mind a number of possibilities. Suppose that the next time the major came to the Royal Duke, Joe jostled him and shouted that his pocket had been picked, having stealthily dropped his own wallet into the major's pocket.

He was saved from such wild ideas by a startling message that Kell had arrived in Portsmouth, was staying with a Colonel Upjohn, and would be calling on them.

Joe said, "I've heard about him. People call him a colonel, but he's really a lootenant. Or is it the other way around?"

Luke managed to work this out. Colonel Upjohn was the lord lieutenant of the county. It was unclear what *he* had to do with the matter. It seemed to add one further complication to a matter that was complicated enough already, for God's sake.

When Kell arrived that afternoon, he brought one piece of good news with him. He said, "I've heard from Judge Rosenberg. He wrote to me personally. He said, 'I have no hesitation in identifying the subject of your photograph as a man who passed here under the name of Edward Palmer, from Canada. His papers, under that name, were apparently in order. We became suspicious of him, since he seemed to spend his time addressing shop-floor meetings, provoking anti-British feeling, and running an anticapitalist line. But it was only after he had left that we were able to obtain any accurate particulars about him. It seems that his real name is Erich Krieger and that he works directly under Gustav Steinhauer, the German intelligence chief. Incidentally, he has never held commissioned rank in any armed service. Had we known all this in time, we could have charged him, either with traveling on false documents or—a very serious offense in this country and in yours, too, I think—of professing to hold a military rank to which he was not entitled. I hope this will give you the leverage you require. I must add that, on the one occasion on which I met him in England, he maneuvered himself so skillfully that I only caught a fleeting glimpse of his face. I wish I had had the courage of my convictions and told you then what I tell you now'."

"Why, that's grand," said Luke. "Terrific. Now we've got him."

"It takes us halfway there," said Kell.

"But surely, sir, his papers—in the name of Richards—they must be forgeries. And calling himself a major—"

"If we had all the time in the world," said Kell, and Luke could have sworn he saw him looking at his watch as he said it, "then I'd agree with you. Unfortunately, time isn't on our side. Colonel Upjohn gave me a very enlightening character sketch of the two men involved. Sir John Smedley is obstinate, narrow-minded, and proud. Marcher is a tolerably honest policeman, but a weak man. If he was on his own, in the face of this new evidence, I'm sure that he would act promptly and in the way we want. As it is, he will almost certainly find some excuse for postponing action until the chief constable returns. In a way, this simplifies the problem. Smedley must be dealt with."

And that was all he would say.

After he had left them, Joe said, with unconcealed relish, "I've always understood that when it comes to the point, these secret service people don't bother too much about rules and regulations. They go straight for the throat. I wonder what he's planning to do. One of those phony 'accidents,' do you think? Or straight assassination?"

"Something subtler than that, I hope," said Luke.

This was on Tuesday, July 21. The Third Fleet, having completed its test mobilization, had been given a warning order to disperse, an order that Churchill countermanded before it could be put into effect.

On Wednesday night Luke was in observation. He saw the Zeppelins, three of them this time, swinging up out of the night sky to the east. Though the guiding light in the attic was shining steadily, the fact that the port was dark seemed to disconcert them. After approaching the port they had, unusually, swung away to the north, on a course that took them over the built-up area of Southsea.

Luke watched them with hatred and impotence. He had not bothered to read the message that was flashed up at them. However many messages he read, no one was going to do a blind thing about it. Feeble, feeble, feeble. They were going to lose the war. They deserved to lose it. The fleet would be destroyed before the army could reach the Continent. Serve them all right if we became a vassal state and the Kaiser took over Buckingham Palace and Windsor Castle.

Having arrived at this point, he managed to laugh at himself, climbed down, went home, and went to bed.

* * *

On the following morning, having some trouble with the cook, Lady Smedley, who was usually down first, arrived at the breakfast table ten minutes after her husband. He did not seem to have eaten anything. A helping of bacon and eggs was congealing on his plate, and he was staring out of the window.

When she said, "What's happened?" he pushed the letter across. It was headed, "The Office of the Lord Lieutenant of the County" and said, after a customary civility, "It is, as I am sure you know, one of my duties as lord lieutenant to recommend, from time to time, to the Magistrates Courts Committee, the names of nominees as lay magistrates. More rarely, and unhappily, it is equally my duty to recommend to the committee that a magistrate be removed. Recent circumstances have forced me, in the national interest, to take such a step. I have, therefore, to inform you that as from the date of this letter, the Lord Chancellor's Office has withdrawn your commission as a justice of the peace. Please acknowledge."

Quick as a dagger or a bullet and more effective.

Nine wives out of ten would have said, "I did warn you." Joan Smedley was the tenth. Seeing the look on her husband's face, she said, "I think the best course will be to tell everyone that you have resigned, because you have found it impossible to work with Superintendent Marcher."

When Kell called on Marcher and gave him the news, the superintendent, once he had gotten over the shock, expressed his willingness to cooperate in every way. Kell said, "I have to go back to London. I've been away too long already. My assistant, Hubert Daines, will give you any help you need, but I am quite happy to leave it in your hands. I suggest you adhere, for now, to the specific matters mentioned in Judge Rosenberg's letter, which I'll leave with you. There will, of course, be other charges later."

The preparations for taking Major Richards were worked out between Marcher and Daines, Luke keeping tactfully in the background. Late on Thursday evening six policemen, led by the superintendent, closed on Fairford Manor. The drive gate was chained, but anticipating this they had brought the necessary apparatus with them. Once in the garden, Marcher spread his men in a semicircle to cover all ways in and out of the house, advanced with one sergeant, and rang the doorbell.

When this produced no answer, he executed a brisk rat-tat on the doorknob. After a further delay, footsteps were heard approaching, and the door was opened by a middle-aged woman wearing a dressing gown. She seemed reassured by the sight of the police uniforms, switched on the porch light, removed the chain, and opened the door.

"I'm sorry to disturb you, ma'am," said Marcher, "but we've come for a word with Major Richards."

"That I'm afraid you can't have," said the lady. "Tuesday

evening it was. Him and that creature of his, both left. Good riddance, if you ask me."

"Left? How, when, where to?"

"As I understand it, they caught that German-American boat. The one that calls in here every week."

"For God's sake," said Luke, when he heard the news. "Why couldn't we stop him?"

"Can't blame the police," said Daines. "Their papers, as far as anyone knew, were in order. He seems to have made an open booking for both of them some weeks ago. It was one he could use whenever the Norddeutscher boat from New York called in here on its way to Bremen. He must have gotten wind of the order cancelling the dispersal of the Third Fleet and seen the red light. He was too quick for us, that's all."

"Or we were too slow for him," said Luke bitterly.

* * *

That was not quite the close of the Portsmouth episode.

By the end of August, England had been at war with Germany for three weeks. Luke and Joe were in London, having taken rooms alongside Hubert's flat. The first casualty lists from the retreat and the engagement at Le Cateau were starting to come in, and there was no room in the papers for civilian casualties. It was from Bob, in Southampton, that Luke got the news.

He said that the Zeppelins, on their first raid, seemed to have missed the port altogether, perhaps on account of its efficient blackout. They swung inland and dropped most of their bombs on the Southsea suburb. "You will be very sorry to hear," he added, "that Stokes, his wife, and their daughter, Doll, were all killed."

So, with sad finality, did the curtain come down on Act One.

PART TWO

London

8

"If," said Luke to himself, "I suffered from claustrophobia, I'd be mad or dead by now."

Lately he had found himself indulging in one-sided conversation, because there was no one else to talk to. Joe had established himself in his old stamping ground, the dockland area of Southeast London. He said that he was cultivating a new contact. Whether this contact wore trousers or skirts had not been revealed.

"It was very thoughtful of Kell," he continued, trying to be fair, "to bring me into his own office. A compliment, no doubt. And I appreciate that with the rapid growth of his staff—one man and a boy, didn't he tell us, when he started?—now fourteen full-time operatives. Most of them stolen from other departments and with numbers growing almost daily—of course, he's short of space. I appreciate that. But he might have found me something a bit bigger. It's not much more than a cupboard, really."

This was unfair. There was room in it for a table and a chair. Just. There were also rows of shelves along two of the walls. These, like the table, were overflowing with documents. Some were in folders of the dark blue color that Kell affected, possibly to demonstrate his connection with the Metropolitan Police. Some held in elastic bands, some loose. Luke had read all of them at least once; some more than once.

They dealt, among other things, with the cases of the seven spies that Kell had located and the Special Branch had arrested for him in the period between the formation of MO5 in 1909 and the outbreak of war: Lieutenant Siegfried Helm; Dr. Max Schultz; Heinrich Grosse (a.k.a. Grant); Armgaard Karl Graves; George Parrott, the only Englishman; Wilhelm Klauer (a.k.a. Clare); and Frederick Adolphus Schroeder (a.k.a. Gould). But this clutch of birds brought down by his guns faded into insignificance beside the coup that had finally established the reputation of MO5: the rounding up, on the day that war was declared, of almost the whole of the German spy network then in Great Britain.

This had been the result of identifying the barber, Karl Gustav Ernst, whose shop on Caledonian Road had been the post office for letters to and from agents in Great Britain. Armed with a list of their names and addresses, Kell had sat in his office—had slept there during the first few days of August—surrounded by telephones and waiting for the striking of H hour, when a coded message could go out to his allies in the police stations concerned.

"Very good work," Luke agreed. "In a way, too good. It's rather as though someone had invited you to go out fishing and had then calmly announced that there would be no fish available, because he had caught them all!"

Luke laughed bitterly.

"Glad to find you in good spirits," said Kell, who had made a typically silent entry. "Because I've got a job for you and it's one that really needs your attention. You can forget all this stuff"—with a wave of his hand he abolished about a hundred pounds of documents—"though I'm glad you've read it. It'll give you a good idea of what we've been up to. But that's all past. What matters now is not the past, but the future."

This sounded so promising that Luke hitched his chair forward. Kell squatted on the edge of the table. Kell was a man of moods, and Luke could tell, from his voice and from the expression on his face, that this time it was his expansive mood, a mood in which he could do anything, from sending you to interrogate the archbishop of Canterbury to dispatching you, at a moment's notice, to the Outer Hebrides.

He said, "No doubt you realize that if our lords and masters had moved just a little bit quicker, and you had had Aunt

Dora with you in Portsmouth, that dangerous ruffian Krieger would not have succeeded in slipping away. Mind you, though I accuse them of being slow, when they gave their minds to it they did hustle the old lady past the winning post in the course of a single afternoon."

Noting, and enjoying, the look of bewilderment on Luke's face, he said, "I expect you've been too busy to keep an eye on the proceedings of the Mother of Parliaments. I was referring to the Defense of the Realm Act, a very useful *omnium gatherum* that has sharpened our claws wonderfully. If someone is found now on a forbidden site, or behaving suspiciously anywhere, he has got to prove that he wasn't indulging in espionage or similar activities. The boot's on the other foot. You could have had Krieger inside in a brace of shakes, Smedley or no Smedley. In fact, under the new act, you could probably have clapped old Smedley under hatches for lending help and assistance to the enemy."

"A lovely thought," said Luke. He was still feeling bitter.

"No good crying over spilled milk. What we've got to do now is work out what our old friend Steinhauer in Berlin will think up next. Something artful and unpleasant, no doubt. Particularly now that he's got Krieger alongside, prompting him."

Luke said, "He can't be best pleased at having lost the whole of his organization in this country."

"*If* it is the whole of it."

"I noticed that you had twenty-two names on your list and pulled in only twenty-one. Is that the missing one?"

"No, no! Number twenty-two was Willie Kay. A totally insignificant character. He happened to be in Berlin when the net closed. No doubt he was running some errand for one of the bigger boys, so he slipped through, and good luck to him. No. The missing man—the one we *must* lay hands on—is *der Vetter.*"

"The cousin? Whose cousin?"

"No one's in particular. That's just a name he's been given. He crops up more than once in the correspondence we intercepted. And there's one thing we noticed about him: Whenever his bosses wanted to get in touch with him—to send him instructions, or ask for information—the message was always a verbal one. Someone, not specified, was to speak to *der Vetter* and ask him to write to "the usual address." So, not very helpful. But since those careful precautions were taken, *in his case only,* it's easy to see that he was an important man. We'd heard whispers about him before. They said that he'd been here a long time. Five or ten years, maybe more."

"If he's buried as deeply as that," said Luke, "he won't be easy to dig out."

"*Nil desperandum.* You unearthed the *richt Kannonier* for us. I'm sure you'll find him."

"Can you give me any idea? Any lead?"

"Certainly." Kell removed the files from the table by sweeping them onto the floor. He replaced them with a long, double sheet of paper he had brought in with him. "His name's on this list—somewhere."

Luke gazed in horror at the double column of names that occupied, as he saw when he turned them over, both sides of the four large pages.

"What are these people?" he said, trying to keep the note of apprehension out of his voice.

"It's part of my national register of aliens, which I compiled by circularizing all chief constables, asking them for the names of anyone they thought might be likely to indulge in espionage or other conduct harmful to the state. They responded enthusiastically."

"They did indeed," said Luke. He was starting to count.

"Don't bother," said Kell. "I can tell you the answer. This is the return for London and the home counties. You'll find 949 names on it."

"What are those letters against the names?"

Kell's half smile showed for a moment. He said, "That's our private classification system. You may find it helpful. Let's start at the top. 'AA' stands for 'absolutely Anglicized.' They're the real white-headed boys. 'A' is simply 'Anglicized.' Nothing known for or against them. 'AB' is 'Anglo-Boche.' I'd call them doubtful. The next lot are 'B,' which means simply 'Boche.' Not necessarily German, you understand, but

definitely hostile. A lot of Irishmen in that category. Then, at the bottom of the ladder, 'BB.'

"Bad Boche. Bloody Boche. Boche bastards?"

"Whatever you fancy. Definitely, maybe actively, hostile. Just not enough evidence to run them in."

"Even if they can't be charged, couldn't they be interned?"

"In the end, I imagine, public pressure—or public panic—may drive us to intern the lot, 'AA' to 'BB' inclusive. But me, I'd rather let them run, so that we can find out what they're up to—*if* any of them are up to anything, which, in the majority of cases, I'm beginning to doubt. After all, we've got fairly wide powers now. We make them all register with the police. And we can keep them out of certain prohibited areas. Anything else worrying you?"

"What's worrying me," said Luke, "is that this man *Vetter* could be in any of those categories. In fact, most likely, in the top one, 'AA,' if he's buried himself so deeply."

"Very possibly," said Kell blandly. "So get out your little spade and start digging. Oh, yes—one other thing: Your friend Joe"—it was one of Kell's most endearing habits that he referred to everyone, however junior, by their given name—"has proposed a new recruit for us. A man called Ben Lefroy. Do you know him?"

"I know about him. He was security officer to the Portsmouth and Southampton Chemical Works. It was well below his ceiling, so he chucked it and came up to London."

"Below his ceiling?"

"He had a degree in chemistry and physics from London University. He got the sort of research job he wanted, at the Silvertown Chemical Works. Joe had kept in touch with him and found him lodgings—with a spare room, when needed, for himself. He seems"—Luke tried to suppress his resentment—"to spend most of his time down there nowadays."

Kell looked at him thoughtfully for a few moments and then said, "All right. I'll have a word with Ben. Now—is there anything you want to help you in your *Vetter* hunt?"

Luke said, "I did think of one thing. You mentioned the letters you intercepted. Were copies of them made before they were sent on?"

"They were photographed if they seemed important. In other cases, only the relevant information—names, addresses, and so on—were extracted."

"Could you give me authority to take over the copies that were made?"

"Certainly. They're already complaining at Mount Pleasant that the work is swamping them. They'll be glad to get rid of the old stuff. I'll give you a letter to the head man, and you can go along and collect them. You'd better take two large suitcases with you."

* * *

Since arriving in London, Luke had seen very little of Hubert Daines. This, he thought, was a pity, since, in the absence of Joe, he would have welcomed the presence of his second most long-standing friend.

After all, but for Daines he would never have joined MO5 and would have continued his career as a policeman—possibly been an inspector by now, with an inspector's position and responsibilities. But in time of war the police had become, somehow, demoted. They were no longer in the front line. Their main job, equipped as they were with the armory of Dora, seemed to be the harrying of suspicious people of foreign ancestry, most of whom were turning out to be excellent and patriotic citizens.

Luke's thoughts were running on these lines when Hubert walked in. Though he was brown and fit, there was a look in his eyes that Luke had not seen before. A look of controlled apprehension. He wondered what he had been up to. He might find out, by asking questions, but he had been long enough in the Intelligence Police to realize that the asking of questions was not encouraged. The doctrine of "need to know" was already firmly established.

Spotting the two suitcases, Hubert said, "Typical. You've wangled yourself a holiday."

"Not so," said Luke. "The call of duty." He explained the object of his forthcoming visit to Mount Pleasant.

"Watch your step," said Hubert, "or you may find yourself run in."

"I can think of no reason why I should be arrested."

"People have stopped following the dictates of reason. The population of this island, with a few honorable exceptions, thinks of only one thing: discovering and arresting German spies. Their neighbors, casual acquaintances, someone behaving suspiciously in the street—"

"Surely they also think a bit about what's going on in France."

"Nothing's going on in France. It was exciting enough for the first month or two. Now the armies have dug themselves in and spend their time spitting at each other. The real action and excitement's all here. It's like Boy Scouts rubbing two sticks together. Rub a spy and a counterspy against each other and you'll soon see the sparks fly."

"I haven't seen much action myself," said Luke sadly. "Have you?"

It was clear from his tan that Hubert had been leading an open-air life.

"I've been in Ireland. Action? Certainly not. Ireland's a nice, quiet place. The people have reverted to their prewar occupations: hunting, fishing, and drinking Guinness."

"An example which you were glad to follow."

"The particular sport I was engaged in could rather have been described as stalking. I was looking for a man called Daryl Forbes, who is either a very dangerous man, or a remarkably stupid one, who opens his mouth too wide. Before the war he was a regular contributor to the *Irish Citizen*, under the name of Loki."

"I think I read some of his efforts."

"Then you'll remember that they were remarkably unfriendly to the British. Urging soldiers and sailors to exercise their rights. In any other country he'd have been put away for treason long ago. As soon as war was declared, he decamped. Heading for Ireland. I was sent after him, to see what he was up to."

"And did you?"

"No," said Daines sadly. "He was altogether too quick and too slippery for me. Then I heard, on the best authority, that he'd come back to England. So I came back, too. I'm on my way to Fleet Street to see whether the *Irish Citizen* can give me a lead."

"Journalists are famous for *not* giving away their sources. Irish ones are probably more close-mouthed than most."

* * *

As he jolted over the streets of London in a horse bus on his way to Mount Pleasant, Luke was thinking about what Hubert had said, not about the Irish. They were a chronic affliction. In one way the coming of war had been an advantage: It had put the insoluble problems of Ulster into cold storage. No. It was what he had said about spy mania.

It was true. It was a fantasy, a hobby, a preoccupation that had grown steadily since the first days of the war. It had been blown to fever heat by the sinking of the cruisers *Aboukir, Cressy,* and *Hogue* by a German U-boat. *Things like that did not happen to the Royal Navy.* Clearly, then, there had been treachery. The whereabouts of the cruisers had been betrayed. By messages, flashed or tapped out—somehow.

Kell, who had many contacts in the Admiralty, had expounded the sad truth to Luke. "The sea was so rough that the destroyer escort had been left behind. It was thought that if it was too rough for destroyers it would be too rough for submarines. It wasn't."

But this was not the sort of explanation that the British public found satisfactory. A farmer in Norfolk had been arrested for sending signals out to sea by means of the sails of his windmill. Ha! That was more like it.

When he reached Mount Pleasant Luke found two overworked members of MO5 in a room that had been allotted to them. Until six months before, both had been schoolmasters. They had been selected for this particular job because they were German-speakers. The table behind which they worked was piled with letters, some opened, some still unopened. Luke picked up a check that had fallen on the floor. It was received apathetically. He wondered whether it would go back into the right envelope.

"Before the war," said the older of the two men, "I gather

it wasn't so bad. About half a dozen letters to be dealt with each day."

"Opened carefully," said the younger man, "and carefully resealed. Now apparently it doesn't matter so much if these people know their mail is being examined. So what do they expect to get out of it?"

His complaint seemed well founded. When the examination had been concealed, the authors might have been indiscreet. Not now, surely?

He found photocopies of the prewar letters in one of the cupboards, crammed the copies into his suitcases, and departed. When he reported what he had seen, Kell said, "I realize they're shorthanded. If I had a single man to spare I'd send him along. And yes, I do think it's worth keeping up the inspection, even if they can't be as careful as their predecessors were. The Germans think themselves cleverer than any other of God's people. Sooner or later they'll slip up." He added, "Anyway, they've got a cushy job compared with their friends in the trenches."

Kell's two sons were still too young for military service, but, like all fathers, he could see the dread day approaching.

* * *

Hubert Daines, meanwhile, was heading for Fleet Street.

The *Irish Citizen* had an office on Stag Court, one of the tiny alleyways that run north from the street. It was not an impressive outfit. The girl in the front office suspended her midday meal of sandwiches, examined Hubert's card, and rang a bell. This produced a fat man in shirtsleeves who introduced himself as Mr. Portlach, the editor. He asked, in tones that were not truculent but were not noticeably friendly, what he might be able to do to help Mr. Daines.

"In private, if you please," said Hubert.

Mr. Portlach now examined the card more carefully and said, "Ah. I see. Well, come into my office. We can be quite private there." He offered Hubert a chair and perched on the edge of the desk, swinging one leg, while Hubert explained what he wanted.

"Always happy to help the authorities," said Mr. Portlach,

massaging one of his many chins with his forefinger. "Only thing is, I'm afraid we shan't be a lot of use to you. You've got to realize that we're only what you might call the British terminal. All the real work's done in Dublin. We get the finished product and try to sell it."

"And this man Forbes—or Loki, as he calls himself—does he never put in an appearance?"

"Here?" said the editor. His surprise seemed quite genuine. "What would he come here for? He deals with our head office and he's paid by them."

Hubert said, "I suppose you realize that if the stuff Forbes is churning out is treasonable—and it's beginning to look very like it—then you could get into trouble, bad trouble, for reproducing it and selling it here."

The idea did not seem to worry the editor a lot. He said, "I suppose that's what you might call an occupational hazard. If the government wants to make a whipping boy out of me, because I'm handy and the real villain isn't available to be whipped, that's up to them. In this job, we often have to suffer for the sins of others."

"No one wants you to suffer," said Hubert. "And I can make a suggestion that will get you out of any trouble. All we want is to locate Forbes. He's said to be in this country. Very likely he'll be in touch with you. Might write, or telephone, or even turn up in person. If you contact us quickly—the number on that card's manned day and night—and if that enables us to lay our hands on Forbes, we'll count it quittance for anything else."

"Well, that's a fair offer," said Mr. Portlach. "I do have certain contacts. I could sound them out."

When Hubert emerged from the half light of Stag Court into the afternoon sunshine of Fleet Street, the man who had been propping up the wall at the entrance to the court levered himself into an upright position, crossed the street, and spoke to a man on the pavement. This man swung off behind Hubert. He made no effort to catch up, but seemed content to keep him under observation.

* * *

From Joe's point of view one of the pleasures of plowing a lonely furrow was that it enabled him to regulate his own timetable. He liked to get up late, and go to bed when the day had no more interest or excitement to offer. He was finishing his breakfast as the clock of St. Stephen, Silvertown, was striking eleven. At this moment, to his surprise, the door opened and Ben Lefroy came in. He had heard Ben leave the lodging they shared a full four hours before and had turned over comfortably in bed. He had not expected him back until the evening.

"Wassup?" he said. "No. Don't tell me. Let me guess. You've mixed something with something it didn't ought to have been mixed with and it's blown up."

"Nothing like that."

"Then why are you looking like a billy goat in stays?"

"At the works—last night—we had a burglary."

That didn't seem to Joe to be anything to get worked up about. He said, "Fear not. You'll get it all back from the insurance. Probably make a profit."

Ben wasn't really listening to him. He said, "It was horrible. Three men broke in—or rather, they didn't have to break in—seems they'd gotten hold of a door key from somewhere. Fred Hardistone was the only man on duty. They'd managed to disconnect the alarms before he could set them off. They tied him to a chair and soaked his trousers in gasoline. One of them held a light near his trousers and said, "Do you give us the strongroom key, or do we toast your legs?"

"And I've no doubt," said Joe, "that he did just what I should have done: handed over the key in double-quick time. What do you keep in the strongroom, anyway?"

"Chemicals and drugs mostly."

"So that's it. They were looking for drugs."

"Wrong. When we checked this morning we found that all they had taken was sulfuric acid. Three large carboys of it."

"Strange choice," said Joe, putting the last piece of buttered toast into his mouth and speaking through it. "What next?"

"Before they left, they lashed Fred up tighter, gagged him with cotton waste and sticking plaster, and departed. When our people found him in the morning he was nine parts dead."

"And couldn't describe the men."

"Not even when he'd recovered. They were masked, you see. He thought that two of them were Irish."

"Sounds like the Killarney Boys," said Joe. "We shall have to do something about them. They're getting out of hand. However, cheer up. I've got some news for you." He pushed a letter across the table. "The old man wants to talk to you. Luke has been telling him about you. He thinks you might be useful to his department. Just what you might call a temporary attachment, so pull yourself together, boyo, and try to look less like a depressed poultice-basher and more like an alert and courageous secret service man. More like me."

* * *

A week later, at four o'clock on a dismal November afternoon, Hubert Daines, picking up the office telephone, recognized the voice of Mr. Portlach.

"I've got some news for you. Secondhand, but reliable, I think. The man you're looking for has been at 3 Glenister Road, E16, for the past day or so. My informant added that if you want to catch him you'd better get a move on. He'll soon be on his way back to Ireland. I expect he feels safer there."

Hubert thanked Mr. Portlach warmly and then sat, for a few minutes, thinking about it.

Kell's instructions had been clear:

"If Forbes is in this country, locate him, and keep him under observation. Hopefully, he'll lead us to men we want more than him. If he tries to leave the country, we'll have to think again. Until then, let him run."

Keep him under observation? For God's sake! It would need a team of three or four men to do that. Maybe Special Branch would lend a hand. The immediate thing was to confirm Forbes's whereabouts.

He located Glenister Road on the map. It was one of a tangle of little lanes north of a small patch of green called Royal Victoria Gardens that ran straight down to the river. It was within a stone's throw of North Woolwich Station, the terminus for passengers using the free ferry.

When Hubert got there, it turned out to be as uninspiring a piece of London as it had looked on the map. The few passengers who had come with him as far as the station struck off for the pier, where the ferry was waiting.

There was little suggestion of royalty about Victoria Gardens, a dank patch of turf intersected by gravel paths. Hubert knew from the map that if he circled it, going north, then turning to the east, he would find the street he wanted.

The third one along was Glenister Road. There were no streetlamps. It sloped downhill into a pit of darkness. The door of No. 3, the second house on the right, was open. Striking a match, he tried to read the names on the board inside the hall. All of them seemed to be married ladies. Two on the ground floor, right and left of an unsafe-looking staircase; two more on the first floor, two more above that. Six respectable females. How was he going to find out which of them housed the man he wanted? It was while he was wondering about this that he realized he was not alone. Three men had come into the hall behind him. Before he could make a move to save himself, a savage blow on the back of his neck had shut out sight and sound.

As Hubert slipped to the floor his assailants proceeded, with the speed and silence of men who knew what they were about, with the job of disposing of him. They had brought with them a sack of the type used by Smithfield porters. One end had been weighted with oddments of iron and stone. When Hubert had been inserted into it, the open end was knotted securely. Two of the men picked it up and carried it the ten yards up the lane to the road. The third man had gone ahead to prospect for trouble. By the time they arrived he had the garden gate open, and when he gave them the all clear, they staggered across the road, carrying the sack.

At the far end of the garden, past the railing, at the foot of a sloping embankment, the Thames ran by, in full flood. Here they halted. What was holding them up was the ferry, which still waited by the pier. Until it was out of sight across the river they dared not complete the job they had in hand.

It was at this moment that a new character came onto the scene. He was a man near six and a half feet high and broad in proportion. They recognized him at once: Big Tim Brady, a character feared and respected on the waterside from Southwark Steps to Barking Creek.

He strolled up, stared at the men and at the sack on the ground, and said, "Phwat goes on here?"

There was a moment of silence before the leader of the men said, "Private business, Tim. Nothing to do with you."

"Anything at all what happens around here," said Big Tim, "is something to do with me. And why? Because I'm the big man in these parts. People have learned to treat me with respect. They've learned the hard way."

The man who had spoken before said, in tones that demonstrated that fury was beginning to overcome discretion, "Like I told you. This is our business, no one else's." Out of the corner of his eye he could see that the ferry was moving off. "If you want the truth of the matter, we're disposing of a load of rubbish."

As he spoke, the other two men were edging slowly around behind Tim. None of them was as big as he, but if he was looking for a fight, at those odds he should have it.

Tim seemed unperturbed by this development. He seemed to be listening. "Rubbish, is it?" he said. At that moment the sack had given a convulsive jerk. "Lively rubbish, ain't it?"

Having heard the police patrol advancing along the path, he added, in the confident tones of a law-abiding citizen, "What you've got in that sack will interest the boys in blue, I don't doubt."

By the time the policemen arrived, Tim was busy unknotting the cord around the neck of the sack.

9

Luke was attempting to solve a problem.

On the outbreak of war, the barber Karl Ernst had been arrested, charged with espionage activities, and sentenced to seven years' imprisonment. His twenty-one correspondents had been luckier. They had merely been interned. It was copies of letters to them that Luke had collected from Mount Pleasant. He had noted in particular the nine cases in which the recipient had been entrusted with verbal messages for *der Vetter*.

All nine had been questioned about this. They had replied, with suspicious unanimity, that since they neither knew who *der Vetter* was, nor where he was to be found, they had been unable to comply with the instruction, which they assumed had been given to them in error. Their interrogators had not believed a word of this. But since the use of judicial torture had been abandoned in England in 1640—a great mistake, Kell thought—there was nothing further they could do.

Luke was now approaching the problem as a mixture of geography and geometry.

The plan he was drawing covered the part of London that lay south of the river, between Greenwich Park on the west and Erith Marshes on the east. He had marked on it, with a small cross in red, the addresses of those nine correspondents. From them he had drawn a tentative series of lines inward. He had hoped that he could arrange them so they met at a single point, the center of his imaginary circle.

Kell, who had come in and was looking over his shoulder,

said, "Your problem can never be solved by a Euclidean construction. The points you have drawn do *not* fall on the circumference of a circle. Therefore you cannot ascertain its center."

Luke said, "All I had really hoped for was that it would give us an approximate location for *der Vetter*. What it has demonstrated, so far, is that he is, or was, south of the river and in the district SE7, SE18, or SE2."

"Allow me to correct you," said Kell. "Had your lines miraculously converged at a single point it would not have demonstrated even that."

Luke could see that he was in his schoolmasterly mood that morning. This was almost as dangerous as the friendly and expansive mood. When he donned the mortarboard, if you wanted to avoid having your knuckles rapped, your observations had to be sensible and your replies well considered.

"Knowing the elaborate precautions that our quarry has taken to dig himself in out of sight, can you suppose that he would have disclosed his whereabouts to *nine* of his subordinates? Unthinkable. Clearly the center of your imaginary circle—if it could have been plotted—would have located a single, trusted go-between who could pass messages on to him—either directly, or maybe through a further intermediary. We are dealing with very careful, experienced people. Not with a troop of Boy Scouts."

Luke agreed that they were not dealing with Boy Scouts.

"Allow me, then, to turn to more immediate matters. First, what news of Hubert?"

"I saw him yesterday. He has a very stiff neck, but is recovering. He hopes to be out of the hospital by the end of the week."

"He is lucky to be alive," said Kell coldly. "Going off on his own like that, without asking for help, or even leaving a message. It was the act of a novice, a tiro."

"I did wonder whether we could proceed against that editor, Mr. Portlach. After all, he led Hubert into the trap."

"Quite impossible. All he has to say is that he was given the address, in confidence, by a third party and that he had no idea it would lead to trouble."

(Not many marks for that answer.)

"What we should be devoting our attention to is something different: the *reason* for the attack, the *motive* behind it. Well?"

"It did occur to me that Hubert might have been seen visiting the *Irish Citizen*. It could have been deduced that he was making inquiries about Forbes."

"It's possible." (Five out of ten.) "I understand that the local police head—I've forgotten his name . . ."

"Chief Inspector Horniman, at the Albert Dock Station."

"Of course. I'd forgotten. You served in that division. You know Horniman?"

"Yes, sir. A very sound man."

"Then we must treat his opinions with respect. He says that, in his view, both the attack on Daines *and* the robbery at the Chemical Works were probably—he won't go farther than probably—the work of the same people. A collection of Irish scallywags from the docks who call themselves the boys from Killarney. Did you ever encounter them?"

"Not directly. I knew about them. Not really an organized gang. A pack of dangerous louts who would get together to do different jobs—"

"If they were dangerous, why were they not apprehended?"

"The difficulty was getting evidence. They usually wore masks. And on other occasions, when they might have been seen, people were afraid to testify against them."

"So. A reign of terror," said Kell, pursing his lips and looking more like a schoolmaster than ever. "Then let us move on to the next question. The really important one."

He paused. Luke wondered what appalling poser was coming.

"These Killarney boys, as you call them. Being Irishmen, no doubt they are ardent proponents of home rule."

Luke felt that it was safe to nod.

"We know that their fellow countrymen are preparing for an open strike. Rebellion against the hated English oppressors. Very well. The reason for the Irish helping our German enemies can be divined. They look to them for help in their own struggles. Help in the shape of arms and explosives. Maybe a few junior officers and NCOs from the German Army would increase their power of resistance. You agree?"

"I'd have said that what they'd be mainly looking for would be a shipment of arms. Irishmen prefer to fight their own battles."

"You may be right. The distinction is not important. The basic fact is that the Irish have a very adequate *motive* for supporting the Germans. *But what do the Germans look to get from the Irish?* Trouble in Ireland? That was going to come, whether they helped or not. No, no. They are realists. They must have bargained for some more immediate and valuable return for their efforts."

"Could they not be counting on a similar sort of trouble here?"

"Absolutely impossible. Out of the question. Think what you're saying." (Nought out of ten. Black mark.) "Do you suppose that, with this country on a war footing, any form of public protest or disturbance would be tolerated? Marches and demonstrations? Nonsense. They would simply be identifying themselves as traitors and placing their own heads on the block. Think again."

Being unable to think of an appropriate answer, Luke said nothing.

"Are you so busy," said Kell impatiently, "that you get no chance to read the papers? The responsible ones? *The Times?*"

"Yes, sir. When I can."

"Then no doubt you will remember the leading article that appeared last week. Clearly an inspired effort, based on facts culled from the high command in France. Indeed, it could not have been expressed more clearly if it had been signed by General French himself."

"Yes, sir. I think I did see it."

"Then you will have noted that now that trench warfare has started, the vital matter, to both sides, is the supply of shells—Heavy-caliber shells in particular. At the start of the war we were a full year behind the Germans and are now making desperate efforts to catch up. If those supplies could be interrupted, or seriously diminished, it might cost us the loss of the battle that is now impending. Even the loss of the war. That would be something worth paying for, wouldn't it?"

"Yes," said Luke. He had not thought of it before, but as Kell spelled it out, it seemed obvious.

"Then tell me this: Where are our main reserves of ammunition and explosives held?"

Luke was about to blot his copybook still further by admitting that he didn't know, when Kell answered his own question. He placed one thick finger in the middle of Luke's map.

"The Royal Arsenal. Go and see them. Ask for Colonel Lemanoir. He'll be expecting you. Satisfy yourself that he appreciates the danger of an attack. What precautions are they taking? Are they alive to the desperate importance of protecting the stocks they hold and the further stocks they are beginning to accumulate?"

* * *

Colonel Lemanoir, with his poker-back stance and his vast blond mustache looked, at first sight, like a typical stupid guardsman. The impression did not last. Luke soon discovered that he was intelligent, agreeable, and cooperative. Much of his approval stemmed, no doubt, from the fact that the colonel knew and approved of Vernon Kell.

"First met him when he was with the Staffordshires in India. Remarkable chap. Knew four foreign languages already. Soon picked up Hindi and Urdu. Brilliant. Can't have gotten his brains from his father, who was a stupid soldier like me. Must have inherited them from his mother. She was the daughter of a Polish count, did you know?"

"No, sir. He doesn't talk much about himself."

The colonel chuckled. "Know what he called himself? A Yarmouth bloater. Just because he happened to have been born when his parents were in Yarmouth on holiday. A pretty inappropriate nickname. Now, let's run through it again. You can really divide us into three sections. First there's the school and the office block—which we're sitting in at the moment. Behind us is the Military Store Department. That's the big building you can see through the window and where we keep the bulk of our ammunition. We do all our testing there, too. Then, to the east, as far as the canal, that's what we call the Gun Yard. We keep the pieces under cover—you can just see the roofs of the sheds."

"I suppose it wouldn't be difficult to cross the canal?"

"Easy. When the tide's out you could paddle across it. That's one of the reasons why my predecessor had that wall put up."

It was a handsome brick wall, circling the Military Store Department and the office block, nine feet high, with a walkway inside it, six feet up.

"Our guards use that. They can patrol the whole wall. Only two doors in it. One in front. That's the one you came through. The other is at the back, opposite the shipping pier. Both locked at night, of course."

Luke thought that the arrangements looked efficient and pretty well marauderproof. Helped by a batten of overhead lights, the guards on the inner footway would be able to detect the slightest movement inside the enclosure.

"Do you keep all your explosives in the Military Store Department?"

"We used to. Can't house it all now. We're turning out new stuff every day. So what we did, we built three or four magazines along the riverbank, between the canal entrance and Dundee Dock. Would you care to see them?"

"I'd like to do that," said Luke.

They walked across the Gun Yard, crossed the canal by a wooden bridge, and went from there along a path that led out onto the marsh.

The new magazines were squat, concrete boxes, sunk to half their depth in the ground, each with a double steel door in front.

"It's dispersal that's the real safety factor," said the colonel. "To get at the whole of our stock, an intruder would have to break open a number of different boxes."

"Under observation from the wall."

"Exactly. As long as those lights were functioning, I wouldn't fancy his chances of opening even one of them. What the devil was that?"

It had come from the direction of the Isle of Sheppey, a rumbling explosion.

Luke and the colonel stood, staring at each other, as the echoes died away across the marshes.

10

"Fate," said "Blinker" Hall, "has played many dirty tricks on me in my life, but none dirtier than this one. I was appointed, last week, to head the Naval Intelligence Division—as I'm sure you heard." Kell nodded. "Two days ago I took up my duties, to be presented, immediately, with one of the most important matters that has faced the division since the outbreak of war."

Kell made a noise that expressed surprise and sympathy. He said, "We all heard the explosion, but as there was an immediate blackout on all news—quite rightly, I'm sure—we've heard no details."

"Yesterday afternoon H.M.S. *Bulwark,* one of our fifteen-thousand-ton battleships, at anchor off Sheerness, was almost completely destroyed by an internal explosion, which also killed five hundred men and officers."

"And no one has any idea what caused it?"

"Plenty of ideas. No proof. The story we're putting about—which is the truth, as far as we know it—is that there was an explosion in the ship's magazine."

"And as to what caused it . . . ?"

"A dozen explanations, from an electrical fault in the hoisting gear to a stoker dropping a lighted cigarette."

"And you don't believe any of them. You think it was deliberate sabotage."

"It's a horrible thought. But, yes, that's what I do think. And I'm devoid of ideas as to how to prove it. That's why I've come to you, to pick your brains."

Kell said, "Well, I can give you a few preliminary ideas, most of which you'll have thought of already. If the explosion was organized by a German agent, he must have suborned at least one member of the crew."

"I'm afraid you're right. Have you any idea, at all, where such an agent might be located?"

Kell said, "We're progressing—if that isn't too grand a word—in two fields and suffering from an acute shortage of manpower in both of them. A lot of my best men have been drafted into the Intelligence Corps in France. And I nearly lost another good man when Hubert Daines was roughly handled by some of the dockland Irish. He'll be out of the hospital soon, but will need a bit of leave before he continues as head of our investigations in the East End. It's a promising field. More promising still if I could equip him with a proper team. I'm better off than I was, but still desperately short-handed for all the work I'm supposed to do." Kell snorted. "I'm sure my opposite number in Germany has two or three hundred trained men at his beck and call. Daines has been struggling along with two men and a boy. Luke Pagan—I think you met him . . ."

"Found him on a rock," murmured Hall.

"And his friend Joe Narrabone, formerly with Pagan in H Division of the Metropolitan Police."

"Lost a leg in the Leman Street explosion, didn't he? Ex-poacher and bad boy of the village." Hall had clearly done his homework. "Who's the other one?"

Kell explained about Lefroy. When he had finished, the two men sat in silence for some time, each busy with his own thoughts.

Hall said, "You mentioned two fields."

"The other one is the Mount Pleasant sorting office. We're still patiently examining the in-and-out mail of possible suspects, but I'm not convinced that two men can handle the job properly. They photograph and file any letters that look interesting, but, as you can imagine, since war was declared extreme caution has set in. What I'd like to do is not just photograph the letters, but test them for possible writing in invisible ink."

"They do that, do they? I suppose there's some method of developing it."

"Several different ways. They might be using lemon juice, or saliva, or even diluted milk. The lemon juice can be brought out by applying a hot flatiron. The saliva by having ordinary ink brushed lightly over it. And—what did I say was the third?"

"Diluted milk," said Hall. He had been making notes. He found details of this sort fascinating.

"Oh, yes. That's one of the most difficult methods. The writing is totally invisible in any light, and to bring it out you have to dust it over with graphite powder. You can imagine that with our present staff we have little time for refinements of that sort."

Hall said, "Suppose I was able to find you three or four intelligent naval officers—they'd be men who were too old for active service, or may be crippled. Would you be able to use them?"

"My dear fellow," said Kell. "Manna in the wilderness. I'll use any number you can spare." As Hall rose to go, he added, "I've been invited to visit the Explosives Testing Center on Duck Island. That's on—let me check—yes. Thursday afternoon. Would you care to come along?"

"Delighted," said Hall.

"One thing they're investigating is the possibility of dropping bombs onto selected targets from the air. I suggest that you find out—Antiaircraft Command will be able to tell you—whether there were any Zeppelins over Sheerness at the time of the *Bulwark* explosion, or even a day or two before it."

Hall said that he would do this. He looked a little happier than he had on arrival.

When Luke went, on that same afternoon, to report the results of his visit to the arsenal, he found Kell in a relaxed and equable mood. More than relaxed. He was positively glowing with pleasure. The offer that Hall had made him, if it could be developed into full-scale liaison between the Naval Intelligence Division and MO5, would more than double the efficiency of both.

He listened to what Luke had to tell him and said, "It sounds pretty watertight to me. Could you spot any loopholes?" For a precise speaker like Kell, such a mixing of metaphors was a further indication of geniality.

"Not really, sir. Just one reservation: The sentries who were manning the footway behind the wall were mostly old soldiers. Eight-hour shifts, with a dog watch every twenty-four, is not an easy stint, even for a young man. When I mentioned it, the colonel produced an argument that I found difficult to shout down. He said, 'Men in the trenches serve longer hours than that and aren't half as comfortable.' Which is true, of course. Here they can get hot baths when they want them, and, I believe, a supplementary ration on account of the work they're doing."

"I suppose that's right," said Kell. "As long as they don't fall asleep on the job. I've set up a meeting on Thursday afternoon with Major Cooper-Key, the chief inspector of explosives. You'd better come along. I'm hoping he'll be able to give Hall some theory to account for what happened to the *Bulwark.*"

* * *

The Explosives Testing Center, on and under Duck Island, was a humpbacked construction of concrete blocks with a number of sandbagged enclosures around it. The ducks, after whom the island had been named, had long since departed to a less disturbed home.

The presiding deity, Major Cooper-Key, was not unlike a member of the grallatores, or wading birds, being long and thin and equipped with a prominent beak well adapted for poking under stones. Sitting beside him was Dr. Duprès, the chemical analyst; a perfect contrast—tubby, balding, and with thick-lensed glasses wedged onto a snub nose.

"I've got two theories for you," said the major. "One has been worked out by my department. The other is the brainchild of my friend." Dr. Duprès ducked his head briefly. "The attack, as we see it, might have come from above or from below."

(*"Über und unter,"* the German naval officers in the Royal Duke had chanted.)

"My own theory is of a mechanical attack from above. It presupposes a visit from one or more Zeppelins."

Hall said, "I've checked with AA Command. They tell me that two Zeppelins were over Sheerness the day before the explosion on the *Bulwark."*

"When you say the day before, do I assume that you mean the evening before?"

Hall said, "That's correct. The first sighting was at 2035 hours. It would have been dusk, but not yet dark. Why? Does something turn on it?"

"Yes, Captain. I think it does."

The major picked up the curious object that had been on the table in front of him. It was a fat, metal tube, about eighteen inches long and four inches round, with a small propeller at one end. Grasping it firmly, the major unscrewed it and held it up for their inspection.

As far as they could make out, the interior was in two sections, divided by a membrane.

"This little joker was thrown into an ammunition ship in New York and found on top of the cargo when it reached Liverpool. When I tell you that the ship had been berthed alongside a German boat, you can guess how it landed up where it did. When we found it—it's empty now, of course—one of these chambers contained sulfuric acid, the other high explosives. The membrane prevented them mixing prematurely. Here"—he inserted one finger and lifted a small metal arm—"is a spring-loaded igniter. The device that holds it back is controlled by a small rotating wheel, rather like the wheel that governs the mainspring of a watch. When you have fiddled the wheel around the requisite number of times, the device is armed and ready."

"I follow that," said Hall, who had been listening carefully. "But why didn't this particular one detonate?"

"Sound mechanics, poor chemistry," said Duprès. "The sulfuric acid mixture wasn't strong enough to eat its way through the membrane."

"Second objection, then," said Hall. "How would it get

onto the *Bulwark?* And even if you're going to suggest that a treacherous sailor or stoker was induced to put it into the magazine, I can't believe he'd have been clever enough—or brave enough—to open it and fiddle with the control wheel."

"That's the really ingenious part about it." The major sounded as pleased and proud as though he had invented the bomb himself. "We'll suppose that in the case of the *Bulwark* it was dropped from a Zeppelin. If attached to a small parachute, its descent would be leisurely. Plenty of time for the propeller, which would have been going around"—he twirled it with his finger—"to turn the wheel so that, by the time it landed on the *Bulwark,* it would be armed and ready. Then, as soon as the acid—a stronger mixture this time, no doubt—had eaten through the membrane, it would detonate handsomely. If a single spark reached the magazine, the ship would be destroyed."

"Sounds a bit hit-and-miss to me," said Hall. "How could they be sure that a single bomb would land on the ship? Or if it did, that it would end up in a place where it could do serious damage?"

"No one suggested a single bomb," said Cooper-Key. He was provoked by this skepticism and though, as a major, considerably junior to a captain R.N., did not hesitate to show it. "Half a dozen could have been loosed and escaped detection in the dusk. However, since you find my suggestion farfetched, allow me to hand you over to my colleague. Perhaps you will find his ideas more convincing."

The professor said, "What has been demonstrated to you is the *possibility* of an attack from above. I think you were wrong to dismiss it." He looked severely at Hall, whose unconvincing attempt to look contrite was nearly too much for Luke's self-control. "So let me offer you the alternative: an attack from below."

He produced from his briefcase what looked like a thin stick of barley sugar.

"What I have here is a piece of caustic soda that has been coated with varnish. Before I explain how it *might* have been used"—a further severe look at Hall—"allow me to clear certain preliminary points. Matters of naval routine, about which you will, of course, know much more than I do. First, what armament was being carried?"

"In the *Bulwark?* Six- and eight-inch guns."

"I'm obliged. The ammunition, then, would be in the normal two-part form. The projectile and the cordite charge would be delivered separately to the gun turret."

"Certainly. By mechanical hoists, operating on opposite sides of the turret."

"Just so. And if a continuous and sustained program of firing was contemplated—in practice, or in actual battle—I imagine that there would be a number of projectiles and charges in the turret."

"Yes. In racks, behind the guns."

"Then, one final point: The magazine from which they came would be—I speak comparatively—a cool place."

"Not just cool. Temperature-controlled."

"Yes. And the turret?"

"That, of course, is quite a different matter. It's ventilated, but after a period of firing it does get extremely hot. If discipline allowed it, the men at the guns would work stripped to the waist."

"Just as I visualized it," said the professor happily. He picked up the pencil-shaped object and said, "This device can lie among TNT, quite innocuous, for months on end. *But,* when heat is applied, directly or indirectly, it will burst into flames—which would detonate not only the charge to which it was attached, but also the other charges around it. And if even one of the hoists leading down to the magazine happened to be open . . ."

He broke off. A long silence ensued. Then Hall said, speaking so unwillingly that the words seemed to be wrenched out of him, "I must confess, Professor, that I find your theory the more probable of the two. Hideously probable. A dishonest or suborned member of the crew could, I suppose, carry such a thing in his pocket. Yes? And it would be the work of a moment to insert it in one of the cordite charges—possibly when he was assisting to stack them in the magazine. Then all he would have to do is wait until that particular charge was used."

Kell said, "We know now that the *Bulwark* explosion occurred when the ship was leaving Sheerness on a training course, which was to involve firing practice. The day was an unusually hot one, and if charges had been stacked ready in the turret, then trouble was very likely to occur. But don't these facts give us a chance of locating the man concerned? Knowing what was likely to happen, wouldn't he have made some excuse to stay off the ship? Compassionate leave, hospitalization, a visit to the dentist . . ."

"Yes," said Hall, "we can check that."

"Also, now that you know the two possible ways of attack, you'll be able to take steps to guard against them. If Zeppelins are overhead, don't concentrate all your searchlights on them. Have at least one of them focused *on the ship*. And check all charges, both in store and before using them. That should give you a margin of safety."

"Until the buggers think of something else," said Hall. But he said it so softly that only Luke, who was sitting just behind him, heard it.

11

After this spate of activity, the pace slowed and, before anyone was quite expecting it, Christmas was on them.

A sad Christmas for some small people of no national importance. Into their mailboxes was dropped, in the place of Christmas cards and good wishes, a buff envelope, with its terse message signed by their "obedient servant" from the War Office who "regretted to inform" them. News that took a minute to read and years to forget. A husband or a son had crossed over Jordan into the promised land.

By a strange turn of fate, the people who seemed happiest about the advent of Christmas were the men in the trenches. To the horror of commanding generals, they had seized on the occasion to meet their enemies in no-man's-land and shake hands with them.

Unofficial football games had been played among the shell-holes, and *Heilige Nacht* had mingled with *Noël, Noël.* Clearly the thing had to be stamped on. How could a man shake hands with someone one day and bayonet him the next? Moral fiber would be dangerously slackened. Fraternization became a court-martial offense and was successfully stamped out.

So, as the year turned the corner and as an icy January became a damp and depressing February, both sides braced themselves for the next act: the first studied, methodical offensive. A decisive victory now could end the war. Afterward, the chance would have gone. It would be too late. And the key to success, as Kell had impressed on Luke, was ammunition: bullets, shells, bombs, trench mortars, grenades.

True, the output was beginning to increase, but slowly. New factories had to be built and tooled up, and men had to be found to replace the skilled hands who had hurried to the colors at the start of the war. If the pitifully small existing stocks could be attacked, even partly destroyed, this would be a deadly blow.

And such an attack was coming. Kell was sure of it. If he could divine the enemy's plans, he could take steps to counter them. At the moment, he was lunging blindly, in the dark. He thought about the Royal Arsenal. For the Germans, with their love of the *Schwerpunkt,* the *Angriffslustig,* the bold and aggressive attack on the main objective, it was such an obvious target. And what Luke had told him about its defenses was only halfway encouraging. The surrounding walls might be high, but if the men on them were getting on in years, tired out by long spells of duty . . .

Kell shook his head angrily. He knew that it was on occasions like this that bad mistakes were made. Better at the moment to concentrate on small things he could do. Train his little army and have them instantly ready for action.

Special Branch had temporarily assigned two of their hard men, Kirchner and Durkin, to MO5 to give it some badly needed muscle. Joe had been allowed to disappear from time to time, sinking deeply and more deeply into the half world around the Victoria and the Royal Albert docks. Ben Lefroy had been granted a leave of absence on two afternoons a week so he could improve his schoolboy knowledge of German.

Kell had given him the names of three language schools. "There used to be a dozen and more in London, but a lot of them have closed down, and others have become bashful about teaching German. More credit to the ones that have been honest enough to keep it up. The obvious one for you is the Abbey Wood Tutorial Service. Easy to get at. It's on Southern Railway from Woolwich."

To it Ben had dutifully proceeded, armed with a letter of introduction from Kell. Joe, who had taken an almost paternal interest in Ben ever since he had joined them, was proud of the speed with which he had picked up a new language.

"Quicker than Luke," he said. This was tactless, but tact was never Joe's strong point.

Luke had spent the months of winter and early spring in a tedious checking and rechecking of the names on Kell's list. Somewhere—he was sure of it—somewhere hidden in the jungle of East London was the man it was becoming so desperately important to find.

Snowdrops and then primroses made their timid appearance, and a few buds showed on the skeleton branches of the trees. And life went on—calm on the surface, tense and anxious below it as a climax approached that, it seemed, they could do nothing to circumvent or hasten.

Toward the end of March a tiny gap opened in the clouds—a patch of blue, small but encouraging.

The team that Hall had attached to Mount Pleasant was made up of two commanders and one lieutenant commander, all in their early forties. Their systematic but uninspired attention to the work they had been given may have explained why they had been passed over for promotion. The arrival of a fourth helper had ruffled the surface.

The newcomer was Sublieutenant Burnhow, a boy of twenty, who had been on deck on the *Bulwark* when the explosion occurred. He had been thrown into the sea and picked up, with a shattered left arm that had to be amputated at the elbow. He had been a young officer of ability and promise, and now that his career in the navy had been aborted, he turned with savage energy to a job he hoped would help hunt down the enemies who had tried to destroy him.

His three seniors observed, with concealed dislike, his habit of working twice as hard as they did.

One of the files of copied correspondence that had been handed over to him included a number of letters to and from a Mr. Goodison, the manager of Leslie Lindsell and Sons, sanitary engineers and fuel stockists, who had an office and a yard in Bostall Wood. The letters had come in for inspection only because Charles Goodison, before he changed his name, had been Gustav Gottfried. To avoid insult and obloquy, many innocent citizens had taken a similar step on the outbreak of war. Mr. Goodison had done so six months earlier, which might suggest that he had private information that war was coming. Admittedly somewhat slender grounds for suspicion. His correspondence with Messrs. Zeeman, metallurgists and mining agents of Stockholm, had, in the past, dealt only with details of lead piping and brass fittings and continued to do so, in the dullest possible way.

Previous investigators seemed to have read the letters rapidly and decided that they were harmless. Burnhow, having leafed through the copies of the earlier correspondence, was now patiently treating each new one that came in, with all of the three known methods of restoring invisible writing. His seniors watched him sardonically, wondering why he was wasting his time.

In the last week of March his patience was rewarded. Scrawled down the fold of a letter from Zeeman he was able to read, "Let 105 know special product on its way to you."

This seemed important enough to Burnhow for him to bring it personally to Kell, who examined his offering with the excited attention of an entomologist faced with a hitherto unknown beetle.

Burnhow, who was meeting Kell for the first time, murmured that he hoped he found it interesting.

"Not just interesting," said Kell. "Extremely important. You've read all the earlier correspondence. You know the background. So what do you think it means?"

"It seemed to me that Zeeman was supplying Goodison openly with lavatory fittings and something different under cover."

"Such as what?"

"Something he couldn't get in England. Or couldn't import openly without paying a large import duty. Or perhaps something illegal."

"Drugs," suggested Kell gently.

Burnhow was young enough to blush. Drugs had been the first thing he had thought of.

"Whatever it is," said Kell, "we've both got work to do. I'll investigate the firm. You keep your eyes peeled for further messages."

The result of Kell's investigations arrived three days later in the form of a memorandum. Burnhow was interested to see that other copies had gone to Naval Intelligence, to the Criminal Investigation Department at Scotland Yard, and to the Department of Trade and Industry, with thanks for their assistance.

The firm of Leslie Lindsell & Sons was founded in 1850. Control passed from father to son and son to grandson. Leslie III, who lost money by mismanagement, was happy to sell the assets and goodwill in 1908 to Gustav Gottfried. Gustav calls himself manager—he lives over the shop—but he's clearly the owner. The name ''Lindsell'' was retained by him as part of the goodwill. After this change, the business, which had been chiefly confined to the installation and repair of household water systems, was enlarged. The firm started to manufacture all forms of lavatory equipment. It also became a fuel stockist, a business that needs money, patience, and storage space. All types of household fuel, coal, wood, paraffin, and so on are purchased cheaply, from sources here and abroad, in spring and summer when there is little demand for them, and sold at a large markup when winter sets in.

Kell had scribbled at the bottom of Burnhow's copy, ''Gottfried/Goodison arrived in this country in 1905 from Bavaria. Nothing known against him. Applied for and was granted naturalization in 1910. Original classification A. I've demoted him to AB: Anglo Boche, doubtful. Keep me informed.''

The certainty that he was on to something and that the management was happy about his efforts sustained Burnhow through an empty two weeks of fiddling toil. Then he landed his second fish.

''I was hoping for something a little more decisive,'' said Kell. He was discussing the new message with Luke, who had been deploring his own lack of progress. Together they read and reread the straggle of blackened words:

''Tell Tyr he will get suitable supplies from you in time to do the necessary.''

It was not easy to read, having been written inside the fold of a double sheet of paper.

"He'd have needed to smooth it out flat before treating it. And it's the trickiest of the three methods. The writing's done with a small paintbrush in watered milk. Quite invisible in any light until brushed over with graphite."

"Impressive," agreed Luke. "Nine people out of ten would have missed it altogether."

"Very impressive," said Kell. "He's too valuable to take chances with."

Luke was unclear what he meant, but had learned that when you didn't know what to say, you said nothing.

Kell leaned back in his chair, gazed at the ceiling for a long moment, and then, "You and Joe spent years together as policemen in one of the roughest parts of London and learned a little—not much, but the elements of self-protection. *You must not judge everyone by yourselves.* Here we have two young men working for us—Burnhow and Lefroy—one of them brought up in the nursery of the navy, the other inside a laboratory. They know as much about the real world as my cat, Melinda. Less, really. She's a very knowledgeable animal. So what follows?"

Luke opened his mouth and shut it again.

"What follows is that we must look after them. As we could have looked after Hubert Daines if he'd behaved sensibly and told us what he was up to. We're not without resources. As well as Kirchner and Durkin, Special Branch have lent us a third man, Merchison. A Scotsman who was, I believe, formerly a bouncer in a nightclub. They are messing together in a flat in Poplar that I've got for them. Here's the telephone number. Write it down. If you need help, phone them. They'll be doing a number of jobs for me, but promise, if possible, to leave one man behind to answer the telephone. I've told Burnhow and Lefroy about them." Kell smiled austerely. "Both seemed surprised that such precautions should be necessary."

* * *

Basil Home Thomson, old Etonian, son of an archbishop, was a rough-looking character with poached eyes, a drinker's nose, and an offensive shrubbery of black mustache. He had ruled Dartmoor Prison with a rod of iron for five years and had been rewarded for his efforts with the appointment as assistant commissioner of the Metropolitan Police, in charge of the CID. Although later their different temperaments were to drive a wedge between them, at the moment he and Kell were on friendly terms and able to work together.

This was just as well since, with "Blinker" Hall, their hands were on all the principal levers of national security. They were sitting in Kell's operations room considering the third and the most promising of the messages that young Burnhow had produced for them.

It had been found in the margin of the latest letter from Zeeman, in answer to one from Goodison. Copies of both of these letters were in front of them.

The letter to Zeeman was largely devoted to business, containing a listing of various pipes and sanitary fittings that Goodison required and the prices he was prepared to pay for them. It concluded by expressing mounting dread of the Zeppelins, whose visits to East London had left behind a trail of damage and casualties.

"Only yesterday two bombs were dropped in Plumstead, less than a mile away from us. It would indeed be a crippling blow to our business—no less than to yours—if our premises suffered a direct hit."

In his reply Zeeman had agreed that such a disaster would be calamitous for both of them, but he could do little more than express sympathy and hold out hopes that the worst would not occur.

The marginal note, in invisible ink, was more specific. A great deal more specific:

"The eagles have orders to respect both Tyr and Vulcan. They will in the future avoid SE2."

The three men stared at it greedily.

Hall was the first to speak. He said, "It's as clear as living daylights. Goodison—Vulcan—is in this business up to the neck. Why, Zeeman is promising him preferential treatment by the Germans! Doesn't that condemn him out of hand? We should go straight alongside and board him."

Basil Thomson shook his head. "He's a small fish," he said. "Don't let's jerk the hook out of his mouth. If we play him carefully he'll lead us to the man we really want."

Both looked at Kell, as though for a casting vote.

"I agree with B.T.," he said. "We want Wotan."

"Come again?" said Thomson.

"Wotan, or Odin. Call him what you like. The father of the gods. You remember that journalist fellow called himself Loki. Now that we have Vulcan, the god of thunder, and Tyr, the god of war, doesn't a sort of pattern begin to appear? A neat, tight little group of Teutonic mythmen planning mischief. As I said, the only one missing is Wotan."

"*Der Vetter,*" suggested Thomson.

"Could be. Yes. Wotan and *der Vetter* might well be the same man. Lay *him* by the heels and we've a chance of finding out what they're up to in time to stop it."

Hall said, "What I'm afraid of is that they're arranging another *Bulwark* explosion, and that's why I'd like to get my hands on the one character we do know about and shake the teeth out of his head. However, if you can persuade me that we've a blind chance of getting through him to the man at the top, I'll go along with it."

Thomson said, "Those three messages, considered together, suggest to me that Goodison, who operates under the name of Vulcan, is really only a middleman—"

"Hold it," said Kell. "That reminds me of something. When young Luke was carrying out a piece of mail geometry, based on the previous correspondence"—he explained about this—"I told him that the only result he could hope to get out of it was to locate the middleman. The one person who knew the way down to where *der Vetter* had buried himself."

"I think that's probably right," said Thomson. "Let's take it one step farther. If the 'suitable supplies' are to pass to Tyr for treatment and back to Vulcan for use, that suggests to me that Tyr and Vulcan must be situated fairly close to each other."

"Confirmed by message number three," agreed Kell.

"Clearly they're both in SE2. Bostall Wood is in the south-west corner . . ."

By this time a map of the district was spread on Kell's desk. It was of a scale large enough to show individual streets.

"Could be worse, I suppose," said Kell. "Luckily the northern half, up to the river, is Erith Marshes. No buildings there. And a lot of the southern half is Abbey Wood and Bostall Wood. Really there are only three built-up areas: one to the west and one to the north of Bostall Wood, and one to the east of Abbey Wood."

"And," said Thomson coldly, "with thirty or so little streets in each—with an average of, say, twenty houses in each—okay. I have a sizable force of detectives available, but if you think they're going to search nearly two thousand houses, I'm afraid you'll have to think again." He added, "Once, when I was doing some exploring in the forests of New Guinea, I got properly lost. My guide wasn't worried. He said, 'Go back to the last place you recognize and use your magic box.' He meant my compass. 'It will soon take us where we want to go.' "

"If you mean by that," said Hall, "that we start at Goodison's place in Bostall Wood and move out on a succession of bearings through the built-up areas, it would take a long time and might not get us anywhere in the end. Now, when you were lost at sea—which happens more often than you might suppose—what you did was go forward on a known line and keep your eyes open for a cross-bearing."

"Speaking as neither an explorer nor a sailor," said Kell, "my views are simpler. What I think we want is one further stroke of luck. Talking of which, a kind friend has sent me a bottle of Highland malt whiskey. I was wondering whether either of you would care to sample it."

He was not kept wondering for long.

12

It might, in fact, be counted a stroke of luck that Luke should have spotted the story in the *East London Gazette.* It was a paper he read only occasionally, when nothing more exciting was available, and it was tucked away on the back page amid much war news.

"END OF A REIGN" was the headline.

It recounted that an uncrowned king of the district, one Tim Brady, having consumed a quantity of liquor at Benbow Tavern, was making his way back to his house on Arthur Street. He seemed to have been taking a shortcut, across the triangle of little-used railway lines on the west side of the Timber Yard, to have missed his way, and slipped into one of the two dry docks, offshoots of Royal Albert Dock. He must have hit his head as he fell, and when he was found, by men going to work the next morning, he had clearly been dead for some hours. The author concluded this ten-line account by saying, in the sanctimonious tone commonly adopted by the press, that even though Brady was trespassing on private property, he was surely entitled to expect some sort of barrier around these death traps.

The copy of the *Gazette* was dated April 20, and it appeared that the accident had taken place three days before. Luke, who read the report late at night, showed it to Kell first thing the next morning.

Kell said, "You don't like it. Why? People do drink too much and fall into pits."

"I don't believe it was an accident. It was much too convenient. Those Irish dockies survive only because no one will testify against them."

"And you think they were afraid that Brady might be planning to turn King's evidence?"

"Maybe not. But could they be sure? He could identify them. And he'd seen them getting ready to throw Hubert into the river in a weighted sack. Attempted murder. A very long sentence. They daren't risk it."

"So you think they laid for him when he came out of the pub? Knocked him on the head and left him in the dock?"

"I think it's very possible."

"And you think it's important to us to find out?"

"Yes, sir. I do. If it was that gang of Irishmen, I think the sooner they're dealt with the better. They near as a whisker cost us Hubert. And the fact that they're on the loose is obstructing our work in that area."

"Then certainly see if you can put them away. Have a word with that policeman—Horniman, was it?—and take Dr. Spilsbury with you. He's a very busy man just now, but he'll oblige me if I ask him. He'll clear up the two points that seem to matter: Was Brady in fact as intoxicated as the paper makes out? And was the blow on his head one that he could have suffered from a fall, or must it have been delivered manually? He's very good on points like that."

Bernard Spilsbury was busy. He was the principal medical witness in the King against George Joseph Smith, christened by the papers "The Brides in the Bath Case." But he canceled some minor engagements and made himself available two days later for a visit to the Albert Docks Police Station.

Chief Inspector Horniman received him respectfully and introduced him to the coroner's officer, Sergeant Michaels, previously a member of his own force. Horniman said, "We'd like to know the truth as much as you do, but I'm afraid it's too late. Even Dr. Spilsbury, whose name and fame are well known to us, won't be able to make any useful deductions from a pile of ashes."

They both stared at him.

Spilsbury said, "Are you telling us that Brady's been cremated already?" He sounded incredulous.

"Yes, sir. Yesterday morning."

"That was extraordinarily quick, wasn't it? Six days after death. Involving cremation. Were the proper formalities observed?"

"I understand that the matter was in order."

"Surely the coroner would hold an inquest—"

"In this case the coroner apparently decided"—he looked at Sergeant Michaels, who nodded—"that since the facts were so clear, a formal inquest was unnecessary. He was prepared to certify accidental death."

"Who is this speed merchant?"

"He's only been recently appointed. A Dr. Lightfoot."

"Ambrose Lightfoot?"

"Yes, sir. You know him?"

"I knew of him when he was in the medical school at St. Mary's. Even then he was notorious for skipping over difficulties. The other members called him 'Fairy Lightfoot.' Not intended as a compliment. But however anxious he may have been to hurry things on, Brady couldn't have been cremated without the medical referee's certificate."

"Quite so, sir. But as well as being coroner, Dr. Lightfoot *is* the medical referee. Many of our doctors have joined the army, and it was necessary to combine the two jobs."

Spilsbury said, "Oh. I see." An awkward silence followed.

Then Horniman said, "Please don't think I'm offering excuses for what must look like indecent haste, but the fact is that the Coroner's Department has been rushed off its feet lately with cases resulting from enemy action. We've had seven people killed in the streets. In each case the coroner gave his certificate without formality. He did it, he said, to spare the feelings of the family."

"What about Brady's family?"

"Inquiries were made, but none could be traced. He seems to have been a lone fighter."

"He's fought his last fight now," said Spilsbury dryly. "And I'll tell you what surprises me more than anything else: As you know, the whole idea of cremation was subject at first to public hostility. The Home Office disliked it. The Roman Catholic Church was against it. Even the medical inspector of burials was one of its harshest critics. It only scraped through by agreeing that it should be subject to strict controls, which is why crematoriums are normally anxious that everything should be in apple-pie order. Which one was this?"

Horniman said, "It was the East Plumstead Crematorium, and when I was having a word with the manager I got the impression that he didn't like the situation. But faced with those certificates—"

Speaking for the first time, ex-Sergeant Michaels, who had seemed increasingly unhappy as the conversation continued, said, "If you'll excuse me interrupting, sir, I got the impression that the coroner may have been put under some sort of pressure."

"Explain that," said Horniman sharply.

"Well, sir, to speak frankly, Dr. Lightfoot doesn't give me the impression of being a very courageous man. And you know how people talk. Seems that two of that Irish crowd—the ones they call the Killarney boys—were spotted coming away from his surgery early on the morning after the body was discovered. If they'd said to him, 'We know you can give the necessary certificates, so don't hang about. Unless you want to be the next person found in a dry dock—' "

"If I'd been told about this," said Horniman, "of course I'd have stopped the cremation."

"It only reached me this morning," said Michaels unhappily.

Spilsbury, who had looked at his watch more than once, said, "Whether Fairy Lightfoot was being stupid, or whether he was being cowardly, the story ends the same way: in a pile of ashes. Since I can't help you, I'd better be getting back to some work I can do. Are you ready?"

Luke said he was ready.

Spilsbury said, "It certainly wasn't your fault, Inspector. I'd put in a report if I thought it would do any good."

Next morning Luke was sitting writing when Joe looked in. He had discarded his crutches and was relying on a rubber-tipped stick with a horn handle. He seemed to be in high spirits. He spread himself over the desk, knocking over an inkpot that Luke caught deftly, and said, "I've had an idea."

"Splendid," said Luke.

The gloomy tone did nothing to deter Joe. He said, "I'm letting you have it hot off the grill. And I'll tell you why. Old Kell thinks I'm a halfwit."

"He doesn't really. It's just that he can't appreciate your native cunning."

"Exactly. So what I thought was, I'd explain the idea to you and you could pass it on to the skipper as your own. Then he might take it seriously."

"And if he thinks it's stupid, it's me who gets kicked."

"Stupid?" said Joe indignantly. "It isn't stupid. It's right on the top line. It came to me when I woke up this morning. That character who calls himself Tyr. I said to myself: Why did they call him different things in those two messages? 'Let 105 know special product on its way to you.' Then, 'Tell Tyr he'll get supplies . . .' It must be the same man. Why two names?"

"When we were dealing with those Russian terrorists—do you remember? Most of them used three or four different aliases. It was meant to confuse everyone."

"All right," said Joe patiently. "But *why* 105?"

"The Lord alone knows. Some sort of numerical cypher possibly. What did you make of it?"

"You know what everyone says. That Fritz is a clever boy nine times out of ten, but the tenth time he makes a real number one balls up. I think that's what he did here. He called Tyr '105' *because that was the number of his house.*"

Luke was saying to himself that if he tried that one on Kell the old man would blow his top. But he was very fond of Joe, and Joe was so pleased with the idea that he had to pretend to take it seriously.

He said, "We know that Tyr is somewhere in SE2. Right? And if you look at the map you can see that none of the streets in it is long enough to have more than twenty or thirty numbers."

"Of course I thought of that," said Joe smugly. "I'm not stupid. But there *are* two long streets: Woolwich Road at the bottom and Abbey Wood Road across the top. I tried Woolwich Road as I came along. By the time I got to West Heath the numbers were up to '80,' but then it becomes Bostall Hill and the numbers start again. I was going to try Abbey Wood Road next. Would you care to come along?"

Luke was on the point of saying, "I might as well be doing that as sitting here," but changed it to the more tactful, "It's a lovely morning, so why not?"

Joe picked up the rubber-tipped stick and they set off.

"What I noticed in the other road," said Joe, "most of these little side streets, they like to number the houses on both sides at the end as though they belonged to the main road."

"Feeling, no doubt," said Luke, peering at an undistinguished-looking little house, "that No. 30 Abbey Wood Road was a more imposing address than No. 1 Crumpshall Street."

There were so many openings, some genuine streets, some merely courtyards, that the numbering was up to 80 before they reached the bend in the road from which they could see the spire of St. Augustine's Church. According to Luke's map, this marked the point where Abbey Wood Road became Picardy Street.

"Not many more houses now," said Luke. They could see a cluster of half a dozen buildings on the right of the road, but that was all.

Then they spotted the Crescent.

This was a new construction, a half moon of street leading off Abbey Wood Road and rejoining it a hundred yards along. The houses in the Crescent were markedly superior to any of the others they had passed.

"Getting into posh company now," said Joe. "Upper-class twits, no doubt. Shuvvers and 'ousemaids."

Luke was not interested in the owners of the houses. His eyes were glued to the gateposts. "They've carried on with the numbering," he said, trying to conceal his excitement. The last house on the main road had been 90. From where they were standing, they could see that the five houses on the left of the Crescent started with 91 and, presumably, reached 99. After that there was a gap. Then another five houses before the Crescent rejoined the main road.

"Odd numbers on the left," he said. "Which means that 105 must be the third house *after* the gap. Right?"

"Bang on," said Joe. "Diddun I tell you? Come on. Don't let's hang about."

For Luke had come to a halt.

He said, "If that house *is* the one that Tyr—whoever he may turn out to be—is using, the last thing we want to do is rush up and stare at it. What we've got to do is stroll past it, keeping our eyes to the front and talking hard."

"Fair enough," said Joe. "What'd you like to talk about? I heard a good story the other day about a sailor who was getting married. His intended was a black girl—"

"Hold it," said Luke. "We seem to have lost some numbers."

By this time they had reached the gap, where a pair of iron gates guarded a private driveway. And the next house beyond the gap was 107! After staring at it blankly for a few seconds, the solution occurred to them. Peering through the latticework of the gates, they could see that there were two houses on either side of the drive. It was one of those compact upper-class developments that was becoming popular.

The gates, which seemed to have been more for show than protection, were unlocked. They went through, and sauntered past the houses on the left, which were numbered 101 and 103, the ones opposite being 102 and 104. The end of the drive curved sufficiently to conceal what lay beyond it. But Luke was now in no doubt. Joe had been right all along. He wondered what sort of house 105 would turn out to be. A modest two-up and two-down, or one of those mansions that Joe despised?

"Slower, slower," he said.

"Like I was saying," said Joe, "the girl was something he'd picked up in Jamaica and brought back with a load of pineapples. But she was a girl of spirit. She wanted everything done just the way they done it in Jamaica. Trouble was, the parson wasn't used to the marriage customs of 'eathen wimmin—"

Then he stopped. They could both see it: two impressive gateposts fronting a considerable building. On the nearer one the number 105. On the farther one the words "East Plumstead Crematorium."

* * *

"Then you think you've located Tyr?"

Luke could not tell, from Kell's expression, whether he believed him, or disbelieved him, or was adopting his normal stance of impartiality.

He said, "I did think so, sir. On our way home Dr. Spilsbury said a lot more to me than he did to Inspector Horniman. He said more than once how very surprised he was that the crematorium had allowed itself to be hustled out of its normal program. But if the man in charge was secretly on the same side as the Irish ruffians, then of course he'd have been willing to do whatever they wanted."

Kell said, slowly, "On balance, I'm inclined to think that you're right. Not entirely for the reasons you've given. Other factors have emerged. When I got your note I asked our friends in the Home Office to run a quick rule over the man in charge of the crematorium—one Andrew Robb. Quite an interesting character. Real name Anders Raab, from Munich. Arrived here in 1905. Does that stir your memory? Applied for nationalization in 1910—"

"Aren't those the dates—?"

"The same as Goodison. Exactly. They came here in the same year and were both naturalized five years later—that is, as soon as the law allowed. I've been sent a copy of the naturalization committee proceedings. Immediate acceptance. Both with spotless records. Both holding down good jobs, and both had learned to talk fluent English. Raab had some reputation as a sculptor. Miniature *objets d'art.* He'd given an exhibition in Munich in 1903. Are you thinking what I am?"

"It looks like a little nest of undercover agents, carefully planted. Did 'Loki' arrive at the same time?"

"His first journalistic outpourings started at about that date, but it's not him I'm interested in. He was too openly hostile to be dangerous. No. It's the third man, *der Vetter*—the master gardener who has bedded these plants down so carefully. He's the one we want. And if Robb really is the contact man, the only one who knows where their leader and organizer is hidden, then Robb must be most carefully watched. We are negotiating for an attic apartment in No. 109—that's the second house along from the gateway at the top of the Crescent. It has a good view of the crematorium house, side door, and back door. That's your observation post to be manned in all daylight hours. You, Joe, and Ben can share it out among you. Right?"

As Luke rose to go, Kell added, "And will you please offer Joe my sincere congratulations."

Luke said, "It's odd that his instinct has always been better than my reasoning."

"That may be true," said Kell. "But don't stop thinking. Thought rules the world. Or so I've been told."

Kell smiled almost genially. He could feel that things were moving in his direction.

* * *

"Have you any idea what's become of that journalist?" asked Hall. He and Kell had fallen into the habit of visiting each other on alternate Tuesdays.

"Which of the scaly tribe are you talking about?" Kell had suffered a good deal from the press in his time.

"Real name Daryl Forbes. Calls himself Loki."

"Ah, the god of mischief. Yes. His name cropped up yesterday when I was talking to Luke. I said that he was the least important of the gods in this particular pantheon."

"Because he's the most open?"

"So outspokenly hostile to our state and institutions that I did wonder whether he was deliberately laying himself open to imprisonment—or at least to internment."

"To save his skin?"

"Exactly."

"And now, apparently, he's disappeared."

"He was always a bird of passage. Across to Ireland and back again. And moving about in both countries, though I'm tolerably certain that he's here now. Our new regulations about leaving the country are stringent."

"Here, but in hiding."

"If not in hiding, at least not publicly announcing his

whereabouts. The only person likely to be in touch with him is that editor—what's his name?"

"Portlach," said Hall, who never forgot the names of his friends, or his enemies.

"We might try to shake *him* down. If you think the fact that Forbes is lying low is significant."

"Just a sailor's myth," said Hall. "When the seagulls hide themselves away inland, it's a sign that heavy weather is coming up from the sea."

13

It was three o'clock on a gray morning when the U-boat, going north, crossed the wide opening of Tralee Bay and nosed its way into the estuary of the Shannon River. The equinoctial gales of late March had spared the western coast of Ireland and expended most of their force on the North Sea. There was a light trough on the surface, which made the U-boat roll a little as it came closer to land, but that was all.

''Nach Steuerbord Kerry, Ed,'' said the U-boat skipper.

The man who was standing beside him on the foredeck was wearing a British officer's overcoat and—oddly enough, if there had been light enough for close inspection—what seemed to be a pair of fisherman's waders. He turned his head slightly and said, *''Ja. Und nach Backbord Loophead.''* Then in perfect upper-class English, ''I must congratulate you on such an excellent and accurate landfall.''

The captain evidently understood enough of this to know that it was a compliment. He smiled briefly and turned to the business at hand.

The hatch in the afterdeck was open, and an inflatable rubber dinghy was being coaxed out of it, lowered over the side and held steady, while a motorcycle was slid down into it and held in position by straps on the gunwale. This did not leave much room for the passenger who squeezed in behind it, further encumbered by a large knapsack he laid on top of the machine.

When he had settled himself into position he said, ''As long as the tide holds, I shall not have to use my outboard motor.

If I have to use it eventually, you will have had plenty of time to back out and submerge."

The captain nodded. They shook hands. No more words were spoken.

For the first few minutes the passenger was using his night glasses to pick up the strip of sand he had seen once before, from above, when out shooting. When he had located it, he replaced the glasses in their case and bent to the oars. He needed them only to steer the dinghy, which was being carried forward steadily on the making tide.

There was an awkward moment when they grounded and the motorcycle, pulling against its straps, threatened to capsize the dinghy. But the passenger had thought out the necessary moves, and five minutes later the machine was unstrapped and beached. Then he turned his attention to the dinghy.

First he detached the outboard motor. It was no great weight, and swinging it in a half circle, he hurled it out into deep water. Next he selected half a dozen of the largest rocks he could handle and packed them carefully into the bottom of the dinghy. Then he opened the valve in its stern and allowed it to deflate slowly, controlling the speed by opening and shutting the valve. As it went down he folded the collapsed sides inward, over the stones, finally fastening them down with the gunwale straps.

The dinghy was now no more than a large, weighted, rubber bag. Stepping out into the sea protected by his fisherman's waders, he dragged it with him as far as he could go, gave it a gentle push, and watched the bubbles as it sank. The ebb tide would roll it out into deeper water.

The path that led up from the beach was steep but practicable. Alternately pulling and pushing the motorcycle, he inched his way up it, glad to reach the turf at the top. Here he paused for breath before going down to get the knapsack, which he had left on the beach.

By now the light was coming back into the sky and there was no time to lose. He changed the soaked fisherman's trousers for a more orthodox pair, which he extracted from the knapsack along with a small flask of brandy.

"Time for a nip," he said, "to celebrate a safe landing. *Viel gluck.*"

He fastened the knapsack onto the back of the machine, which carried the blue and red identification of the Royal Engineers, and pushed it forward onto the road, which paralleled the clifftop at this point. Then he kicked the motor into life and departed sedately, in the growing light, in the direction of Limerick.

* * *

Joe and Ben were occupying a chair each, set back from the window, in the attic of 109 Abbey Wood Road. Both were equipped with field glasses, through which, from time to time, they inspected the premises of the East Plumstead Crematorium.

The chapel was a slant-roofed building with a row of uninspired stained-glass windows. It had, as Joe had seen on his previous visit, a large double door in the west side, out of sight from where they sat, opening onto the driveway, which led, through ornamental pillars, out onto the road.

The crematorium building was hidden by the chapel. All they could see of the crematorium was the door at the east end, which gave access to the furnace room and the top of a stubby chimney showing over the roof of the chapel.

"Clear enough, innit?" said Joe. "There's some sort of opening in the wall of the chapel so they can shove the corpse straight through into the furnace."

"Inhuman," said Ben. "What's wrong with being buried in a nice churchyard?"

"Cremation's neater and cleaner," said Joe.

Before this well-worn argument could develop, their attention was switched from the crematorium to the house at the back.

This was clearly the residence of the director, Mr. Robb. They had in view both the door at the side of his house, which gave access to the living rooms, and the back door, which opened onto the kitchen quarters. A green van had now drawn up.

"Baker," said Ben. He looked at his watch and made a note

of the time. A fat woman waddled out of the kitchen, accepted three loaves from the baker's boy, exchanged insults with him, went back inside, and slammed the door. Ben embarked on a more interesting topic. He said, "I was wondering how you were getting on with Rosemary."

"Rosemary?"

"The girl who works for Goodison."

"Oh, you mean Rosie. She's a very nice girl. Simple, but nice."

"How did you—I mean—how did you get going?"

Joe deduced, from the way in which the question was put, that Ben's experience of girls was limited. He thought it was time he had some elementary instruction. He said, "If you want to get started with a girl, there's one part of her body you have to concentrate on. And I don't mean what you're thinking. I mean her stomach. All girls are hungry. Most of the time. So take 'em out and stuff 'em with toast and cakes. That's the first step. Next, see if you can locate some other girl on the premises, or thereabouts, and take *her* out."

"I follow that," said Ben. From his close attention he might have been listening to a professor expounding on a chemical experiment. "That's to make her jealous, I take it."

"Right. The old green eyes. And what's more, it gives you two strings to your bow. You may find number two more attractive, in which case you can drop number one. If she's not so hot, you ask number one out again. By this time she'll be panting to come. But"—here Joe shook a finger at Ben—"don't make a common mistake: Don't pretend you haven't been out with number two. Talk about her, as much as you like. That's the way to sharpen up number one."

"Hold it. Oh, it's just the mailman."

The mailman knocked at the side door, which was opened by the gardener-handyman, whom they presumed to be the husband of the kitchen lady. He took delivery of some letters and three parcels—heavy, by the way they were handled.

Ben, after making a careful note, said, "I suppose you've done a lot of this sort of thing, you and Luke."

"Oh, we was a great pair. The pride of H Division. Luke attended to the roo-teen. I supplied the inspiration. The man we was working for—Fred Wensley—'e was nuts on this sort of job. The secret of success, he used to say, is continuous observation. Once I sat in a damp hole for a week looking at a soap factory."

"That doesn't sound very exciting."

"Nor it wasn't, until it turned out the factory wasn't only making soap. It was turning out dynamite as well. Another time it was a bit more comfortable. We was up in a tree. We was after a sod what called himself Major Richards. A real snake. The sort of man who wouldn't come in the front door until he'd got the back door wedged open."

"Did you catch him?"

"We had him all lined up. Then a pompous bloody nit what happened to have the ear of the local police, made us hold off. Consequence, he got out and back to Hunland, where he is now, no doubt, patting himself on the back, God rot him."

Ben moved back to the topic that interested him more.

"Those girls," he said. "Did you get anything useful from either of them? They were working for Goodison, and it seems from these two messages that what they call 'the special product' went first to him. Then he sent it on to Robb here, for some sort of treatment."

"Maybe in those three boxes we saw the mailman handing in."

"Could be, yes."

"And we shan't find out by sitting on our arses half a mile away. What we've got to do is—oh, hold it. Here's the dustman."

To: *Field Marshal Lord Kitchener, His Majesty's Secretary of State for War*
From: *Sir John French, GHQ British Forces, Amiens*
Dated: *May 18, 1915. Confidential*

Sir,

As I reported in my 095 of May 12, the attack by the French Tenth Army in Artois, after initial success, was brought to a halt on May 10. I have now been requested to attack, in support of a further projected advance by the French, the location suggested being Aubers Ridges in the Lys Valley.

While regarding the idea of two converging attacks as tactically sound, I have, in duty, to point out one fact.

The artillery preparation for the French attack lasted for five days. My ammunition reserves are such that my CCRA, General Burch, has calculated that at the most all we can afford is a preliminary bombardment of forty minutes.

I am driven to the reluctant conclusion that unless a further supply of shells and, in particular, of heavy-caliber shells, reaches me shortly and can be guaranteed to continue on a regular basis, I shall be forced, in reliance on the escape clause granted to me when I assumed command, to inform the French quartier général *that any sustanined action would endanger the forces I have the honor to command and that I would therefore be unable to cooperate with them.*

I am sure you will appreciate the serious results were I forced to take such a step.

While the above letter was being written, Daryl Forbes, who called himself Loki, the god of mischief, was sitting on the veranda of a bungalow at Walton-on-Thames, enjoying the May sunshine. The swallows had arrived and were building under the boathouse eaves. On the river, which ran past the foot of the lawn, two swans were paddling easily against the current.

An oasis of peace in a lifetime dedicated to strife and toil.

The bungalow belonged to a Mrs. O'Malley, a lady well past middle age but constructed of that strong Irish bog oak that defies the passage of the years. She had come to England from her native County Galway at the turn of the century and had spent the past fifteen years expressing her detestation of the British ruling class and helping any Irishman who needed help.

She had known Daryl for forty years, and on the recent occasion when he had come from Ireland to England, fully expecting to find a warrant for his arrest awaiting him at disembarkation, he had turned to her for asylum and comfort, both willingly given.

He had not stepped outside the bungalow since he arrived, and he could be sure of his hostess's discretion. He was not so totally sure of Mr. Portlach. It was only because the editor had insisted that he had given him his address. He was in his hands, for he knew that the *Irish Citizen* was the only paper that would print his articles, and that only because they were acting under direct orders from Dublin.

He did not think that Portlach would go out of his way to betray him—why should he?—but he was a weak man, and under pressure from the authorities he might be persuaded to do so. However, a precaution had been taken to guard against even this contingency. After continued inattention to duty, Mr. Portlach's original secretary had been sacked and replaced by a younger and more intelligent girl, Annette, who was the daughter of Patrick O'Hegarty, a leading light among the Killarney boys.

"A Killarney girl," thought Forbes with a smile. She could be relied on to warn him if danger impended.

He was smiling at this comfortable thought when Mrs. O'Malley came out of the house with a tumbler of pink and frothy liquid and waited to see that he drank it. She said, "Finish it up. Every drop. Remember what the doctor said: You're to be careful of yourself."

Being careful of himself was something he had never found easy. The private warfare he had been waging with his pen for so many years had made him many enemies and much trouble. And had he achieved anything? Had not the time come for honorable retirement? Time to swim with the stream?

As though in answer to this thought the two swans that had been forging slowly upstream swung around, headed downstream, and were quickly out of sight.

* * *

At midday on the day that the letter from General French reached Whitehall, Luke arrived at 109 Abbey Wood Road to relieve Joe, who was glad to get back to his quarters. The affair with Rosie was going well, but like all newly bedded plants, she needed regular watering.

When the two watchers were settled in their chairs, and Ben had shown Luke his notes and brought him up to date as to the visitors to the crematorium they had observed, Luke said, "I hope Joe has been improving your tactical education."

"Oh, he has. Very much so."

"On what lines?"

"Well, it was mostly about girls and how to get alongside them."

"That wasn't exactly what I meant," said Luke severely. Although he was less than two years older than Ben, and Joe was actually a few months younger, both had gotten into the habit of treating him as a promising boy who needed surveillance and encouragement. In an effort to assert himself Luke continued the conversation in German, abandoning this only when he found that Ben was more fluent than he was. For which he felt compelled to congratulate him.

Ben said, "Most of the credit must go to Mr. Mills."

"The head teacher at the Abbey Road tutorial place?"

"David Mills. He's actually almost the only teacher left. Two young men he had have joined the army. There are some women who come in at odd times to teach French and Spanish, but David looks after everything else himself."

"Sounds a competent man."

"He's all of that. And what makes him a good German teacher is that he isn't a German. If you follow me. He's had to teach himself, and that makes it easier for him to pass it on."

"I hadn't thought about it like that," said Luke. "But you could be right."

"And since we're talking about the school, there is one favor I'd like to ask you: Couldn't you arrange that I'm not handed over on Tuesdays and Thursdays as though I were a child being taken to school by his mother?"

"Do they do that?"

"I don't know their names, but one or another of them looms up when I leave my place in Silvertown, follows me under the subway, gets onto the train with me, and sits there until we get to Abbey Wood Station. He does let me walk the hundred yards from there to the school without actually holding my hand, but he's on my heels all the way."

"Embarrassing," agreed Luke. "It'd be Durkin or Kirchner. Good men in a rough house, but not much tact."

"It's broad daylight and I'm in the public eye all the way."

"It was Kell's idea, but I don't suppose he meant it to be carried out in such a heavy-handed manner. I'll have a word with him."

"After all, no one follows Joe about. And he's short of a leg."

"One leg or two," said Luke with a grin, "I'm sure he's more than capable of looking after himself. In fact, he maintains that losing one of his legs has increased the strength of his arms—which were pretty powerful already."

Having made his point, Ben relaxed. He said, "I can tell you something else about Joe: He's champing for action."

* * *

"Yes," said Colonel Lemanoir. "I was sent a copy of it, too. Not the letter itself, but a summary of what it said."

Kell said, "And I suppose you can guess why we both got it."

"Surely." The colonel brushed his mustache up with his forefinger and smoothed it down with the back of his wrist. "It's obvious, isn't it? I'm in charge of one of our main ammunition stores, and your duty is to guard against any attack on it. So, if such an attack is made and is successful, we both get our balls chewed off. And if we complain they say 'We did warn you' and point to this letter."

"Typical bloody politicians," said Kell. "However, I must confess, it made me think. You told this young fellow"—he indicated Luke, who was sitting quietly in the corner—"just how you were guarding this place . . . ?"

"I did. And his only reservation, I remember, was the length of the sentries' spells of duty. Shorter now. They've sent me another two troops from the depot."

"Good."

"Good, yes. But is it good enough? The way I was thinking about it was this: Suppose I was a German, or a German sympathizer. What exactly would my targets be? And how should I attack them? To take the first question first: We've got a lot of new factories making shells. By which I mean turning out shell cases. But if they're going to be useful as anything but flower vases, they need propellants and detonators."

"And you're still the main source of these?"

"We and two others. What used to be called the Powder Factory, at Walthamstow and an old established factory at Tonbridge."

"Wouldn't it be simpler if the new factories did the whole job themselves?"

"Much simpler. And before the end of the year I expect they will. But at the moment three-quarters of their staffs are new boys. Keen, hardworking, and totally ignorant. They daren't let them handle high explosives yet—not until they've had time to learn about it, which they will do pretty quickly. And when I said 'new boys' I should have said 'new girls' as well. More than half their intake are women."

Kell thought about it. It narrowed down his problem but made the solution no easier. He said, "Tell me the answer, then, to your second question: How would you set about attacking the three vital places?"

"If they can't get through the walls, there's really only one way open to them, isn't there?"

"Attack from the air."

"Exactly. We've had Zeppelins over most days since war was declared, and they've done a lot of indiscriminate damage. What I was wondering was whether, if they concentrated their efforts, they might be able to smash us. We've got any amount of explosive material stored here, and one direct hit—"

"I don't deny the danger," said Kell. "But what real likelihood of success would it have? The Zeppelins are only difficult to attack because, at the moment, they can fly higher than our fighter planes. But tell me this: What chance would a Zeppelin flying at, say, ten thousand feet—that's almost two miles above the earth—what chance would it have of hitting a pinpoint target?"

"A comfortable thought," agreed the colonel.

Luke was not so comfortable.

His mind had gone back twelve months. He was sitting outside the private dining room at the back of the Royal Duke Hotel in Portsmouth, listening to the German naval officers blowing off steam.

They were describing how they would set about the Royal Navy. *"Über und unter"* had been their war cry. Over and under. The attack from above had been from Zeppelins. The attack from below had been by submarine. Was it a fantastic thought that a submarine, penetrating the triple defenses of the Thames estuary, might discharge a torpedo into the bowels of the Royal Arsenal?

No. It was surely a fantasy.

14

Joe was standing in an open doorway, staring down into a pit of blackness.

It was a blackness that was warmer than the night air around him, a blackness full of silence and a faint and unpleasant smell. It reminded him of something. Was it the smell of the hospital room where he had come back to life after the surgeon had finished sawing off the bottom half of his leg? Or did it go farther back than that? Much farther. To the last minutes of his father's life? His father, who had fought off death, inch by inch, yielding at last with a grunt of annoyance. Exactly the sort of grunt, thought the boy who was watching, that he would have given if he had come home and found that supper was not ready.

And why was he standing there thinking about his youth, instead of going forward into the darkness?

"Get on," said Joe. "Nothing to be frightened of."

The early stages of his approach had been easy enough. The five houses on the north side of the Crescent each had a handsome garden, the first two being separated by a narrow path, which ran up to the garden of the crematorium house. This was bordered, not by a hedge, which would have been awkward for a one-legged man, but by a simple post-and-nail fence. An easy way in. Even more important, an easy way out if he had to leave in a hurry.

To reach the back of the crematorium building he had had to cross an open space in full view of the windows of the house. Although, at two o'clock in the morning, Mr. Robb and his servants would surely be asleep, he had taken no chances but had snaked across the intervening space with his nose inches above the grass.

The remaining question had been: Could he open the crematorium door?

He had watched Mr. Robb go through it twice, once accompanied by his gardener, once alone. On neither occasion had he stopped to unlock the door. But this proved nothing. The door might be unlocked by day, locked by night. Against this contingency he had provided himself with a ring of keys; but when he turned the handle, the door had opened with a series of heart-stopping creaks.

"Get on, you dope. Are you waiting for a huge black thing to jump out and grab you? Once you get the bloody door shut behind you, you can use your flashlight, can't you?"

This seemed sensible advice. He stepped forward cautiously and swung the door to. Then, by the light of his flashlight, he was able to inspect his surroundings.

On the right was the great iron furnace, a monstrous contraption crouching in the corner, ready to spring.

Joe put this thought behind him and continued with his inspection.

Ahead of him was a platform against the wall that divided the crematorium from the chapel. It was a movable platform—easily movable, as he discovered when he put one hand on it to steady himself. It would carry the coffin up to the furnace.

Overcoming the illogical feeling that he might find human remains inside it, Joe opened the heavy iron door of the incinerating chamber. The narrow space inside was lined with firebricks, the ones on the floor being spaced to form a grid. As Joe shut the door he noticed that, though heavy, it moved easily.

Ahead of him a short flight of steps led down.

On the chapel side there were two doors, neither of them fastened. The first one contained the electric control boards, an efficient-looking collection of fuse boxes and switches. These were labeled "Chapel Main," "Chapel Sides," "Crematorium Lights," "Crematorium Power," "House Lights," and "House Power." The first four were off, the last two were on.

The second door opened onto a small workroom. There was a bench at the far end with a light suspended over it, and in a rack against the wall, as fine a collection of metal saws, probes, and cold chisels as he ever remembered seeing.

"A surgeon's kit," he said; "sharp enough to cut through bone," and as he stepped forward to examine them, something touched him on the back of his neck.

He tried to jump around—not a sensible maneuver for a one-legged man—and found himself on his face on the floor. The flashlight, which had fallen beside him, was still working. He put a hand out, picked it up, and turned the light upward. What had touched him was the end of a long, thick spider web.

Joe laughed weakly and scrambled back into an upright position. Doing so, he placed one hand flat on the floor and winced as he cut it on a sharp edge. The flashlight showed where this new attack had come from: On the floor, in front of the bench, were scattered a number of flintlike splinters.

Joe had had enough. The splinters might be important or they might not. He put three of them into his pocket. Then he turned thankfully back, out of the pit that seemed to stink of death up and out into the clean night air.

Half an hour later he was in his own bed. Having taken the precaution of downing half a glass of neat whiskey, he had not slept too badly.

The next morning he was out of bed by nine o'clock—an unusually early hour for him—and after a hurried breakfast took himself along to the house in the Crescent. He wanted to tell Luke about his excursion.

He took the splinters from his pocket and laid them on the table.

"Look like bits of very hard coal," said Luke. "I'll let the old man have them as soon as I can get away this evening."

Ben said, "My German class finishes at four. I'll stand in for you for the last spell if you think it's important."

"I've got beyond thinking what's important and what isn't," said Luke dolefully. "But I'll accept your offer and thank you." And to Joe, "Is there anything else you'd like to tell him?"

Joe thought about it. In daylight, among friends, it was almost impossible to describe the impression that the cellar had made on him. He said, "Only one thing: The place smelled odd."

"Odd?"

"I can't explain it. Except for one thing: There was a sort of smell of coal."

"Not unexpected in a coal cellar."

"It wasn't a coal cellar. The crematorium runs on gas and electricity. There isn't a coal fire in the place."

Luke thought about this.

"Maybe coal's been stored there some time for the house."

"It's got gas on tap and electric power—like I saw . . ." He explained about the switches. "I wouldn't think there's a coal fire in the house either."

It was a mystery, but a minor one. Luke said, "I'll put it in my report. He stirred the slatelike splinters with one finger. "I'll leave it to better brains than mine."

When Ben finally took himself off, Joe hobbled downstairs with him, to continue the interesting discussion they had been having.

"So how's it going?" said Ben.

"Fair to middling," said Joe. "Hard work, but some results. What I really wanted from her was a list of all Goodison's customers. I had to tell a lot of taradiddles to explain why I wanted it, but nowadays she just does what I say and doesn't ask questions."

How splendid, thought Ben, to be able to twist a girl around your little finger like that. He said good-bye and headed off up the Crescent at his best pace. He was due at the language school at midday, and Mr. Mills liked his students to be punctual.

The army officer, who seemed to be having trouble with his motorcycle and was bending over it making some adjustment, straightened up as Ben came past. The officer had evidently managed to locate and correct the fault, and by the time Ben was out of the Crescent and on Abbey Wood Road his machine was functioning again. He mounted it and rode slowly along, giving Ben an ample start and keeping his distance until Ben turned into Fendike Road.

When this happened, he killed the engine, parked the machine, and went forward on foot, keeping a discreet distance from his quarry. When he saw Ben turn in at the gate of the language school, walk up the front path, and ring the bell, he stood quite still.

It was perhaps as well that no passerby glimpsed his face. He might have reported to the police that there was a homicidal maniac at large in the area.

For a few seconds only. Then the good-natured army mask clicked back into place.

* * *

Vernon Kell was sitting in his office, his pince-nez glasses wedged onto his thick nose and a look of painful concentration on his face.

He had cleared his table of all routine matters and was staring at three reports, each in its neat folder. If he looked at them hard enough, could he wring from them the inner truth he was sure they contained?

"Not only must they mean something," he said, speaking too softly for his secretary in the next room to hear him and spread the rumor that he was going mad, "but taken together, and rightly understood, they *must* tell me the truth."

The first one was from Major Cooper-Key, to whom Kell had sent a letter two days before. Major Cooper-Key wrote:

> *You were kind enough to enclose in your letter a copy of the report submitted by Pagan, together with three flintlike shards. Reading between the lines, it seems to be the result of a highly unofficial visit paid by his colleague, Narrabone, to the East Plumstead Crematorium. Illegal, but enterprising.*
>
> *There are, as I expect you know, two different types of furnace used by such places. In the modern type a temperature as high as*

two thousand degrees can be produced by mixing steam and burning coke. Its drawback is that it needs regular stoking. The older, simpler type—which seems to be the one in use here—relies on a number of concentrated jets of ignited gas. It can simply be turned on and left to itself. The temperature produced is lower, and it takes longer to do its job, which is, putting the matter simply, to transmute the dead body into carbonic acid gas.

I mention these points because they underline the possible importance of the shards that were found in the cellar. These are fragments of anthracite, popularly known as stone coal. This is used primarily in blast furnaces and the boilers of ships but is not *a normal household fuel.*

The writer of the report has clearly noticed the significance of this, since he found no coal fires in the crematorium building and thought it unlikely that there would be any in the house. I agree. And if there had been, soft coal would have been used, not anthracite.

Kell had hoped that the writer would put forward his own answer to this conundrum. He was disappointed. The writer stated the facts but drew no conclusion from them.

Turning to your inquiry about possible explosives, you must bear in mind that in this country all forms of explosives have been strictly regulated since the activities of the Fenians were checked at the end of the last century. You told me yourself of an instance in which Russian terrorists were forced to manufacture their own dynamite under the guise of making soap—a most interesting incident that, with your permission, I intend to include in a paper I have been invited to read to the Royal Socity.

The truth is that if anyone requires a supply of explosives powerful enough to arm an infernal machine or machines, he is really driven to import it from some country that is laxer in its regulations than we are. Norway, Sweden, and Belgium are the most likely candidates. If your suspect, Goodison, is the importer, the explosive could easily be concealed in or among the tankage, lead piping, and brass balls that are part of his normal imports. If he is a regular dealer his stuff would be allowed through without any, or any careful, examination.

Kell paused for a moment to think about this. Certainly the possibility existed. The most suspicious customs officer would be unlikely to probe into the component parts of a lavatory. Well, that was a loophole that could be closed.

The report concluded:

> *Which brings me to the question of the type of explosive. Bearing in mind that it has to stand rough treatment in the course of loading and unloading, I think the answer is probably cordite—58 percent nitroglycerin, 37 percent guncotton, and 5 percent mineral jelly. It is a powerful explosive but unusually stable. In a recent test a bullet was fired through a compacted mass of cordite without detonating it. Any other help I can give you, please let me know.*

Helpful, certainly. But not entirely conclusive.

The second report was the one from Luke Pagan that Major Cooper-Key had referred to. The only additional items in it were the result of the watch they had been keeping on the crematorium. Nothing in it that was not normal and aboveboard. Except—what was it?—yes, the mailman. On a second occasion he had delivered three heavy parcels. Was that important?

At the back of his mind, while he was reading these reports, lay the three messages that Lieutenant Burnhow had riddled out. He had no need to think about them consciously. He had read them so often that they were part of his subconscious memory.

The third one was straightforward. It had enabled them to locate Goodison and Robb and had established the connection between the coal merchant and the crematorium. The first two were more difficult. The key to understanding them, as he was beginning to realize, was to differentiate between the "special product" and the "suitable supplies."

When he had first read the messages he had assumed that they were the same thing. Now he was not sure. "Let 105 know special product on its way to you." This meant that Robb had been worrying that regular supplies of the "special product" might not be reaching Goodison from his foreign supplier. So what was it? It seemed, from Cooper-Key's report, that it might be cordite.

Then Robb had started agitating again.

He was to be told not to worry. "Suitable supplies" would reach him from Goodison in time for him to "do the necessary." So what were the suitable supplies that Goodison was to send him? Could they be in the six large parcels that had been observed? Very possibly. But what were they?

A further thought: If Robb was in a constant fret about the availability of special products and suitable supplies, was it possible that he was in charge of the whole enterprise? That the blame would fall on him if it failed? That he was, in fact, *der Vetter?* How could he have been more deeply and safely buried than by establishing him as head of a crematorium?

Yes, it was possible. Kell turned now to the third document, which was an odd postscript to the others. It was from a Lieutenant Samuels, R.N., port control officer at Dun Laoghaire, and was a copy of a letter which had gone to Superintendent Patrick Quinn of the Special Branch. It said:

> *A curious problem, which might have repercussions at your end, has recently cropped up here. As you will know, since the outbreak of war, all persons entering or leaving Ireland have been very carefully checked and noted. Two weeks ago a Captain Marriott, R.E., left by the daily steamer from here to Holyhead. It seems that he had been spending part of his leave with friends shooting in County Wicklow and was on his way back to rejoin his unit. His papers were in order and aroused no question. But this odd point has now arisen. It appears from the routine checks we make from time to time* that there is no record of his entry into Ireland. *We have searched back for two months, which should be more than sufficient to cover a few weeks' shooting leave. We are puzzled by this discrepancy and feel that Captain Marriott should be located and questioned. A copy of this letter is being sent to Customs and Excise and to MO5.*

Kell sighed. If Captain Marriott was, as Lieutenant Samuels clearly suspected, an enemy agent, landed by submarine, he would have been supplied with two or more different sets of papers and would by now be Captain—or Major—or Colonel the Lord knows who. The Special Branch, as part of its duty of guarding important visitors, was expert at picking up the trail of dangerous infiltrators. They might be lucky enough to lay him by the heels.

It did not seem to be part of his own problem.

* * *

Annette O'Hegarty was worried.

When her father had gotten her the job as secretary, typist, and general assistant to Mr. Portlach—which he had seemed able to do without much difficulty—his instructions had been clear: She was to arrange her own desk so that she could hear anything said to, or by, the editor. If on the telephone, no problem. The line came through her. If in person, the door left open an inch or two should be good enough.

Routine espionage. Any girl could do it.

Until today nothing very interesting had transpired. This morning it was different. The two men who had arrived were oddly formidable. They had given her a card, to take in to the editor. As far as she could see from a quick glance, it contained only a set of initials in one corner.

When she handed the card to Mr. Portlach and started to explain about the two men, he had cut her short and had come out with her into the anteroom. Both men were standing. One of them said, "Mr. Portlach?" The editor nodded. "We have something to tell you. Since it's confidential, could you ask this young lady to remove herself to some other part of the building?"

She had seen, with astonishment, that the editor was not prepared to refuse this outrageous request. He had smiled weakly and said to her, "Perhaps you could sit for a bit in the conference room. You'll be quite comfortable there. I don't suppose we shall be long." That was where she had sat for nearly half an hour, alone with her thoughts and fears, until she heard the footsteps of the two men departing.

When Mr. Portlach came to get her she thought he looked like a man who had had a severe shock. But there was something else there as well. It was as though the shock had released a spring and restored an element of unsuspected determination. His voice was quite steady when he continued the dictation of the letters that the arrival of the strangers had interrupted.

Then he said, "I've two more letters to do. I'll be writing them myself while you are typing the others. They'll be ready for you by the time you've finished. Then I'd like you to take them all straight down to the post office."

One of these handwritten letters was, she noted, addressed to the chairman of the *Irish Citizen* at his Dublin office. The other was to Mr. Portlach's solicitor—his lawyer. She would dearly have liked to have read them and had, on more than one occasion, managed to open a badly fastened envelope to inspect the contents. But on this occasion, as she explained to her father, the envelopes were firmly fastened down and sealed with the editor's private seal.

Her father was more interested in the men than in the letters. He said, "What did they look like? Do you think they were policemen?"

Not exactly policemen, she had thought. Men with some sort of authority.

A colleague of her father's, a squat Irishman called Nick Mansergh, said, "If you ask me, it's plain as pie. They scared the poor bugger out of his wits and he's quitting. And once he leaves, you won't see him for dust."

"You may be right," said O'Hegarty. "And if you are, maybe, before he goes, we ought to impress on him the virtues of silence."

"A short, sharp lesson to take away with him," agreed Mansergh with a grin.

That was on Wednesday.

At four o'clock on Friday Mr. Portlach informed the two members of his staff—his secretary and a cleaning lady—that the office would not be reopening on Monday. He handed each of them a month's salary in cash, with a further month in lieu of notice and when they had departed placed his few remaining papers in the stove. As soon as they were well alight he went out, locking the inner and outer doors of the office behind him. The keys went into an envelope which he had prepared, addressed to his solicitor, and this he posted in the box at the end of Stag Court, together with a brief note addressed to Daryl Forbes c/o Mrs. O'Malley, Watersmeet Bungalow, Walton-on-Thames, informing him that any future contributions should be sent directly to Dublin.

He felt a lightening of his heart as he performed these closing ceremonies.

The shortest way to his flat on Neville Court was across Gough Square and along Pemberton Street and Harding Road. These were small and little-used byways, and he met no one until he emerged onto Great New Street. This, being a shortcut between Farringdon Street and Fetter Lane, was more used, and he was not surprised when he found a group of three men engaged in conversation and blocking the pavement ahead of him. Looking back, he saw a fourth man emerging from Harding Street. Mr. Portlach had been subconsciously aware of footsteps behind him ever since he had left the office, but he had been too busy with his own thoughts to pay much attention to them.

The men ahead of him stopped talking as he came up, but made no move to let him pass. Two were on the pavement, one in the roadway. The only other people in sight at that moment were a man and a woman on the opposite pavement, and a small boy who was amusing himself by clattering a stick along the railings.

Mr. Portlach stopped. He had no alternative. The way ahead was blocked. One of the men said, "Off on holiday, mister?"

Mr. Portlach muttered "None of your business" and edged out onto the road. He had a cold feeling that he had run into something it might be difficult to get out of. He saw that the man and the woman had turned their backs and were moving off fast. Whatever was going to happen, they wanted no part of it. The small boy had stood his ground. He thought that some sort of excitement might be coming up.

It was O'Hegarty who had spoken. He gestured to the two men, who stepped out into the roadway after Mr. Portlach. One of them put out a hand, grabbed his tie, and gave it a sharp tug. As the editor jerked forward, he kneed him in the stomach.

"Gently," said O'Hegarty. "Gently. We don't want to take him to bits. This is just a reminder of the value of a man keeping his lips buttoned. And of what might happen if he opened them too wide."

"Like this?" suggested Nick Mansergh and slapped the editor's face with his open hand.

"Or this?" said the third man and kicked him on the shin so hard that he uttered an involuntary cry and folded forward onto his knees. Upon which the second man, feeling perhaps that he had not made his point sufficiently forcefully, swung his boot. The kick landed on the side of Mr. Portlach's face.

"Now, just you stop that," said a new voice.

The Irishmen had been so intent on what they were doing that they had not noticed the arrival of another character. This was a slight young man, dressed in corduroy trousers and jacket, bareheaded, and carrying a light cane. He repeated, "Just you leave him alone."

O'Hegarty stared at him for a moment and muttered, "Christ, what are you doing here?"

"Seeing fair play, Pat."

At this moment two men erupted from the side road. They were Kirchner and Durkin, whose job it had been to follow and protect Mr. Portlach. The reason they had gotten so far behind was simple and discreditable. They had run into a young lady known to both of them and had stopped to exchange compliments with her.

Now they made up for lost time.

Both carried short sticks with heavy heads. Kirchner, without pausing for an instant, hit Nick Mansergh hard on the head. As he went down, O'Hegarty shouted from the pavement, "Run for it!" and belted off. The two men in the road paused for only a second before following him.

The small boy looked upset. The felling of one man and the arrival of two others had leveled the odds at three-all. Just right, he thought, for vigorous action. He felt shortchanged.

The young man now came to help Durkin, who had an

arm around Mr. Portlach and was trying to get him back onto his feet.

"Got one of them anyway," said Kirchner, prodding the prostrate Mansergh with his toe.

"If you're interested in the others," said the young man, "I can give you their full names and their addresses. I fancy that's a policeman just turning the corner. Let's hand over this fallen warrior—his name's Mansergh, by the way—and give the police particulars on the others."

Mr. Portlach was swaying on his feet, the blood running down his face.

"Aggravated assault, or some such charge."

* * *

When Captain Lewin, formerly Marriott, approached the Abbey Wood Tutorial Service on Fendike Road, he did so quite openly. His arrival attracted no attention. Before the war many army officers had been pupils there. Most of them were now busy elsewhere.

The maid who admitted him said that Mr. Mills had received his telephone message and was expecting him. The captain smiled gratefully. An officer and a gentleman, as she told her friends afterward.

As soon as the study door was shut behind him, the captain marched up to Mr. Mills, who had scrambled to his feet, bent his head forward, and said, very quietly, "I take it that this room is soundproof."

"Certainly. Even if there was anyone interested in eavesdropping. I see no reason why there should be."

"Good," said Erich Krieger, pulling up a chair and seating himself. He had made no move to shake hands, and his manner was that of a senior officer addressing a subordinate. "I am paying you this personal visit because Operation Asgard is nearing its climax and there are one or two points to be settled before the whistle is blown. First, as to the disposition of Tyr and Vulcan."

Mr. Mills, who was a careful user of language, thought that the word "disposition" accurately expressed what was in

Krieger's mind. He thought of Robb and Goodison as parcels to be forwarded somewhere.

He said, "Yes. They have done good work. They will have to be looked after."

"Very well, then. Here is an envelope for each of them. They will find in them identity papers, including a passport, money, and instructions as to where to go when they reach Ireland. Now, as to you—"

"I see no reason to run. Safer to sit still. Movement attracts attention."

"A sound army principle," agreed Krieger, "with one proviso: that there is no single scrap of paper, in the coal shop or the crematorium, that connects you with them."

"There could be nothing with Goodison. He knows nothing about me. Robb is different. He has been my sole contact with the rest of the group. All messages have gone out and come back through him. It is quite possible that he has papers that mention my name. However, I assure you that he will see that every scrap of paper is collected and destroyed before he leaves."

"Together with the spy who has gotten so close to you?"

Mills stared at him.

"You were not aware, then, that a young man who has connections with British Intelligence has inserted himself into your school?"

"You are talking about the chemist, Ben Lefroy?"

"I am."

"Are you sure?"

"Am I sure that he has connections with British Intelligence? Yes. I saw him recently in conversation with one of their operatives. But whether he joined your school to spy on you or simply to learn German—of that I am not sure. *But it is a matter on which we cannot afford to take chances.* Youngsters have sharp ears. He may have picked up some suspicion of your connection with Asgard. If he has, a further vital question poses itself: Has he passed on these suspicions? If he has not done so, then once he and every incriminating scrap of paper have disappeared, you will be as safe as you were before. If he has passed on his suspicions, you will be in danger.

Extreme danger. Had you not better change your mind? I have papers for you. You could vanish with the other two."

Mills said, "No." He said it with the firmness of a man who had thought it through, had made his mind up, and was not to be shifted. "I cannot desert my post. Not at this moment. You know, of course, of the action that is planned in Ireland."

"I not only know about it. We have been affording it all the help in our power. Arms, ammunition, explosives. And the service of a helper who has been organizing volunteers in our prisoner-of-war camps."

"If I stay here, I, too, may be able to help them. Help them in their work of pulling down the British bullies who have been treading on our necks for six centuries. I would count personal risk as nothing compared with the chance of playing the smallest part in that crusade."

"A fanatic," thought Krieger. There was no room in his cold mind for fanaticism, but he could recognize it and use it when he met it. He said, "Very well. I respect your decision. One final matter: When does Lefroy next come to you?"

"On Thursday afternoon. From four to six."

"Excellent timing. On this occasion, could you offer him a little extra instruction? Say, until eight o'clock?"

"I could. But why?"

"Because by that time it will be getting dark."

He saw, from the look on Mr. Mills's face, that he understood what was meant.

"Consider," he said, "the work that you and your two associates are engaged in." He was still speaking softly, but the steel edge was showing now. "If it is successful, it may mean the difference between winning and losing the battle that is now impending on the Western Front. Even if we win, the number of our young men who will die will be counted in thousands. If we lose, in tens of thousands. How heavy does one life weigh on such a scale?"

Mills shook his head. He could find nothing to say.

"Very well, then. I will explain exactly what I have in mind."

He spoke, uninterrupted, for ten minutes and did so with the assurance of a man whose own plans are well in hand. He was attached, temporarily, to the B Mess at Woolwich and was due to leave, on that Thursday, with a party of other R.E. officers joining their units in France. He was happy at the thought that he would be on the other side of the Channel when Operation Asgard reached its final bloody conclusion.

Before Mr. Blundell, in the East London Magistrate's Court.
The King against Patrick O'Hegarty, Dennis Macardle, Nicholas Mansergh, and Patrick Dunphy. Charged with committing grievous bodily harm: contrary to Section 18 of the Offences Against the Person Act of 1861.
Being an application to commit the case to the High Court for hearing.

COUNSEL: (To the witness) Your name is Arthur Merriman and you are currently serving in France as a second lieutenant in the Royal Warwickshire Regiment.
WITNESS: Lieutenant, actually.
COUNSEL: I apologize. I should have said lieutenant. And at the time of this offense you were on fourteen days' leave?
WITNESS: Correct.
COUNSEL: Before you joined the army, in September 1914, you were in charge of Loading Pier No. 5 in the London Western Dock and the four accused had worked under you for some time?
WITNESS: For six months in the case of Dunphy. For more than a year in the case of the other three.
COUNSEL: And you identify all four of them as having taken part in the assault on Frederick Portlach. (To the Magistrate) An assault, sir, that the medical evidence has shown to be a savage one.

Counsel for the defense, being asked if he had any questions, indicated that he would reserve his questions for when, and if, the accused were committed.

The magistrate, having found a prima facie case established, remitted the case to the Central Criminal Court. He said that the application that had been made for bail would be refused. He then pointed out that there was one important point to be considered. Addressing the witness, he said:

"I am informed that in view of the pressure on the calendar

it is unlikely that the case will reach the Central Criminal Court before late June, or possibly July, by which time you will have served for several further weeks in France. I have no doubt that an application for your attendance in Court will be readily granted. What I have to consider is the possibility—Mr. Blundell hesitated—that you will no longer be available.

Witness: *You mean that I may have copped a packet.*
Mr. Blundell: *That is the possibility I had in mind. And that is why you should consider making a formal deposition. The Crown solicitors will assist you with the wording.*
Witness: *(Apparently delighted with the idea) Then it can be read as my funeral oration.*

Joe's waking in the morning had, by now, become a well-established routine. At about seven he would be roused, unwillingly, from the depths of sleep by the sound of Ben, who had the next-door room, getting up. Then Joe might catnap until he heard feet clattering downstairs and the clack of the front door. After which he would turn over in bed and sleep until conscience, or hunger, got him out of bed at about nine-thirty. Recently they had taken two steps to simplify life: They had reduced the watching team from two men to one, covering the twelve hours of daylight in two spells of six hours. This gave each of them one complete day off out of three and enabled Joe to preserve his comfortable morning routine except on the day on which he had the first spell of duty. Also, they had not now so far to go. They had moved into new lodgings, on Paroma Street, halfway between the attic observatory and the language school.

On this occasion Ben had sent out none of the usual signals, and when Joe stomped down to breakfast there was still no sound from his room. No reason for him to be up. He did not take over from Luke until midday. But a worm of uneasiness had begun to stir. It had been Joe who had lured Ben into MO5, and he felt a corresponding responsibility for his welfare. He had not been happy when—at Ben's own insistence—the protective screen of Richner, Durkin, and Merchiston had been withdrawn. As soon as he had finished breakfast he went upstairs to look into Ben's room.

His fears crowded back. The bed had not been slept in.

It took him less than ten minutes to reach the attic observatory, where he found Luke, sitting at the window, his eyes glued to a pair of binoculars.

Before Joe could speak he said, "Something's going on. Ten minutes ago I saw that gardener-handyman drive off, and he had a trunk in the cart and the old woman with him. And yes—there goes the young one. Something wrong there."

"I'll say there's something wrong," said Joe savagely. "Ben's disappeared."

"Disappeared?"

"Never came back last night."

The note of fear in his voice sobered Luke. This was a crisis. He was in charge. Must think. He said, "There's a telephone downstairs. Get hold of our heavies. Any of them who are there. Bring them here quick."

During the half hour that it took to get Kirchner and Durkin he never took his eyes off the chapel and the house. He saw no sign of movement. Joe said, "Go the back way. The way I went before." Luke nodded.

The windows of the house were shuttered, and the silence was so absolute that Luke found himself whispering. He said to Kirchner, "You watch this door." It was the door leading into the chapel from the back. "Joe, you take a look in the cellar."

"For anything in particular?"

"Yes. Have a look at those power and light switches. If they're *all* off, we'll know they've left."

The cellar door was unlocked. Joe kicked it open and, armed with a small pocket flashlight borrowed from Kirchner, went carefully down into the darkness.

When Luke and Durkin reached the front of the chapel they saw a van parked in the forecourt. There was a pile of luggage in the back. The big west door was ajar. Luke eased his way through, into the small antechamber. It contained only a few chairs and a notice board, with a list of services on it. Examining it quickly, Luke saw that there had been two on the Tuesday and one on the Wednesday. Thursday, and all the days after it, were blank.

Luke turned to point this out to Durkin, who was standing in the doorway. He said, "If there's no service, why've they lit the bloody furnace?" It was true. A belch of black smoke had started to rise, slowly but steadily, out of the chimney.

Luke stared at it for a few moments, trying to rearrange his ideas. Then he walked across, opened the door that led into the chapel, and went in.

At the far end, between the front row of chairs and the altar, was a platform on wheels, which ran up to an opening in the wall between the chapel and the furnace room and was closed by a steel shutter. On the platform lay one of the simple plywood coffins of the type used in cremation. But Luke had eyes only for the man behind the platform. It was Andrew Robb, but not the English businessman; not even Anders Raab, the German. This was Tyr, son of Odin, god of war. The first look had been surprise, but that had disappeared. There was nothing now in his engorged face but rage and defiance.

As Luke and Kirchner walked forward he touched a switch in the wall and the steel shutter slid up, letting in a gust of overheated air.

"You can feel it?" said Robb. "Yes. You can feel it, because the furnace door is now wide open. I have only to press down this lever and the rollers will send the coffin through into the fire. They are stronger than you are. Nothing you can do will stop it. You understand me?"

Luke nodded. The coffin, he could see, was clamped down onto the rollers.

"And you wish to save the life of the young man who is in it? Alive, I assure you."

Luke nodded again. He was unable to speak.

"Then I make you this offer. I require five minutes' start. Only five minutes. How many years has this boy to live? If you give me your word, I will accept it and you shall have your friend back."

Luke saw that Robb's hand was on the lever. He had no

doubt that he was speaking the truth. The rollers and clamps would send the coffin through with a power they could not counter. He was about to say something—anything—to postpone the decision, when the door at the back opened and Joe came through. He gave a thumbs-up sign and said, "Don't worry. I've turned off the power."

For a moment Luke could not grasp what Joe was saying, but Robb understood him and backed away from the platform. Kirchner, who had produced a clasp knife, inserted the blade under the thin cover of the coffin and levered it up clear of the pins that had been holding it. They could see Ben, cradled in a nest of papers and most clearly dead.

For a moment no one moved.

Then Robb, seeing that Joe had left the door open, spun around and darted toward it. Joe, who was holding an iron bar in his right hand, allowed Robb to go past him and then swung it in a vicious backhanded swipe, driven by all the strength of his arm and backed by all the fury in his heart. It hit Robb at the top of his spine with such force that it nearly severed his head from his body.

Kirchner, more used to violence than the other two, was the first to move. He came around the end of the platform and looked down at Robb, who lay in a slowly oozing puddle of blood. He said, "Killed trying to escape. Right?" Leaning forward, he picked up the envelope that had slipped onto the floor. The passport had fallen out of it. He said, "Give him the five minutes he was asking for and I guess you wouldn't have seen him for dust."

"But who?" said Luke. "How did he? When did this happen?" He was finding it difficult to speak.

"If I might make a suggestion," said Kirchner. "Have a quick look through the papers this type was trying to burn and you'll probably find the answers."

* * *

That same morning Kell was having one of his weekly meetings with Basil Thomson. It was clear that Kell was pleased with himself. "Two strokes of luck," he said. "First, we've got rid of that gang of Irish bullies. For a good long time, I should say."

"Good luck for us," said Thomson. "Bad luck for them. That they should have run up against the one man who could identify them."

"And someone they couldn't hope to intimidate."

"Right. You said two lots of luck."

"For some time now we've been examining the letters in and out of that newspaper office. The very last one that the editor mailed gave us the address of Daryl Forbes in Walton-on-Thames. The local police have now got him under discreet observation. He seems to have settled down very nicely. They'll tell us at once if he tries to move on."

"It's even better than that surely. Now that the English edition of the paper has folded up, he'll see no point in writing further articles. It was England he was preaching to, not Ireland. He's lost his pulpit."

"Two up and one to play," said Kell. "It'd be game, set, and match if I could only make out what Robb and Goodison are up to. But the damnable thing is"—he indicated the pile of documents on his table—"that it's all there. Under my eyes. If only I could read it. The key's in those first two messages. I'm sure of that. I spent two whole hours yesterday thinking about them. Have you ever tried thinking about one thing for two hours?"

"Certainly not," said Thomson. "After ten minutes my thoughts would be going around in a circle, chasing each other up their own posteriors. So what conclusion did you come to after that feat of mental gymnastics?"

"I came to this conclusion: To find the answer, you've got to take a general view of the matter before trying to pick out the details."

"Wholesale first, retail later," suggested Thomson.

"It was rather that you had to look at the background before you could focus on the foreground. You understand me?"

"No. But don't stop."

"Right. The background is in Germany. No question about it. I can see the hand of Steinhauer pulling the strings to make his puppets dance. What's more, he can send them messages, through Zeeman, in Switzerland, to Goodison in London. He must have sensed that Robb was getting fidgety. Were things going quickly enough? Would he be ready in time? Goodison is told to calm him down. Tell him that the 'special product' is already on its way to you. And tell him that you'll be letting him have 'suitable supplies' in plenty of time for him to do his bit."

"That's tolerably clear," said Thomson. "It would be clearer still if we had any idea what things he was talking about."

"I'm more and more convinced that the 'special product' is some form of explosive—probably cordite. I could ask Customs and Excise to make a special examination of anything coming from Zeeman. But I don't want to alert Goodison until we've got the whole picture."

"Very well. Let's assume that the 'special product' is cordite. In that case, what are the 'suitable supplies'? Am I being simplistic if I point out that Goodison is a fuel stockist? In the ordinary way what he would *supply* would be coal."

"Heaven preserve my wandering wits," said Kell. "Of course. Not just coal. Anthracite."

The words seemed to sound an echo.

"Slivers of anthracite. A bench of tools. Robb was working on lumps of anthracite that Goodison sent him. That must be right."

"Not forgetting," said Thomson, "that Robb, in his youth, had been a sculptor. What he was producing was a novel sort of bomb."

The two men looked at each other. Before either of them could speak, the door burst open and Hall was in the room. He was white with fury, so angry that he could hardly speak.

He said, "While we've been piddling and twiddling here, they've done it again."

"Done what?"

"Destroyed another ship. The *Princess Irene,* with most of her crew and some dockyard men who were working on her. You may be happy to sit talking. I'm not. I've brought half a dozen of our own dockyard policemen, and if you won't get off your bottoms and pick up that sod Goodison and twist him till he squeals, why then I'm quite ready to do it myself. And my men won't be gentle. They had friends on the *Irene*—"

"As a matter of fact," said Kell, and the coldness and heavy calmness in his voice took some of the steam out of Hall, "we were planning to go around there ourselves. We've just worked out what we're likely to find. We'll explain as we go."

When the two naval tenders squealed to a halt outside the coal merchant's shop there was no stopping or delaying the wave of men who broke over it. The youngster who opened the door was swept aside. Any door that was shut against them was kicked open. Goodison was alone in his office. He started to say something, then stopped. Tried again and failed again.

Hall said to the naval contingent, "Take this place to pieces. Particularly the fuel stocks. You know what to look for."

As they streamed out of the room, Hall marched up to Goodison, who was on his feet now but silent. When Hall spoke, their faces were only inches apart. He said, "The laws of England contain one section that you may have overlooked. The crime of treason is still on the statute book. It includes damaging or setting fire to His Majesty's dockyards or the ships in them, and punishment for it is specified in the act. Not an honorable death, in front of a firing squad. That's too good for traitors. The penalty for treachery is hanging. You understand? To be dropped through the floor with a rope around your neck, your arms strapped to your side, and a hood over your face. And if we could cut you down and hang you twenty times it would be less than payment for the work you've been doing."

Goodison backed away from the fire and fury in Hall's voice. Kell thought he was going to faint. But he managed, somehow, to get back to his chair.

At that moment a sergeant came in, followed by two men. Each of them was carrying, with extreme caution, a lump of anthracite, roughly the size and shape of a small pineapple. "I think this must be what you're looking for, sir."

Kell said, "Let me have it. And lend me your knife."

He inserted the blade gently, and the two halves of the lump came apart. Both halves had been hollowed out, and both were empty.

Hall said, "Cordite in one half—sent from Stockholm by Zeeman—sulfuric acid in the other—stolen for them by their Irish friends from that chemical works. A thin membrane to separate them, which the acid would eat through in due course. If inserted in a furnace the heat would destroy the membrane and activate the cordite at once." He weighed the lump of anthracite thoughtfully in his hand. "As pretty a little time bomb as ever slid unsuspected into the boiler of a ship."

"Or of an ammunition factory," said Kell. "Take this man away. Handcuff him and throw him into one of the vans." He grabbed the telephone. There were so many people he had to contact urgently. The Royal Arsenal, the powder factory, the premises at Slough, all dockyards, all ports in which coal-fired ships might be found. If any had received fuel from Landsells their furnaces would have to be raked over and every lump of coal, in furnace or in store, examined.

"We can only pray," said Hall, "that we aren't too late."

* * *

"Well," said Luke flatly, "so now we know."

The first two or three papers from the coffin had shown them the truth. *Der Vetter,* Wotan, the director of Operation Asgard, was the soft-spoken, intelligent, helpful head of the Abbey Road language school, David Mills, into whose hands outrageous chance had delivered Ben. Now that all the papers had been removed, from around and under him, he looked small and lonely.

Joe, after glancing at him, had not spoken a word but had wandered off, out of the chapel and into the anteroom. When the others joined him they found him sitting, cross-legged, on a chair and staring at nothing in particular. Luke, spotting a telephone on the shelf above his head, said, "Is it working?" Joe said, "No," but it was clear from his tone of voice that he meant that he didn't know and didn't care. His mind was far away.

Luke found that it did work, was put through to Kell's office, and listened to it ringing interminably. Finally a girl answered. She said, "There's no one here but me. They've all gone."

"Gone? Where?"

The girl said she didn't know. They'd pushed off with a crowd of sailors. She then replaced the receiver firmly.

Luke was still staring at the instrument when Kirchner said, "If I might suggest it, don't you think we ought to be getting after Mills? If he's been supplied with a set of papers like the other one, he might be difficult to stop. My van's parked around the back—"

Luke said, "While you're fetching it, I'll have a word with Inspector Horniman. He can take over here."

As they were driving the short distance down Abbey Road to the school, all four crammed together in Kirchner's tiny vehicle, Luke said, "We'll be too late. He'll be gone."

Durkin said, "I wouldn't be on it. He'll be there and he'll put up a fight—I hope."

Kirchner said, "He'll be there, but he won't fight." Joe continued to say nothing.

Kirchner came nearest to the truth.

When Mills saw them pile out of the van and guessed what they had come for, he opened the drawer of his desk, took out a service revolver, placed the barrel carefully in his mouth, and pulled the trigger, scattering his brains over the wallpaper behind his desk.

* * *

It was only after a week of mixed and strenuous work that Kell found time to sum up for his two young assistants. Four of the anthracite bombs had been found in the last delivery of coal to the Royal Arsenal—two each in the coal stores at the powder factory and Slough. Clearly they had been intended to detonate at the same time, if possible. An explosion in any one of the three places would have been a disaster.

Kell said, "If all three had gone up it wouldn't have been a disaster. It'd have been a catastrophe. A close-run thing.

Closer than I like to think about. However, now that you have disposed of Robb—"

Joe, who seemed to have recovered some of his spirits, said, "Yes, I disposed of him."

"It has been accepted that he was trying to escape and that you had no option. Mills has killed himself. Goodison is being held on charges that will, almost certainly, lead to a capital sentence. With the removal of Wotan, Tyr, and Vulcan we may assume that Operation Asgard has gone into—what shall we say?—involuntary liquidation. However, there's one man who would have been a more valuable prize than those three together: Erich Krieger. Palmer in Canada, Richards in Portsmouth, Marriott in Ireland, and Lewin—as we've recently discovered—at Woolwich. From which he left for France a week ago with a party of officers who were rejoining their units."

"No doubt he's back in Germany by now."

"I wouldn't go so far as that. Let's say he's certainly back across the Channel, absorbed safely into a million other soldiers and perfectly camouflaged."

Luke and Joe looked at each other. There was a note in Kell's voice that seemed to offer a hint of the opening they were looking for.

Luke said, in as casual a tone as he could muster, "Didn't you once tell us that a number of your men had been drafted into the Intelligence Police in France?"

"If I said that, it was, regrettably, true. I have lost a lot of good men."

Joe gave him a look that said, "Go on. Don't fluff."

"We did wonder," said Luke, "whether an attachment, a temporary attachment, might be arranged for us."

"It might be. But why?"

"Well, sir, you said that Krieger would be a valuable prize."

"And you think that you might be able to locate him."

"He won't have been able to change his appearance all that much. And we examined him, night after night, at his card table in that house above Gilkicker Point—"

"The last time *I* saw him," said Joe, "he was fiddling with his motorcycle outside that house in the Crescent. He had his back to me and was bending over the machine, so I didn't recognize him, but I'm sure it was he—"

"Oh, why?"

"Because he recognized me. Must have done. And saw me talking to Ben, and that's why—"

"Stop that!" said Kell sharply. "If anyone's to blame, I am. I picked out that language school for him. All right. I agree there are few people more likely to spot Krieger than you two. I'm not making any promises, but I'll think about it. And I've got a piece of news for you: Hall tells me that the navy has scored a fine success in the North Sea. It's not been announced yet, so don't splash it about. Two of our cruisers engaged and sank the German armored cruiser *Kobold.* She went down with all hands."

"*Über and unter,*" said Luke softly.

PART THREE

Le Touquet

15

Luke was perched on the top of Mont St. Frieux, five hundred feet above the sea. From this inconsiderable height he could look down on the largest reinforcement camp in France.

It was divided two ways.

Laterally by the Canche River, which ran from Montreuil to the sea. Lengthways by the D940 from Hardelot to Berck-Plage and the railway that ran alongside that road. This produced a pleasing pattern of four, roughly equal, quarters. The northwest quarter was an area of shrub and sand dunes that stretched from where he sat to the outlet of the Canche River. In the left-hand corner he could see the court-martial prison and detention camp, a massive construction girdled by ten-foot wooden stakes and a double entanglement of barbed wire. It looked strong, but no stronger than it need be, thought Luke, holding delinquents and deserters from all parts of the British line. There were men in the detention block awaiting armed escorts. Some of them were under sentence of death.

The northeast quarter, in and around Étaples town, housed the base camp, a tented city planted around playing fields. The headquarters building, a block of recently constructed flats, contained the rabbit warren of offices that seemed to spring into existence as soon as the British Army settled. The overall commander of the base, Major General Eustace Foxley, seldom visited it. He left all routine matters to his adjutant, Captain Edwards, and spent most of his time fishing.

The southeast quarter, on the other side of the river, was the Kingdom of Q. It was based, sensibly enough, along the railway from which spurs ran to its four main sections, vast depots of clothing, ammunition, food, and drink. These were almost as carefully protected as the prison.

Finally there was the southwestern quarter. Much of it was taken up by the sprawling seaside town of Le Touquet. Most of the officers had found billets there, and the large Hôtel Bristol and the smaller Hôtel Le Manoir had been taken over as officers' messes. A villa in the southern outskirts of the town was the base hospital, with a number of convalescent camps strung out along the shore. From where he sat this was out of Luke's sight, but he could see the tops of the trees in the Forest of Merliment, a wild area that ran down all the way from Le Touquet to Berck.

He wondered how many officers and men this mushroom city contained. Several thousand at least. And among them one man who might be there. One man whom he and Joe would have given a lot to locate. The difficulty of the job seemed to depress Joe more than it did Luke.

He had enjoyed the weeks he had spent at Boulogne under the genial command of Colonel Knox-Johnson, who was busy, under General Macdonough, in forming and training the Intelligence Police, a remarkable collection of Oxbridge dons and London City men who managed both to shock and to impress the army hierarchy.

When it was realized that Luke was a fluent French-speaker, he had been given the job of sorting out the crowd of Belgian refugees, many of whom seemed willing—sometimes too willing, he thought—to help the Allied cause by returning to their own country as spies. Some of the more promising were given a short course of training and were returned to Belgium by a roundabout route. Across the Channel to England; to Holland by the Folkestone–Flushing ferry; and back over the Dutch–Belgian border. The last leg of their journey had become more difficult since the Germans had erected an electric fence, but there were ways over it and under it.

Outstanding among these Belgians had been the sagacious Max Pieters. He was not offering himself as a spy but as a source of information. He knew both sides of the line. Head of the famous jewelers' shop in Brussels, with a host of German and French customers and friends, he had been able to foresee more clearly than Paris or Whitehall the right-handed sickle sweep of the German Army and the inevitable occupation of Belgium that would follow. He had, in good time, transferred his money to a Swiss bank and the bulk of his stock to his branch establishment in the holiday resort of Le Touquet.

He had been there himself when war broke out and was now keeping a close eye on things. Had he detected the least likelihood of the German Army breaking through the locked trench system, he would have made all the necessary preparations to move his stock to London. Like many Belgians, he was more attached to the English than to the French. Maybe it was a case of distance lending enchantment to the view.

Luke had spent long hours talking to this cynical old man. Becoming confident in his discretion, he had told him, in general terms, what had brought him to France.

"If you are looking for a top-ranking German agent," said Pieters, "you won't find him in Boulogne. It is nothing more than a railway station, men coming and going, all firmly controlled by the army. Boulogne and Calais are places in which you dare not relax your grip. If you lose control of the Channel ports you lose the war."

"Then perhaps you can suggest where I ought to be looking."

"You say that this man can pass, unquestioned, as a British officer. He has the uniform, the papers, the correct manner. But—and this is surely the important point—he *must* confine himself to the back areas. If he approached the lines, it could only be on the basis that he was rejoining his unit. He would be detected at once."

"You mean that he's reasonably safe in a transit camp or a base camp—where the units are mixed and no one is over curious about his neighbor."

"A base camp or a convalescent camp would suit him well."

"And you have such a place in mind?"

"Certainly. The place I have in mind is your base camp at Le Touquet. Having a shop there, I have been well placed to study it. And it seems to me to offer the greatest possible number of chances to a man whose mission it is to remain hidden and to stir up trouble. You may imagine that, because you have brought over a number of military policemen and set up a strong prison, you are in control. If you think that, I advise you to go and see for yourself. It is a curious area. The chalk pits and corridors of the forest of Merliment have never been properly explored. A primitive area, into which you have, by force of circumstances, crammed a crowd of desperate men. Men with nothing to lose and ample places to hide in. Did you know that recently the police recaptured in Étaples a deserter who had been on the run since the opening of the war in August 1914? You must get Colonel Harper to tell you about it."

"Colonel Harper?"

"Dan Harper. The provost marshal. A good man. I have no wish to denigrate the soldiers of an ally, but some of the other senior officers are—what is the word you use—deep pits? No, dugouts."

When Luke had repeated the gist of this to Knox-Johnson the colonel had said, "I've never been entirely comfortable myself about that place. You'd better do what your jeweler friend suggested. I'll organize you a temporary commission in the C.M.P.s. When you've assessed the situation report back here. Harper will let you know if there's any serious trouble in the offing."

Trouble? thought Luke, looking down at the base camp; at the men playing soccer on the two playing fields; at the hurdy-gurdy crowd around them; Crown and Anchor schools; three-card tricksters. It was like Epsom Downs on Derby day.

Some of them were reinforcements, waiting to go up to the line; some were convalescents well enough to be allowed out, or who had simply removed themselves from the camps on the shore, to enjoy life before, if lucky, they were sent back to England, or if unlucky, back to the trenches. The camp commandant, Major General Foxley, whom Luke had met once, briefly, had expou ed his creed to him: "As few restrictions as possible. Most o em have earned a holiday. Let them enjoy it." If this ha en a camp in England, adequately staffed, it might hav n an acceptable policy of laissez-faire. In this corner o ce it was, Luke thought, bloody dangerous.

Climbing to his feet, L out on the five-mile tramp to Étaples station. For the t he walked on the railway tracks, which was easier the sand and coarse grass. The C.M.P.s had taken ov tion hotel, and Luke had been allotted a room at the ad previously housed a minor member of the hote sibly a housemaid? It was small, neat, and seclude ed him perfectly. He changed from his outdoor clo ice dress and went down to the anteroom, wher o men drinking and talking. One was the bla spoken A.P.M. David Longhorn, who had som putation as a disciplinarian. The other, Robert a liaison officer from the French Police Judi

"Poor old Dan," Longhorn was rt bleeds for him."

"Why?" said Luke.

"He's been invited—which means headquarters mess. Which means tha a table with Foxley at one end and Lan the listening to Porteous, Lipholzer, and S t at exactly how they'd have won the war er, charge."

Luke could already identify the names. La in ng the quartermaster general. Porteous, Lipholzer, mith were majors and were in charge of three of s depots.

"Have you not omitted someone?" said Dujardin. there not four depots?"

"So I did. I forgot Puppy."

Puppy, thought Luke, must be Major Yapp. Identifiable, at first sight, as that dangerous type, an occasional hea drinker. Not the best guardian for store QD, which contai

not only the army's reserve supplies
Royal Army Medical Corps reserves
Dujardin said, "Doubtless we v
count when the colonel return
"No such luck. Dan is too
officers. And here is Corpo
ready."
It was a good dinner
but he went to bed d
He wished he wa

Next mornin
the main r
Touquet.
only re
east,
ign

alcohol but also the
medication and drugs.
et a blow-by-blow ac-
soldier to criticize senior
e, to tell us that dinner is

ld have raised Luke's spirits,
It was not a happy ship.
Boulogne.

* * *

fter breakfast, crossing the river by
strolling through the streets of Le
enjoying the autumn sunshine. The
war was the sound of gunfire to the
ground grumbling they had learned to

own, he struck out northward, across the
a point at the corner of the forest that he
n as a useful observation post. From it he
se hospital and the three convalescent camps
g the shore. His eyes were fixed on the south-
presently he saw a figure detach itself from the
the camp and come stumping toward him, using

not need his field glasses to tell him who it was.
d perch on top of a bloody mountain," said Joe, who
ting from the exertion of crossing the rough ground.
untain," said Luke. "It's hardly a hill. A hillock, per-

illocks to you," said Joe, seating himself carefully. Get-
, up was sometimes more difficult than sitting down. "I
e it you're living, as per usual, in the lap of luxury."
"Comfortable enough. What about you?"
"Nothing to write to the papers about. Would you believe
it, when I arrived, the sergeant in charge offered me a ham-
ock; I ask you, a hammock for a man with one leg. Luckily
ur pal, the chief doctor, came along and sorted things out."

"Colonel Deeming, that would be."

"I take it he's in the know."

"Yes. He's been briefed about you."

"He's fixed me up with a bed, a nice wound stripe, a couple of corn cakes, and made me an honorary corporal. I spend my time dishing out food, handing out mail, and evading questions about my war service. Luckily, they mostly think about themselves. Question number one: Can they wangle themselves back to England? Question number two: What's for dinner?"

"Along with your not too arduous duties, I take it that you've been keeping your eyes and ears open."

"Both," said Joe. "Eyes first. Take a look around you. What do you see?"

"Acres of sand, thousands of trees, and millions of bushes."

"Ah. That's because you've only got what you might call superfissual vision and don't know what's underneath." Joe thumped the ground with his stick.

"No. Tell me."

"Solid chalk, and in the chalk there're miles and miles of caves, one leading into another. If you knew your way through them you could go all the way from here down to Berck without surfacing once. I said, *if* you knew your way. If you didn't—well, one of our brighter invalids thought he'd do a little exploring. They found him ten days later. What was left of him. Plenty of rats in those caves, thankful for fresh meat."

"Ugh," said Luke. "What else have you found out?"

"Oh, I haven't been wasting my time. It's an interesting part of the world, this is. Full of life. There're two villages on the coast. Doonyer—can't pronounce them—and Easy."

"Dunière," said Luke, who had been examining the map, "and Ezé. What about them?"

"They're fishermen and smugglers, and if I wasn't being polite, I'd say pirates. And you know how it is with neighbors, spend all their time quarreling. Seems there was some dispute about fishing rights, which ended in a fight. One killed on each side. It evened out. Now, if they meet, they don't talk. They just spit at each other."

"And which side are you on?"

"Oh, I'm a Doonyer. And I'm in good with their head man. *Grand-père,* I call him. It's a name something like that. He's got a beard down to his waist and he's lost one arm, which gives him a sort of fellow feeling with me. He owns most of the fishing boats and the only pub in the place. It was through him I picked up Pepin. Though, actually, he's an Easyite, not a Doonyer."

Joe's ability to make unlikely friends had always impressed Luke. He said, "Tell me about Pepin."

"He's a monkey. A monkey in human shape."

"A French boy?"

"A youngster, I'd call him. Not a boy. He's from Alsace, and he don't like the Germans. He hates them. On account of what happened to his father. He was foreman of a gang of workers in one of the coal mines. When the Germans took over he refused to work for them, so they shot him. After which Pepin removed himself with his mother and came across here. One of his relations is in the Easy fishery crowd, so he soon made himself useful: mending nets, fishing for bait, repairing tackle, you name it."

"Sounds a useful sort of chap."

"You're all of that, aren't you, Pepin?"

A voice close behind him said, "Pleezeter meecher."

Luke spun around and saw a brown face looking at him from the middle of a bush.

"I taught him to say that," said Joe. "At the moment, it's about all the English he does know, but he seems to understand my French—that is, if I go slowly. He pointed at Luke and said, *"Mon amee."*

"Ah, si, votre copain, dont vous m'avez parlé. Sans doute un brave garçon." The face-splitting grin with which Pepin accompanied this seemed to cast some doubt on the total sincerity of the compliment.

"One thing he can do," said Joe, "as you may have noticed, is slip in anywhere without calling undue attention to himself. That way he picks up useful odds and ends, one of which I'll pass on to you at once. Seems that the Easy crowd are in with certain villains up your end of the town. See what it means? It's a nice little back door if they need it. A boat trip down the coast to Spain. Once they're there they'd be safe enough.

Luke nodded. He knew about Spain's odd notion of neutrality.

"But there's a snag: The Easy boss is a smooth character called Moulin. That's the French for mill."

"Yes," said Luke patiently.

"Well, old man Mill isn't in the job for peanuts. He's got a scale of charges. To go down to Spain would cost you five hundred Jimmies, or whatever that comes to in francs, or marks, or dollars, for that matter. He's an all-around financier."

"Five hundred pounds," said Luke thoughtfully. "How's a runaway going to get hold of that sort of money?"

"One way would be by selling booze, wouldn't it? Great market here for booze. Pepin told me that one of his Easy friends told him that liquor was leaking out of the Q stores like water out of a sieve."

Pepin, who seemed to have understood that drink was being discussed, smacked his lips.

Luke said, half to himself, something that sounded like "Puppy Yapp," and aloud, "Yes. Thank you. I'll be looking into that. And for all the other information."

He was not as interested in the fishermen and their feuds or the leakage of liquor as in the possibilities of Pepin. An assistant who could maneuver inconspicuously was something he had been looking for since he arrived at Le Touquet.

It was a pleasant thought to balance the unpleasant ones.

16

Major General Eustace Foxley was feeling pleased with life. He was strolling along the southern bank of the Canche, heading for the colonial-type mansion that served him as a personal residence.

One of the reasons for his complacency was the three fine speckled trout in his landing net. The purple queen lure, which he had tied the evening before, had justified the time and trouble he had spent in its construction. Also, the sun was shining. And his troublesome charges were, for once, behaving themselves.

Credit for this must go to Colonel Harper and his C.M.P.s. He did not like the colonel but hoped that he was broad-minded enough to appreciate a professional job, adequately carried out.

At first he failed to recognize the young man who was walking toward him. He was dressed as casually as the colonel himself. Flannel trousers and an open-necked shirt. A soldier or a policeman off-duty? Yes. A policeman, he thought, as the man came closer. Hadn't Harper introduced him when he arrived? An odd name. Pagan. Good, he had remembered it. Captain Luke Pagan. Absurdly young and naive-looking for a C.M.P. None of that hard-bitten look he associated with policemen. Tiresome fellows most of them.

This one unloosed a charming smile on the general as he bade him good morning and congratulated him on his catch.

"Fine fellows, are they not?" said the general. "You must be the latest addition to Dan Harper's crowd. If you have the time, perhaps you'd walk back with me. I'd like to hear the latest news from Sing-Sing."

Luke turned around willingly and fell in beside the general. At this point the track swung away from the river, and they were crossing the frontage of the German compound. It was not nearly such an elaborate affair as the detention camp. A single strand of barbed wire seemed more to delineate the area than to keep the prisoners in. Having sidestepped the war, they had little incentive to escape back to it. Well fed and organized by their own N.C.O.s, they served as a useful, unpaid labor corps that in return for extra rations did most of the routine work in the four big Q stores. The ones who were sitting or lying closest to the wire rose politely to their feet as the general passed.

"Good men," he said, "and clever craftsmen. If you've a moment I'll show you something they made for me."

He led the way into the hall and through it to the room at the back, which was lined with books.

"My study," said the general. "Not my books, of course." He took down from a shelf a model of a frigate under full sail. The detail was meticulous.

"It's lovely," said Luke. "It must have taken no end of time and trouble."

"I'm sure it did. But when all's said and done they haven't much else to do in their spare time. Yes, what is it?"

An orderly had appeared at the door. "It's Major Porteous, sir. He'd like a word with you."

"Show him in," said the general, adding, with a smile, "As you see, I'm not allowed a lot of spare time myself. Come in, Pat. What's up now? If it's official business we'd better turn this young man out."

Major Porteous, who was a stout, red-faced Hampshire man, said, "It's official business. But since I believe—am I right?—that this young man is a policeman, he might as well hear what I've got for you. He can report it to Dan, who may feel that he should take—well—should take appropriate action."

"You're making me nervous," said the general jovially. "Let's have it without the trimmings."

"Well, sir, you remember that when I took over the QA store"—he turned to Luke—"that's 'A' for ammunition, there was a certain amount of awkwardness."

The general did remember it. The previous head of QA had been a dipsomaniac wished on them by a commanding officer who was frantic to get rid of him. Once installed, he had proceeded to drown his sorrows in further libations of cognac and had finally been removed, incapably drunk and strapped to a stretcher.

"As you may imagine," said Major Porteous, "his records were in no sort of order. I had a snap check made and I *think* I got a full record of what QA *ought* to contain. The trouble was that just at that time stuff was coming in and going out almost daily. We had to reequip the First Army after Aubers Ridge and Festubert. So that, one way or another, I wasn't sure that the record was complete. It was the best I could do. Two days ago, having a little more time on my hands, I had a thorough check made and it did seem to me that I was short of more than thirty rifles and several boxes of ammunition."

"You seemed to be short, but you're not sure. Right?"

"Fairly confident, sir. I've got a good storeman now."

"It's worrying," said the general, who sounded far from worried. "And I'll let Dan know. Rifles aren't in a seller's market around here. Most of the men are only too glad to have done with them, for the time being."

Major Porteous departed, looking unhappy. Luke said, "I wonder, sir, if you could explain about these stores—what they've got in them and how they're run. It would be very helpful."

The general, who was clearly attracted to the good-looking, deferential young man, said, "Better to see one of them than to talk about it, wouldn't it be?"

He led the way, down a path through the bushes and out into a wide-open space that backed on the road and railway. Here were the four main stores, each of them a substantial construction of vertical timbers roofed with corrugated iron.

"When I took over," said the general, "I suggested to the Q.M.G. that we put each one of them in charge of a different corps. QA, ammunition, is staffed by the infantry—the Middlesex Regiment is on duty at the moment. QB, food, by the Guards. QC, clothing, by the Royal Army Service Corps. And QD, drink, by the R.H.A. As you know, horse gunners have a reputation for smartness and efficiency. I see the B.S.M. out in front there. If you'd care to look over it I'm sure he'll be happy to open up for us."

Since it was the store that he was most anxious to see, Luke expressed his delight at the idea. The man who answered their hail and unbarred the door in the massive wire barrier could only have been a sergeant major. His brick-red, deeply lined face announced a man who had done most of his service under the tropical sun and had learned to accept difficulties and responsibilities as his daily lot.

"B.S.M. Forgan," said the general. "Our *maître de chai.*" When the B.S.M. looked blank, he translated it for him. "Our cellarmaster."

"That's right," said Forgan. "Enough drink here to sink a battleship. If you'd follow me . . ."

There was a corridor running lengthways down the building, with a number of strong-looking doors on either side.

"They're all arranged the same."

He unlocked the first door and they could see rows of slatted shelves with boxes lined up on them. A card, tacked to the edge of each shelf, had two columns: one headed "In" and the other "Out."

"That way, I can see, at a glance, what should be here."

"Excellent," said the general.

Forgan relocked the door and led them to the end of the corridor, which opened out into an office where a pale young man was seated behind a desk, calculating figures. He did not get up when they came in.

"Bombardier Light was an accountant before the war. Right?"

The bombardier nodded. He looked as though he wished he was safely back in the London City office that the army had press-ganged him from.

"Do you mean to say," said Luke, "that you two look after all this?"

"We're the brains of the establishment," said Forgan with a

grin. "When stuff's coming in or going out, and cases have to be shifted, we use the Jerry prisoners. And we've got our own transport." Through the window they could see a driver thoughtfully polishing the windshield of an army truck. "Otherwise, yes, we do it all ourselves."

"Under Major Yapp," said the general sharply.

"Yes, sir. Of course, under Major Yapp."

"Where is he?"

"The M.O. has confined him to his quarters, sir. A stomach upset."

The general was clearly about to comment on this when the same orderly appeared, this time with a written message.

"Good heavens," said the general. "I'd almost forgotten. We've got a French general coming around and I've got to be nice to him. I'll have to love you and leave you. If you want to look around the other stores you're very welcome to do so."

Luke thanked him. What he really wanted was time to think about what he'd seen. If Pepin was right and there was a regular leak from this tightly organized and guarded store, he wondered how it operated.

He was still wondering about it the next day when he set out on his customary morning walk. This time he went north of the river, crossing the playing field area, and making a laborious way upward over the loose gravel and the bushes and dwarf trees of the wasteland that fringed the base camp.

After fifteen minutes of exhausting effort he sat down, avoiding an offensive crop of thistles and concentrating his thoughts on the liquor store.

Apart from casual assistance from the German prisoners it seemed to be staffed by one major, one sergeant major, one bombardier, and one truck driver. From the point of view of security this taut organization was both an advantage and a disadvantage. If there had been a large staff of storemen, checkers, and handlers, that would have meant an increased chance of one of them being dishonest. On the other hand, if one of them was dishonest, there would have been an increased chance of his dishonesty being spotted by one or another of his fellows and reported.

He considered different permutations and combinations of villainy in the liquor store.

Suppose that "Puppy" Yapp, a known drinker, was helping himself to a regular supply of filched liquor. The wide-awake and efficient sergeant major would soon find out about it. After which the major would be under the sergeant major's thumb.

Or they might be in the racket together. If they were, they would be pretty safe. *Quis custodiet ipsos custodes* was one of the few Latin tags he could remember from his village school. The head teacher had used it and explained what it meant when he had found his assistant becoming a lot too familiar with one of the boys.

On the other hand, might the racketeers be the pale and ineffectual-looking Bombardier Light, hand in glove with the truck driver, Gunner Whitehouse. That seemed possible. He understood that when the liquor was being distributed on Tuesdays and Fridays to the different recipients, the two men went out together. Since Light was keeping the books, it would be easy for him to have additional bottles, or even cases, loaded onto the truck and to dispose of them profitably, sharing the proceeds with Whitehouse. He would then fake the records.

Or might the German prisoners—? At this point his thoughts were diverted by a rustling, as of a small mammal or a snake, making its way toward him along a fold in the ground. As he watched, the tangled hair of Pepin came in sight. He seemed unwilling to raise any part of himself from the ground. On the previous occasion he had stood up, quite boldly. True, there had been no one in sight, and he had had the forest behind him as a means of escape. If he stood up now he would have been within view of the playing fields, on which a number of men were strolling.

Luke leaned forward to hear what his messenger had to say.

"Faites attention à une boutique de vêtements dans la Rue de Samer."

Luke picked up the sense of this, though the voice was

husky and the Alsatian accent turned "v" into "f" and "s" into "z."

Having delivered his message, Pepin had initiated a series of wriggling movements that were fast carrying him backward. In another moment, thought Luke, he would have disappeared entirely, like the figment of a dream, barely remembered on waking.

"Hi," he called out. "Stop a moment. *Un instant. Dites-moi le nom de cette boutique. Ou le numéro.*"

Pepin was now almost invisible. Luke thought he heard *"N'y a qu'une."* Then he was alone once more, and only a movement in the long grass persuaded him that he had not imagined the whole thing—alone, with thoughts that were not agreeable. If Pepin felt obliged to take such elaborate precautions not to be seen talking to him, then he himself must be an object of suspicion, possibly of dislike, in this unstable and dangerous community.

If this was true, he would have to proceed with great caution.

Clearly the first step was to take a walk down the Rue de Samer. Not to stroll down it, looking about him. No. To walk briskly down it, as though he had business at the far end.

Although it was a busy street and crammed with shops, Pepin's statement seemed to be accurate. There were bakers, pork butchers and horse butchers, patisseries and shops that simply called themselves "Alimentation" and sold everything from cheese to matches; jewelers, curio shops, an estate agent, and a pinball machine area, but there was only one shop that dealt with clothing.

This was at the far end of the street, divided from the café on its left-hand side by an alley and bounded on the other side by a builder's yard. Being cut off from the other shops in this way, it had an air of seclusion. Secluded, thought Luke, but far from exclusive. Two deep boxes outside were labeled "Occasions," and the clothing in them, rummaged by the hands of frugal buyers, had clearly never been of top quality. Jackets and trousers in one box, shirts and undergarments in the other, with a tray of boots and shoes on the pavement in front of them.

The clothing seemed to be entirely male. Maybe female garments were more discreetly arranged in the interior. But since the windows were of nontransparent milky glass, it was impossible to see. A discreet establishment, evidently, that did not go out of its way to attract attention. Luke was able to make out the name of the proprietor painted on the door: Hercule Serpolet.

Serpolet? Wasn't that French for that most fragrant of shrubs, wild thyme? He wondered what the inside of the shop actually smelled like.

That afternoon he had a word with Colonel Harper. Feeling that the colonel might not entirely approve of Pepin, he simply said that information about the shop had come to him from a friend. When a policeman talking to another policeman uses the word "friend," it has a meaning that inhibits further questions. Harper said he would speak to their liaison officer, who knew most of the local notables.

Robert Dujardin reported to Luke that evening. He said, "It's a rare pair of pigeons you've got your sights on, my boy. The husband is a dwarf, but an immensely powerful one. He used to do an act in the circus, holding by his teeth to a trapeze and swinging a girl from each hand. His wife is a fitting mate. The grenadier, they call her. Six feet high and broad in proportion, with a mustache that wouldn't shame your Guards Brigade. I would say that with this pair your motto should be 'Handle with care.' "

Harper, who was present, supported him. He said, "I've had reports, from time to time, that they might be the town end of a smuggling racket of some sort. But no positive proof of this. And even if it is true, we'd have no authority to act against them unless we could show that their criminality was connected with the army. We could, of course, have the shop watched, very discreetly—"

Dujardin said, "I noticed a *pharmacie* on the opposite side of the road. That is a lucky chance. A *pharmacien* will always cooperate with the police. He requires two licenses: one for the shop, one for his practice. It would be very easy to close him down. The mere threat of trouble would be sufficient. I will have a word with him.

"Short notice," said Luke. "But could you possibly fix it for me by Friday midday? Tuesday and Friday are the important days."

"*Pas de problème,*" said Dujardin.

He was as good as his word, and by midday on Friday Luke was occupying a chair on the first floor of the *pharmacie* of Dr. Lasalle. He had slipped into the shop by a back door and had been escorted upstairs by the doctor.

"If you place your chair just so," he said, "the curtain will mask you from any direct observation. If you want anything further, you have but to ask."

When he had taken himself off, there was nothing for Luke to do but sit still. He thought about long hours spent in observation in other places. A doorstep in a stinking back alley in Whitechapel; a hole in the ground on Plaistow Marshes; on top of a tree on Gilkicker Point. Sometimes comfortable, sometimes hideously uncomfortable. He had repeated to himself many times Fred Wensley's dictum: "The secret of success in police work is continuous observation." It had become part of his own creed.

It was three o'clock in the afternoon and he was nearly asleep when the truck arrived. It slowed as it reached the Serpolet shop. Gunner Whitehouse was driving, with Bombardier Light sitting beside him. Whitehouse was handling the big truck very skillfully. He stopped it just past the entrance to the alleyway, swung it in a tight half circle, and backed it. The alley, which sloped down toward the river, was so narrow that it was barely wide enough to admit the truck, and when it stopped, only the top of its canvas cover was visible.

The two men got out, opening the doors with some difficulty, squeezed past, and went out into the street. They sat down at one of the tables in front of the café. Old customers, evidently: The waiter had glasses of wine in front of them almost before they had settled in their chairs.

Luke was now able, for the first time, to get a good look at Gunner Whitehouse. He had the same brick-red face as Sergeant Major Forgan but none of the lines of worry. A simple soldier, who did what he was told?

While they were drinking, Luke kept his glasses focused steadily on the truck. It was so parked he could see nothing directly, but he did, once, see the top of the canvas cover move, as though something was being done behind the truck and out of sight. But that was all.

Half an hour later, Light paid the bill. The two men edged their way back into the truck, which drew out into the street and drove off.

17

Luke was left with two questions, neither of which he could answer with any confidence.

There was no breath of wind, but the canvas had moved. He was sure of that. Who had moved it? Even more curious, since there was more than adequate room at that point for the truck to park in the street, why the tricky maneuver of backing it down the alley?

Clearly the next step was to examine the rear part of the shop. A glance into that back room might answer a lot of questions.

There was no formal curfew, but most people were in bed by midnight, and it was through empty streets, at one o'clock the following morning, that Luke approached his objective. He had marked out a line of approach through the builder's yard. It involved climbing a fence to get into the yard and another to get out, and it brought him to the back of the shop without coming out into the open.

When he got there he found that the windows of the back room had been painted over on the inside—surely a curious precaution for an honest shopkeeper? Luke had anticipated this difficulty and had brought with him his pocket knife, which was furnished with a diamond-topped glass cutter. He reckoned that he could cut out a small and inconspicuous piece in the corner of the glass and shine his flashlight through it.

Before he could start, things began to happen.

There was a rumbling growl, and a dog hurled itself at him.

Luke swung around and launched a savage kick that rolled the animal over but failed to discourage it. Then he took to his heels. He went head first over the first fence, like an athlete crossing a bar, and rolled as he landed. The dog made no attempt to emulate this feat but contented itself with barking furiously.

By now neighboring windows were being thrown up. Luke, feeling every sort of fool, scuttled across the yard on hands and knees and climbed the fence on the other side.

He realized that he had not only made a fool of himself he also had committed the error of not using his resources properly. Next morning he made contact with Pepin by the simple expedient of stationing himself in full view at the point where he had first met him. Ten minutes later the call of "Pleezeter meecher" signaled the arrival of his assistant.

Pepin listened impassively as Luke spoke. Could he find a point behind the clothing shop from which he could see without being seen?

Yes.

Could he get into observation there at midday next Tuesday?

Yes.

And report what he had seen by coming to this same place on Wednesday morning?

Yes.

* * *

"So that's that," said Harper. "Your informant—I'm assuming he's reliable—"

"Unorthodox, but in my view perfectly reliable."

"Says that he saw Serpolet removing two cases and a dozen odd bottles from the back of the truck and taking them to his shop. And you're suggesting that this is a regular occurrence?"

"Every Tuesday and Friday."

"How long do you think it's been going on?"

"The R.H.A. took over the liquor store three months ago. If Light got busy right away he could have made twenty-six deliveries."

"Even if he didn't, it adds up to quite a lot of liquor. All stored in that back room, I suppose. And sold for cash to people ostensibly coming in to buy clothes."

"With a payoff to Light—and to the driver, *if* he was in it, too."

"I think he must have been," said Harper. "I suppose he might just have been doing what Light told him."

He thought about it. Then he added, "It's going to be tricky, but I've always found that the best way with a tricky setup is to go straight through the middle of it. And the quicker the better. We can dress it up as a health and hygiene inspection. You'd better come, too."

On the following morning Harper stationed two of his men at the back of the shop, marched the other four up to the door, and sounded a tattoo on it. This produced Madame. She was dressed in a scintillating green bed gown and had pointed green slippers on her feet and her hair in curlers. The total effect was of a sleeping dragon aroused from its lair.

When Harper pushed in, she tried at first to bar the way, then retreated, screaming. Her husband came bounding down the stairs and added his shouts, a bass undertone to his wife's treble. The few words that were thrown in suggested that Harper was the illegitimate offspring of a diseased hyena and a glandered jackal.

As for Madame, she wasted no time on words, took a further deep breath into her substantial lungs, and continued to scream.

The door at the end of the passage was locked.

"Quick as you can," said Harper to his assistant, who was carrying a sledgehammer. Two blows broke open the door. They looked in. The room was lined, from floor to ceiling, with shelves, and on all the shelves were boxes and bottles.

"Thank God I brought two trucks with me," said Harper. "We shall need both of them."

Luke noticed that neither the dwarf nor the grenadier was showing any signs of doing what an honest shopkeeper whose store was being rifled would surely have done: going for outside help. The woman's screams and the man's bass accompaniment were collecting spectators, who seemed more amused than hostile. One of the men said, "If any of that stuff's for sale, I'll make you an offer."

Harper ignored him. He was too busy to waste time on chat. His six men and Luke had formed a chain and were manhandling the boxes and bottles along it. In a surprisingly short space of time the back room was stripped.

Ignoring the Serpolets entirely, Harper said, "We'll take all this stuff to my headquarters."

When they saw he was going, the dwarf and his mate fell silent.

Perhaps, thought Luke, they are wondering what to do next.

Not an easy question.

* * *

"Not an easy question," said Major Yapp.

Seemingly recovered from his indisposition, he had come around, at Harper's invitation, bringing the camp adjutant, Captain Edwards, with him. The drinks were arranged around the walls of Harper's office. The cases had been built into a rampart, crowned by a frieze of bottles.

During the ten minutes since Yapp had arrived, Luke's mind had been performing a series of unexpected somersaults. Their starting point had been the deceptive effect of nicknames. If you were lumbered with a surname like "Yapp," he thought, the juvenile humor of the officers' mess would immediately christen the young officer "Bonzo" or "Doggy" or "Pup." And when he had been addressed in this manner long enough it would be easy for outsiders to assume that he was a person of no consequence.

What surprised Luke was that Yapp was clearly in command of the situation and that Harper, Edwards, Dujardin, and even the intolerant and outspoken Longhorn were waiting on his lead.

"When you think about it," he said, "there are two quite distinct problems. The first, and the simplest, is what to do about the Serpolets. I call it a simple problem because, in fact, there's nothing one can do."

He looked at Dujardin, who nodded agreement.

"Any steps against them would have to be taken by the French authorities. If they did move against them, they might argue that the drinks had come into their possession legitimately. Not a point they can take too far, however, since I assume that the bottles are marked?"

Edwards said, "The ones I've had time to examine were, sir. It's a small imprinted 'g.s.' on the label. Difficult to spot, but clearly there when you look for it."

"They would therefore be asked where they got it from. Not an easy question for them to answer. At the moment I think it's a stalemate. They will wait for us to move. If we don't, they'll sit tight. They won't be too unhappy. They've lost their stock, but I'd guess they've made a lot of money. So let's forget them for the moment and think about the more important end of the problem."

He paused to collect his thoughts. Then he said, "I understand that the only person who actually saw the stuff being removed from Bombardier Light's truck—with or without the cognizance of driver Whitehouse—is a witness who would be unlikely to stand up to cross-examination."

"He's a young Alsatian," said Luke. "Doesn't speak much English yet. I don't fancy he'd be keen to give evidence. He's got every reason to hate the Germans, but that doesn't mean that he wants to feature publicly as an informer for the English. If we forced him into court, I think he'd just keep his mouth shut."

"Right," said Yapp. "That's the situation. Until we can *prove* that all this liquor came from the store they were meant to be in charge of, we can do nothing effective about Light or Whitehouse. Next point, then: How do we get that proof?"

He looked around, but no one had any suggestions to offer.

"Come, gentlemen," he said with a smile. "It's not as difficult as all that. A little simple mathematics should produce the answer. When we took over, we signed for the drinks in the store, and since I had to sign the chit, I can assure you that I checked it carefully before I did so. New supplies have come in, monthly, from the Royal Army Service Corps. They may not be the most warlike of soldiers, but there's nothing wrong with their bookkeeping. That gives us the plus side.

Now for the minus side. Two deliveries a week for thirteen weeks. Beer and soft drinks go to the Naval Army and Air Force Institute. As far as spirits are concerned, there are only six authorized recipients: the two officers' messes, the sergeants' mess, the hospital, the convalescent center, and, by special arrangement"—he smiled at Harper—"your headquarters."

Harper nodded.

"So these are the six recipients. In each case a man will have signed for the drinks received. A responsible man. The mess secretary, the hospital and convalescent camp social service workers, and in your case . . . ?"

He looked at Harper. It was Longhorn who said, "In our case, the mess sergeant."

"Excellent. Then all we have to do is to instruct Bombardier Light to visit these six persons, in turn, and to obtain from each a statement of the drinks he signed for since the RHA took over: There should be no difficulty about that. Such records are always carefully kept. Our data are now complete. 'X' for the original contents of the store. 'Y' for the R.A.S.C. deliveries. 'Z' for the outward deliveries. 'X' + 'Y' – 'Z' *must* be the amount now in stock. And any discrepancy *must* be the result of leakage. Right?"

"The only thing I don't understand," said Longhorn, "is why you propose to ask Light to obtain these figures. Won't that simply alert him to what we're up to?"

"Certainly. I hope it will not only alert him, but also alarm him. He cannot falsify the statements. We shall, of course, have made copies of them ourselves. He is not a strong character, and as he sees the figures failing to add up and the net closing around him, he may feel inclined to shift some of the blame from his own shoulders."

"You mean," said Harper, "that Sergeant Major Forgan might be involved."

"Indeed, he might have organized the whole operation."

The others could not tell from the tone of voice in which he said this whether he was serious or not.

18

And so, as September crawled toward October, this curious little campaign continued, a campaign whose object was to discover who was extracting and selling wine and spirits from a government store; a minuscule affair, not to be compared with the campaign that was rolling forward a few miles away, where French general de Castelnau was attacking with two armies on a front of fifteen miles between Reims and Verdun and where the British, under Sir John French, prepared to launch their largest attack so far, with six divisions, at Loos. A campaign in which the gains would be small and the casualty lists, on both sides, appalling.

The casualties in the battle of Le Touquet were on a smaller scale.

The sergeant in charge of the German prisoners had arranged with Bombardier Light to carry into the store three truckloads of cases received that morning from the R.A.S.C. He had half a dozen of his men, lined up and ready, at the place outside the store that had been agreed. Light, as so often, was late, which gave the sergeant food for thought, as he compared the slackness of his captors with the promptness and discipline of their prisoners.

He had been entrusted with a key to the building but not to the individual storerooms. After waiting for fifteen minutes, he had used it to open the outer door and had walked down the central passage to the office at the end. Here he had found Bombardier Light. He was sitting behind his desk, with an army revolver clasped in his hand. The number and the enthusiasm of the flies around him suggested that some time had elapsed since he had used the revolver to blow the top of his head off.

* * *

"So that's that," said General Foxley. "Good marks for Yapp. He said that the culprit would break under the strain, and broken he has."

"Does that mean," said Harper, who had brought the news, "that we acquit driver Whitehouse of any part in the operation?"

"Not proven, I think."

"I find it hard to believe that he could have gone out twice a week, for three months, left his van in exactly the same spot, taken his drink at the same table, and driven home suspecting nothing."

"Difficult to prove that he didn't," said Foxley.

"And why in the world didn't he complain of being made to back his van down a steep and narrow passage when he could so much more easily have parked it on the road?"

"Our men are conservatives. They're used to doing stupid things at the same time and in the same place every day. It's a way they have in the army . . ."

The smile with which Foxley accompanied this declaration of his faith persuaded Harper that he was not going to move the general. Of itself, this did not worry him. He had no particular reason for wanting to see Whitehouse penalized. What was making him uneasy was something more general.

The news of Light's suicide had, of course, gotten out. That was to be expected. What was hard to explain was just why it should have had such an explosive effect. Maybe it was the weather—a broiling and unseasonable Indian summer; maybe the powder was dry and only awaiting the spark. Whatever the reason, the discomfort caused by the news was almost tangible. Officers, going to bed, had started taking their revolvers with them.

General Foxley alone seemed unaffected. Luke had come to be treated by the general as an additional aide, a means of liaison with the military police, particularly useful since it saved him from having more than the minimum contact with Harper. Luke found himself, unwillingly, admiring the general's professional balance, his refusal to move from the placid central course he had selected.

Oncoming events were to test that placidity severely.

When trouble took a long step nearer it was Harper, once again, who brought the news, and the fact that he spoke so calmly emphasized rather than hid the feeling behind his words. He said, "Last night—or rather, in the early hours of this morning—twenty prisoners escaped from the detention compound. They included six men who were awaiting armed escorts. Two of them were under sentence of death. They were all classified as dangerous men. They are even more dangerous now. You will remember, perhaps, that a number of rifles and a quantity of ammunition were reported to you as missing from the QA store. It seems that whoever took them was in collaboration with the prisoners. They are all, now, armed."

"Have you any proof of that?"

"Very practical proof," said Harper grimly. "Two of my C.M.P.s who were on patrol in the area between Le Touquet and the forest encountered them at four o'clock this morning, when they fired a volley over them to demonstrate that they meant business. Sensibly, I think, they made no attempt to stop them, but returned as quickly as possible and reported to me. It was then that the prison break was discovered."

"How did they escape?"

"In the normal manner: by digging a tunnel. I have inspected it. Quite an elaborate affair, some thirty yards long, coming out close to the railway."

"And they were able to dig this tunnel without arousing suspicion?"

"I would imagine they did so without any difficulty at all."

The general looked sharply at Harper, as though he suspected what was to come.

"When I took over the prison you instructed me that I was to confine my attention to seeing that the outside defenses were secure. I was not to harass the prisoners with the sort of inspections and periodic checks that are normal in prison camps and that are usually effective in spotting the signs of tunneling and stopping it before it gets too far."

"Yes," said the general. "I did so instruct you. You may regard that particular instruction as canceled."

Luke thought that Harper, who was furious but containing his fury, might have made some observation about locking stable doors. Instead he said, "I have thirty-five military policemen on various duties in and around the camp. I've applied for more, but so far without success. I could withdraw the ones I have and use them as a posse to hunt down the escapers, but only by canceling their other duties. And in view of the general feeling in the camp at this moment, I'd be happier to have them available under my hand."

"Then what do you suggest?"

"The only course open to us, unless we are going to ask the army for outside help, is to form a strong contingent from camp personnel—say, of company strength; there are plenty of soldiers hanging around, waiting for leave or assignment. Put a good man in charge and comb through the forest."

"I'll think about it," said the general.

And that was all Harper could get out of him before he spun around on his heel and marched out.

The general signaled Luke to stay.

He said, "I'm told that you and your one-legged assistant are often seen in and around the forest. I'd like your view as to whether the escaping prisoners now in the forest will find it possible to go farther. Frankly, if they did, I wouldn't be sorry to see the last of them."

Luke realized the compliment that was being paid to him and chose his words with great care. He said, "From what I have learned so far, sir, of the situation in the south of the forest, I'd imagine that their main chance—really their only chance—of reaching safety would be to make for Spain. They could not, of course, hope to do so, on foot, through France. They would have to persuade the fishermen at Ezé to carry them by sea."

"*French* fishermen. Would they agree?"

"I understand that this particular crowd place the payment of money a long way above the call of patriotism."

"Substantial payments, I suppose."

"I am told that the regular fare is five hundred pounds per person. No doubt they have been getting a share of the money from the illicit liquor sales, but they could not possibly have saved the large sum necessary to pay for a succession of trips. I don't suppose a fishing boat takes more than four or five at a time. That would mean half a dozen trips to accommodate the prisoners alone. And I think there are others ahead of them in the line. Men who have slipped away in the past . . ."

Luke forbore to say that control in that vast, amorphous camp had been so slack that any number of men could have slipped away unnoticed.

"Suppose there are a dozen of them—or even twenty. Where do you suggest that they have been lying up? Living rough, in the forest?"

"The story is that they are living comfortably in a cavern near Ezé, fed by the Ezéites, well paid for their services, no doubt. They'll only be offensive if the money supply dries up. They won't get any more from liquor sales, so they'll be looking for alternative sources."

"It's not a pretty picture," said the general, "whichever way you look at it. But the one thing I don't intend to do is to ask the army for help. They've got more than enough on their hands just now."

As though to underline his words the wind, backing around to the east, brought them the sound of the opening bombardment at Loos.

19

Had Pepin ever been party to a legal document, he would have signed it Pierre Clairambaud. His nickname, signifying, in Alsatian argot, a fox cub, had been attached to him almost at birth. He had no objection. The fox was one of his favorite animals.

The Clairambauds were a well-known Alsatian family. Many of them had left the country when it was handed over to Germany at the disastrous conclusion of the Franco-Prussian War. They had spread across France and had prospered as factors and managers in the vineyards of the Médoc and the fishing communities on the Atlantic coast. Pepin, with his mother in tow, had been happy to light on one of them, François, a many-times-removed "uncle" who had risen to the post of second-in-command under Jacques Moulin of the Ezé fishing community.

Once established, Pepin had made himself useful, particularly as a net mender. As he squatted happily on the quay, mending a net with nimble fingers, no piece of news or gossip had escaped him.

When British troops had arrived, he had seen the desirability of acquiring at least a smattering of English, and Joe, on one of his visits to Ezé and spotting his usefulness, had taken him in hand. His progress had been steady rather than remarkable. From "Pleezeter meecher" he had now attained a grasp of most of the soldiers' normal obscenities.

On the morning after the jailbreak his uncle had approached him with a request.

It was clear, from the tone of voice in which he spoke, that the matter was important to him. Pepin, with an eye to the main chance, would have been delighted to help him. The difficulty was understanding exactly what his uncle wanted.

He referred to it as a "mouser," seeming to indicate a cat or dog skilled in catching mice. A curious request, seeing that Uncle François occupied one of the most up-to-date houses in the village. It was only after elaborate explanations and the drawing of a diagram that he realized that what his uncle had set his heart on obtaining was a Mauser pistol.

He said, "In a great cavern behind the village, English soldiers are in hiding. They are hoping for transport to Spain. One or two have gone already. Others will go when they have accumulated the necessary money. You may have heard something of this already."

Pepin, indeed, knew all about it. His face, however, showed nothing but polite interest.

"Now I will tell you something you may *not* know. It is confidential information, and I pass it on to you only because you must know about it if you are to help me. Recently these men have acquired a great number—a positive arsenal—of weapons. Some were stolen from a British store. But even more were brought by a German officer who was put ashore here, by motorboat, recently."

This was important confirmation of something that had previously been nothing but the vaguest of rumors. It was said that, under cover of night, in the dark of the moon, a German officer had landed. No one admitted to having seen him, or if they had, they were not prepared to talk about it.

"The Mauser pistol is of a type that many German soldiers carry. I have no doubt that there will be one or more in this arsenal." He paused, to answer the question that Pepin was going to ask. "It is a small cave, near to the main cavern, above it, on the south side."

His uncle did not explain how he had obtained such precise information. Pepin had his own ideas about this. He would, no doubt, have bribed one of the escapers, hungry for money to pay his fare, to act as his spy and informant.

"So, if I were to show you a small, well-hidden entrance—

known to me but to very few other people—you should be able to make your way, passing from cave to cave, until you reached the place where the arms are stored."

It was not an attractive project. It was all too easy to miss your way, to wander for days, to lie down at last, a feast for the rats who had been following you so hopefully.

He said, "If I do this—if I get for you the pistol you desire—what do I get?"

His uncle mentioned a sum of money.

"In francs or in gold?"

"In gold."

Remaining impassive, Pepin said that he would give his uncle a final decision when he had thought about it. First, he realized, this tidbit of news ought to be passed on to his new British friends.

He found Joe in conference with Luke and, abandoning any attempt at English, spoke at length in French. He had the full attention of his listeners, who made him stop, from time to time, to repeat what he was telling them.

Finally, after a long moment of silence, his voice dropping almost to a whisper, Luke said, "Do you think it could be?"

"It'd be right up his street," said Joe.

Pepin could see that they were excited, but the last two exchanges, having been in English, had bypassed him. Reverting to French, Luke described their two previous encounters with the man of many pseudonyms whose real name was Erich Krieger; how in both cases he had not been acting as a simple spy, his aim being the disruption of their war effort—first, by guiding Zeppelins onto their fleet base at Portsmouth; then, even more dangerously, by attacking their ammunition reserves.

Pepin did not understand all of this, but he did gather that Krieger was an important and dangerous man.

Joe said, "The boat he came ashore in. When it had landed him, did it go back out to sea?"

"I asked my uncle the same question," said Pepin. "He said that when it had put the German officer ashore, it went back. I think he was lying."

"What makes you think that?"

"My uncle is not very skilled at telling lies. Also, I thought it would have been much more sensible for the man to have kept the boat, in case he had to leave in a hurry. There are a hundred places along the coast, little inlets where it could be hidden."

"And the crew?"

"I think they will have gone with the officer. Even in this fine weather they would not have been too comfortable camping out. They would be happier, and safer, in the cavern."

Joe nodded agreement. Luke's mind was on a different point. He said, "If this is the man we think it is, he is a careful operator. Even before he arrived, contact could have been made for him with certain of the German prisoners. With their help—foolishly trusted as they are by the authorities—it would not have been difficult to organize the developments that have upset our people—the arms theft and the prison break. The overall objective must be to provoke a private war, on such a scale that we would be forced to withdraw badly needed men from the front."

"As I observed," said Joe. "Right up his street."

"You will appreciate how important it is to identify him. Tell me: Do you really think you can reach this arms store?"

"Knowing its general direction, yes."

"And you say that it overlooks the main cavern?"

"Yes."

"So you should be able to identify this German officer and describe him to us?"

"Yes."

"And having done so, find your way back?"

"Yes," said Pepin. "I think so."

20

Staff Sergeant Wilbraham, who was in charge, under Captain Mason, of the main officers' mess in the Hôtel Bristol, was conscious of a feeling of relief when the last of the officers had departed, heading for their billets.

Superficially it had been a normal and agreeable evening—a cheerful babble of talk and an unusual amount of laughter. But Wilbraham was experienced enough to detect the underlying uneasiness.

His last job in England had been running the mess in the embarkation center at Southampton, and he had noted the same thing there. On the night before they were due to cross the Channel, many of the young officers were unusually noisy; but immediately behind the gaiety was the thought of what lay ahead of them.

In this case thoughts centered, perhaps, on an isolated billet on the outskirts of Le Touquet, one they had originally welcomed for its privacy and its distance from the lighted streets. Normally happy to be in bed by eleven o'clock, now they were hanging on until a group was ready to go. It would give them company for part of the way at least.

Wilbraham superintended the clearing up of the mess room, the washing of the glasses, and the locking up of unused, or partly used, bottles, after which he sent his assistants to bed. They had had a long day and were glad to go. Wilbraham relaxed for a few minutes in his sanctum and thought of all the things he had to do the next day and how he was going to organize them. Having arrived at a tentative conclusion, he got up, turned out the lights, and moved into the hall to lock the front door.

As he got there it was opened in his face, and six men stalked in. They were wearing denim overalls and were masked. The leader, speaking good but guttural English, said, "Don't do anything stupid. I have here a silenced revolver, and it will cause me no pleasure to shoot you in the stomach. You understand?"

Sergeant Wilbraham, unable to speak, nodded.

"Good. Then show me into your office. No hurry. There are also four men on guard outside. They will make certain that we are not interrupted."

When they reached the office, a small room that had once been the butler's pantry, Wilbraham, whose legs were feeling weak, was glad to sit down.

"That's right," said the masked man, "make yourself comfortable. Now, to business. We require all the cash that you have. And since you only bank on Fridays, and it is now Thursday, there should be a most satisfactory amount in your safe."

Wilbraham croaked out, "I haven't got the key."

"Who has it?"

"The officer in charge, Captain Mason."

"Who will, no doubt, be back in his billet."

"He left with the last of the officers."

During this exchange the masked man had been eying the safe thoughtfully. It was a moderate-size one, not built into the wall, but standing free.

"We have men who could open it, but not here and now. However . . ."

He signaled to one of his followers, who went out and came back with two more men. He said to the sergeant, "It would be easier if we had some sort of cart. No doubt you have something of the sort. Think." As he said this he raised the gun he was holding very slightly.

"In a shed at the back," croaked Wilbraham. In his early service he had seen a man who had been shot in the stomach, and his one wish was to get rid of the man before anyone intervened and a gun battle started.

The cart was one that had been used to carry bulky items. It had never held anything as heavy as the safe, and it creaked, but survived, as it was rolled down the hall and out into the road where a truck was standing, backed and ready. Two planks formed a sloping approach, and with all eight men helping, the safe was hefted up into the truck.

At this moment two officers, who had been at a party, came strolling past. They were happy but not drunk. They stopped and stared in blank surprise, but had no time to do or say anything before they were knocked down and held down.

"Tie them up," said the leader. "Back to back, wrist to wrist, ankle to ankle. Right. Now roll them into the gutter."

The ten men crowded, somehow, on and into the truck, which drove off, leaving the helpless officers on the road, jerking like newly gaffed fish.

* * *

"I agree with you," said the general. "It was done deliberately, in the most insulting way possible. The object being, I imagine, to increase the tension."

"Hardly necessary," said Major Lipholzer with a smile. "The atmosphere's so thick at the moment you could cut it with a knife."

He was sitting with Major Shoesmith on one side of the conference table, with Majors Porteous and Yapp opposite. Colonel Harper sat at the end of the table, facing the general. The meeting was informal, in the sense that no notes were being taken of what was said, but there was no doubt that it was an occasion of high seriousness.

Shoesmith said, "I've noticed that it is affecting the German prisoners, too. Normally they're quiet enough, willing to lend a hand and not showing any signs of wanting to escape. Now they're getting—I don't know—perhaps restless is the best description."

The general looked at him thoughtfully. Before he could say what was on the tip of his tongue, the genial Major Porteous broke in. "I've been wondering," he said, "all the things that have been happening lately—the missing rifles, the money extracted from the liquor store, the prison break, and now, this barefaced robbery—it all seems to hang together. Can someone be running it?"

"Exactly what I thought myself," said Shoesmith. "The situation is dangerous enough, but doubly dangerous if, as seems to be the case, it's being organized."

"Who by?" asked the general coldly.

"Well, sir, my men have gotten the idea into their heads that an army's being built up in the forest. A hundred men—two hundred—the numbers grow each time it's talked about. But they're certain that Jerry's behind it. If the prisoners broke out and joined them they could take over the camp and massacre everyone in it."

The general seemed more amused than alarmed. He said, "Is that what you think, yourself?"

"Of course not, sir," said Shoesmith hastily. "But it's what my men are beginning to believe. And I don't think they are the only ones."

Colonel Harper, sitting silent, found that he could read the characters of three of the officers quite clearly from the comments they made and, even more clearly, by the tone in which they were made. Shoesmith was an old woman. He was exaggerating the danger in the hope that the general would call in help from the army. He wanted a battalion, or, better, two battalions to shield him from the danger that threatened, and if that meant taking men away from the desperate struggle now approaching a climax at Loos, that couldn't be helped. Security came first, particularly his own security. Lipholzer and Porteous were neutral. They were not intelligent enough to propose any novel solution to their difficulties, but they would faithfully carry out any orders they were given. Yapp, for whom he had recently formed an increasingly high opinion, had not yet spoken. Now he leaned forward to gather their attention and said, "If I might make a suggestion, sir."

"Certainly."

"I respectfully agree with the comments you made earlier. Our role is to hold the camp with the forces we have available, without"—he shot a glance at Shoesmith—"in any way weakening the men who are doing the fighting. But if we are to organize ourselves efficiently, we need to set up a proper chain of command. Apart from a very small permanent staff, the camp consists, in its larger part, of a shifting population of men coming through it. In its smaller part, of men who are not at liberty to move, either because they are hospitalized or because they are in prison; more securely now, we hope—"

Harper nodded. They all knew of the precautions he had taken.

"Then it seems to me that the first step should be to organize this fluid mass into four specific companies so that everyone knows where he stands, and if orders have to be given to him, where those orders will come from. The logical way to do so would be to place each company, A, B, C, and D, under the officer presently in charge of that particular Q store. That will mean"—he smiled around the table—"that we shall each of us cease to be shopkeepers and will have an active command."

"I think that's a very sound suggestion," said the general.

It was clear that everyone except Shoesmith thought so, too. He was looking so alarmed at the thought of this additional responsibility that the general decided he must be replaced as soon as possible.

"I'll get the adjutant to draw up nominal rolls, and I suggest that each of you arrange a muster parade of the men allotted to you and tell them that all future orders will come from you. Meanwhile, I'll draw up a general instruction. I'm open to suggestions, but I think that the minimum requirements are the imposition of a curfew and a direction that men shall carry arms with them at all times. And if that interferes with their sporting activities, so much the better. I think they spend too much time playing games and too little thinking about the war."

Porteous said, "I suggest, too, that they should organize a system, under selected N.C.O.s, of defense of their quarters at night."

"Agreed. We want no more tame handing over of cash. And you might add that while I'm looking for no reinforcements at present, as soon as action at the front does die down,

I shall certainly ask for a battalion to comb through the forest and unearth such secrets—if any—as it may hold."

* * *

After Pepin had taken his normal, unobtrusive departure, all that Luke could do was sit in enforced idleness and await his return. By the evening of the second day he was becoming extremely uneasy. On the previous night he had dreamed of passages in the chalk that twisted confusingly, sometimes turning back on themselves like a snake that bit its own tail. Realizing that he was not going to get much sleep that night, he remembered what Colonel Knox-Johnson had said to him. When he had assessed the position, he was to report back.

He was far from confident that he could assess a state of affairs that had become more complex and more alarming every day that passed. But that did not excuse him from putting in an interim report. Indeed, he would not be sorry to have better brains than his own assessing the position.

After dinner, therefore—a meal presided over by Dan Harper in almost complete silence—he had taken pen in hand. Until he started, he had not realized how tired he was. He tried to sort out his ideas. It was difficult to know where to begin. So difficult that he fell asleep in his chair, waking to stare down at a blank sheet of paper, with the single word "REPORT" at the top of it.

He heard the cracked tones of the station clock announcing the hour of three, straightened up, and set resolutely to work. The short nap had cleared his mind, and the words seemed to come easily enough.

He realized that what he was being forced to describe was a community that had lost its nerve, a community held together by the determination of the man at the top not to ask for outside help.

Not an easy point to put across to his superiors. By the time he had finished and reread what he had written, light was beginning to come back into the sky. Almost the only comment Harper had made at the table was a complaint that the camp lacked a reliable dentist and that one of his men would be going to Boulogne that morning to have an abscess dealt with. Good. He should take the report with him.

It was after he had decided this important point that he heard the sound of footsteps coming up the uncarpeted stairs. The newcomer was taking care to avoid making a noise. It had been a warm evening, and the windows downstairs had been opened for coolness. They should have been shut when they came up, but this might have been forgotten. Reflecting on this possibility, Luke got up, took his service revolver from the webbing holster in which it was hanging behind the door, and waited.

After a moment of silence, the intruder started to call attention to himself by scratching gently on the panel of the door.

Holding his gun in his right hand, Luke used his left hand to open the door and swung it back, stepping aside as he did so.

It was driver Whitehouse who was standing there, looking like such a scared and unhappy parody of himself that it took a moment for Luke to recognize him. When he did so he slid the revolver back into its holster and said, "Come in."

"Shudden have broke in," said Whitehouse. At least, that's what it sounded like, but the words were so jumbled and unclear that it might have been anything at all.

Luke fetched a bottle of whiskey from his cupboard, poured out half a tumbler of the neat spirit, and said, "Drink that up. Go on. It's an order."

Whitehouse summoned up a pale smile and drank the whiskey. When he had finished spluttering, Luke said, "Sit down. Right. Now tell me, quite slowly, what you've come to say."

The whiskey seemed to have done its work. Whitehouse said, "I came along because I wanted someone to protect me."

"Protect you? What from?"

"From what happened to Light."

Luke asked, speaking slowly, "And what *did* happen to the bombardier?"

"Forgan blew his brains out. Light knew what might be

going to happen to him. He told me that he had made up his mind to inform on Forgan. He'd written it all out. All the details and dates and the money he'd made. It was going to the major in the morning. As soon as he handed it in he was going to ask to be placed under arrest. Close arrest."

"And this is the document?"

"He made two copies, in case he was prevented from handing one in."

"I see. And you're saying that Forgan took steps to prevent him?"

Whitehouse nodded. He had started shivering. When the comfort of the whiskey had faded, Luke thought he was probably going to collapse altogether. Just as well that they had it all in writing.

He said, "I'll get you a bed here in one of our cells. You'll be safe enough. I should try to get some sleep."

He found Harper, always an early riser, shaving. He listened to Luke while he scraped his chin with his old-fashioned cutthroat razor, washed his face and hands, and dried them carefully. When this had been attended to he said, "First stop, the QA store. I imagine Forgan will have cleared out, but in case he hasn't, we'll take two men with us. Second stop, Major Yapp's billet. Third stop, the general."

Luke had observed General Foxley playing a number of roles, from the relaxed and happy fisherman, to the captain of a sinking ship determined not to leave the bridge. Now, for the first time, he saw him anxious and uncertain.

It was not the news they had brought with them. He had listened without great interest to the story of driver Whitehouse and B.S.M. Forgan.

He said, "So Forgan's taken off."

Yapp said, "Yes, sir. One of our men spotted him, early this morning, heading for the forest."

He listened with approval to the immediate steps Yapp had taken to replace him. ("Sergeant Drewe, very sound man. Won't be able to get back to active service until they've fixed his arm.") After this he had dismissed Yapp and the adjutant, indicating that Harper and Luke should stay behind.

When they were alone he said, "What I have to tell you doesn't go outside this room."

They both nodded.

"The monthly imprest payment, which was due here yesterday, failed to arrive. When, by six o'clock, it was clearly overdue, our head cashier came to see me. Normally our money supply comes to us from the Central Bank at Montreuil, in the form of cash for our immediate necessities and a credit note, to be lodged with the branch bank in Le Touquet, so we can draw against it. I telephoned the bank at Montreuil, who told me, with some surprise, that the van carrying the cash and note had left Montreuil at two o'clock yesterday afternoon."

This was so unexpected and had such serious implications that neither of his listeners had anything to contribute.

The general said, "If the truck has been ambushed and robbed, we are very awkwardly placed: We can't ask the bank here to sanction future withdrawals until new credit has been arranged. Our cashier tells me that there wasn't much left in the account anyway. And he has only a few thousand francs of ready money in hand."

"Surely, once they know," said Harper, "they'll send more money. Properly guarded, this time."

"That may be their immediate reaction. But I'm not happy that they won't make it an excuse to do the one thing I don't want them to do."

"Reinforce us with troops from the line."

"Yes."

Luke said, "Might I ask, sir, wasn't the money guarded at all?"

"There was one man with the driver. They wouldn't be expecting trouble."

Harper had been looking at the map on the colonel's table. He said, "Do we know which route the truck took?"

"It might have been one of two. The normal way here from Montreuil would be north of the river by the N39. But they could have come south of the river through Valcendre and Trepied. It's a bit longer, but a much pleasanter road."

"More picturesque," agreed Harper. "Goes through two or three lots of woods."

"I noticed that," said the general. And after a moment of silence, "I want you two to tackle this. I've told our head cashier to keep his mouth shut. Apart from you two he's the only man here who knows anything about it."

"When you say 'tackle it,' sir."

"Find the truck. And the men."

"In that case," said Harper, "I'd like to brief one of my men. Sergeant Renishaw. He's half Indian and an expert tracker."

"And he'll keep his mouth shut?"

"Yes, sir, I can guarantee that. He doesn't talk much anyway."

"Very well. As quickly as possible."

They took the main road to Montreuil. Luke sat in front between Harper, who was driving, and the sergeant. They went slowly, to give Renishaw plenty of time. He never took his eyes off the shoulder of the road, even when a fox tried to commit suicide. They reached Attin and the outskirts of Montreuil without him having moved an inch or uttered a word.

They skirted Montreuil to the south, turned right at La Madelaine, and followed the minor D139. Here they were in woodland, with trees on either side of the road, thin on the right, much thicker on the left.

Renishaw raised his hand.

"Here," he said.

When they got out and looked around them, they saw what he had already spotted: a break in the hedge and signs that something heavy had passed through it.

Renishaw, avoiding the break, pushed through the hedge farther along and motioned to them to follow.

The trunk of a newly felled tree was lying along the inside of the hedge.

"If they put that across the road," said Luke, "the truck would have to stop. Mightn't have been suspicious. Tree might have blown down. Any road, they'd have to get out to shift it."

"Follow the sergeant," said Harper.

Renishaw, his head bent forward, led them along a path into the heart of the woods. The recent hot weather had baked it too hard for it to hold any obvious clues, but the sergeant moved along it confidently. It ended in a small clearing. Here there were signs of recent activity—bushes broken down and the earth trampled. Something else, too: two places, side by side, where the earth had been turned and piled up.

"That's where they are," said Renishaw.

"You're certain?"

"Quite certain."

"So what do we do now?" said Luke.

"Return and report."

The general seemed almost pleased that uncertainty, at least, was ended. He said, "The bodies will have to be formally identified, and that"—he turned to Luke—"is something you will have to do. Colonel Harper has just gotten—thank the Lord—the first of the reinforcements he has been pressing for. Fifteen more men and a further fifteen coming after the weekend, which means that he and his N.C.O.s will be busy."

As he said this he was looking out of the window. For the first time in weeks a vanguard of black clouds was rolling up, forming a premature dusk.

"I'll give you the same truck and a man to drive it: a youngster called Perry. He was a friend of the driver of the other van and says he knew the man who was with him by sight. The idea of identifying the bodies upset him badly. You'll have to hold his hand."

"And when we have identified the bodies, sir?"

"I'll have a word with the padre about that. He may think it better to say a few words over them, mark the spot, and let them lie. Then the war graves people can deal with them in due course."

Luke was deeply relieved. He was not as squeamish as young Perry, but the idea of bringing the bodies back with them had been an unpleasant one.

"It's too late to do any more today. Start in good time

tomorrow and you should be able to do what has to be done." He added, rather grimly, "We're up against a time limit. I've been promised interim relief in the form of one week's supply of money. One week. After which anything may happen, so don't waste any time."

By six o'clock on the following evening Luke was back in his quarters. It had been a miserable day. Under an unrelenting downpour he and Perry had grubbed with their hands in the newly turned earth until they reached the two bodies. One of them had been shot cleanly in the neck. Executed after surrender, Luke thought. His face was undamaged. Perry, when he had finished being sick, had identified him as his onetime friend. The other man had been shot in the chest, and a second shot had destroyed his chin.

Perry had agreed, quickly, that he knew him, too. As quickly as possible, to avoid looking at the broken face too closely. After which the muddy earth had to be shoveled back and patted down.

Luke had had the forethought to bring a bucket of cold water in the van, and both spent some time washing their hands; washing away the mud and the memory.

Luke, who felt little desire for food, had made a poor showing at the evening meal and had gone straight up to his room. Here he had found Joe. He was hoping for news about Pepin but was disappointed.

"He's been gone three days," he said. "What on earth can have happened to him?"

Joe said, "Why don't we go and find out. The old man owes you a break. Tell him you want two or three days' leave. Shooting leave they used to call it in the army, diddun they?"

"That's right."

"The rain seems to be clearing. We could take some grub and a couple of ground sheets and make a proper job of it."

"That's exactly what we'll do," said Luke, his spirits marvelously raised by the thought of action. "But we'll have to plan it carefully."

He was thinking about mobility.

Joe had been fitted with the most modern type of false leg available, and continued practice had made him expert in using it. "Can do anything but dance the hornpipe," he used to assure people who asked. But one thing he clearly could not do was a long march, over difficult country, particularly if he was carrying anything.

"As I see it," Luke said, "there are three things we want to do. First, and most important, find out what's happened to Pepin."

"That's a job for me," said Joe. "I know quite a few of the Easyites. I'll call on Pepin's mum. She's got a place—not much more'n a big hut, really—far end of the quay. If anyone knows where he is, or when and where he was last seen, it'll be her."

"Right. Next we want to find a way into what they call the main cavern. Best if we could approach it from behind and find some way to look into it. Then we'd have a better idea of what we're up against."

"Probably a dozen ways into it. Just a matter of finding one."

"That's all," said Luke without smiling. He was daunted by the idea of a maze of underground caverns and passages. "Next thing will be to find a place where we can keep observation on the entrance to the cavern. It'll be somewhere behind the village."

"Kill two birds with one stone if we could see the whole village. The front part in particular. Where the boats are. Mind you, I never done it."

"Never done what?"

"Killed two birds with one stone."

"All right," said Luke. "Now we know what we want. It sounds like a two- or three-day job. We'll start tomorrow evening from Dunière. Must be somewhere there where we can pick up a meal. Leave when it's getting dark, make our way into the forest, and set up camp as close to Ezé as we can safely get. You make your way from there into Ezé. What we do next depends on what Pepin's mother can tell you."

The first part of the program went smoothly. They established themselves in a small hollow full of ferns and surrounded by bushes. There they scraped out two shallow graves and filled them with ferns. Lying on them, they waited for time to pass.

"Early risers, early bedders in Easy," said Joe. "I'll start at eleven. Most of 'em'll be tucked up by that time."

After he had hobbled off, Luke lay on his back, staring up at the sky. The clouds had cleared away, and all the stars were showing. One, larger than the others, was shining steadily. He thought it must be a planet.

As he lay there his mind was following an odd track. It started from thoughts about the power of money. Did the general realize that, armed with the considerable sum they had gotten hold of, a number of the escapers would now be able to pay for the last leg of their journey out of France? And if he did realize it, did he care? The men gathered in the cavern were hard cases. To get money, they had been prepared to kill. Perhaps the neatest solution would be if they all shipped themselves off to Spain.

Neat but unsatisfactory, since murderers would go unpunished.

Could their money buy them safety? It could buy most things. Desirable possessions, great houses, fine clothes. Everything? Everything except love. No money could buy that.

Luke was not inexperienced in these matters. During his stay in London, in the unsettled climate of war, more than one woman had decided that a well-constructed, good-looking young man who seemed to have friends in high places would make a convenient wartime husband. With such a desirable end in view, they had been prepared to sell him their bodies. Afterward, when his total poverty was appreciated, they had scuttled away.

Luke laughed cynically to himself. Such experiences had been disillusioning and unhappy. But surely, he thought, sometime, somewhere he would find or stumble on the true and lovely thing itself.

On this comforting thought he must have fallen asleep. When Joe woke him he looked at his watch and found that it was three o'clock.

Joe threw himself down thankfully on his primitive bed.

He had brought back fresh supplies from Pepin's mother, but neither of them felt hungry.

"Save the food for breakfast," said Luke. "First tell me the news. You located Pepin's mother. Had she heard from her son?"

"We needn't have worried. Seems he's been out and about, all day and every day, and come home at night."

Luke sat up with a jerk.

"I don't understand. Did he get to the cave with the weapons in it? And was he able to see down into the main cavern?"

"Yes, he did all that. Not more'n forty men there, he reckoned. Maybe a few more. And pretty comfortably fixed. The three men from the launch was keeping themselves to themselves in one corner and the officer with them, sort of exclusive."

"The officer? He got a good view of him?"

"Pretty good. Not really enough to identify him. Remember, he'd never seen him. Had only our description to go by."

"Hell's bells," said Luke. "That must have been three days ago. Why the devil didn't he come back and report? He must have known how anxious—"

"When you're talking about Pepin like that," said Joe, overriding him, "I'm thinking perhaps you're not thinking straight."

Whatever Luke had been going to say remained unsaid. It was not only the words, it also was the tone of voice in which they had been spoken. Normally Joe had been happy to follow Luke's lead. Now he seemed to have moved up a step. If not into a position of authority, at least into a position from which he could offer what amounted to a rebuke.

Before Luke could say anything Joe added, "Trouble is, you've bin thinking of Pepin as a Boy Scout. Well, perhaps not quite that, but a recruit to your private army. But he ain't no such thing. He likes me because I'm his English tooter and because I've bin able to get hold of one or two little things for his mother. Butter and sugar, things she can't get hold of herself. And because he likes me, he was prepared to help you. So long as it diddun interfere with his private plans."

"His private plans?"

"Like I told you. He hates all Germans. His main idea is to get back at them for what they did to his father.

"All right," said Luke. "I understand that. He's not a Boy Scout and his one idea is to hurt the Germans. Go on."

"The next bit's obvious, innit? Here's four Germans. They're on what the matlows call a lee shore. If he can locate the launch and remove it or put it out of action, they're up shit creek. In fact, he's in so good with his uncle on account of having got him his gun and his uncle being head of the fishing fleet, he might even be able to prevent the fishermen from helping them. Or at least he could hold them up until the Brits pull their fingers out and come along and clean them all up."

"And he's been looking for that launch for three days? Surely by now—"

"Ah, you say that because you haven't seen the place. The way he describes it, it's like a cake what's bin cut into slices but not served out. Twelve, fifteen, twenty little openings, all covered with bushes and undergrowth, so it's no good just looking at the opening, he has to go right up. His uncle's lent him a rowing boat with a one-man crew. He reckons he's covered half the likely places. He might find the boat first thing tomorrow, or the next day, or in a week's time."

Having delivered himself of this unusually lengthy speech, Joe rolled over and said "Good night."

"Good night," said Luke.

He sounded so subdued that Joe could not refrain from chuckling. The chuckle turned into a snort. Then a snore.

Luke lay awake for a long time, looking at the stars.

Next morning Joe was unusually silent. Maybe he thought he had been speaking out of turn. After breakfasting on the freshly cooked rolls he had brought back with him, they set out to look for a spot that was hidden from sight but that would give them an overview of Ezé.

After an hour of unhurried and patient advance, they hit on an ideal place. Almost on top of a small knoll the earth had been scraped away by a colony of badgers. Digging in their usual thorough way, they had excavated a large hole and deposited a bulwark of earth and chalk in front of it.

Wriggling down into the hole and disturbing the earthwork as little as possible, they found they were able to form an admirable observation point overlooking the village, which seemed to be asleep in the sun. One or two figures were moving on the main street, but the fishing boats were all moored to the quay.

"Odd, that," said Joe. "Could've understood it if a storm had been blowing up." But the sea was calm and hardly showed the faintest ruffle.

"What we've got to do," said Luke, "is see if we can locate the way in from the village to the cavern. It'll be somewhere behind the back row of cottages. Probably not at all easy to spot."

"Unless we see someone going into it," said Joe.

But the back of the village was as quiet and deserted as the front. They waited until four o'clock, then climbed out of their spot and made their way back, trying to direct their path so as to stay, as nearly as possible, over the place where they assumed the cavern must be.

This would not have been too difficult if the ground over which Luke was walking, regulating his pace to Joe, who was hobbling behind him, had been flat and open. As it was, they were forcing their way through the thick undergrowth, alternately climbing up and slithering down the frequent inequalities that faced them.

"Bloody obstacle course," said Joe.

Luke turned his head to express his wholehearted agreement and stood, the words unspoken.

Joe had disappeared.

One moment he had been there. The next he was not.

Luke retraced his steps to the point where he had seen him last and noted, with a sudden sinking of his heart, what must have happened.

Pushing through a belt of overlying shrubs, Joe had stepped straight into a hole. Luke went down, first on his knees, then flat on his face, as he inched forward to inspect it. He had no idea how deep it was. If it went down very far Joe, taken unaware and possessing only one useful leg, must have fallen heavily and might have knocked himself out at the bottom.

He saw that the hole went down almost, but not quite, vertically. It was, in mountaineering terms, a chimney. The procedure for descending it was known to Luke. As you moved down, you had to maintain pressure with the arms and legs against the sides to regulate your descent.

For the first part this technique worked well. Then the chimney started to widen. After a few yards he could reach the other side only by stretching his arms to their fullest extent. After that it was out of reach even to the tips of his bruised fingers. There was nothing to do but turn on his back and start to slide, grabbing at any irregularity that offered. Fortunately this did not go on for long before, with relief overriden by a less comfortable feeling, he found himself on his hands and knees on what looked, in the faint light filtering down the chimney, to be a chalk-walled corridor.

A yard or two along it he found Joe, unharmed but abusive.

"Had to move," he said, "or you'd have bloody landed on top of me. Can't think why you had to come down at all."

This seemed to Luke to be a typical piece of ingratitude.

"What you should've done was get a rope. Then you could've hauled me up. Now we're both bloody stuck."

"Don't talk," said Luke. "Listen."

The acoustics of the place were so curious that it was impossible to be sure whether the noise, which came and went, was the wind, blowing through the crevices and caves, as it might have passed through a succession of organ stops, or whether it was human voices, distant and indistinct.

"Whatever it is, it's in that direction," said Luke. "At least I think so."

He led the way along the passage, which was flat and level. The only thing that changed was its width. At some points the walls were so far apart that the light of Luke's flashlight, which had survived his descent, scarcely reached across to the other side. At other points they crowded together so closely that they had to turn sideways to squeeze through.

As they went, the light brightened and the sounds ahead, now clearly of human origin, grew louder. Luke slowed his pace, crawling around a final turn, which brought them out onto a ledge that formed a sort of balcony above a large cavern. Although there was little likelihood of their being seen, since they were above the light that came from oil lamps disposed on ledges around the walls, they both dropped to their knees before edging forward to study what lay below.

It was a surprisingly orderly scene.

Bedrolls and other belongings stowed along one wall. Men sitting or lying in groups. A soyer stove bubbling in one corner, eagerly watched as dinner hour approached. Only one man was on his feet. It was Sergeant Major Forgan, who passed from group to group, dispensing what sounded like instructions.

One group he steered clear of was the quartet squatting by themselves in a corner. It was with a feeling of great pleasure, though not of surprise—for somehow they had anticipated this outcome—that they recognized their old enemy, Palmer in Canada, Richards in Portsmouth, Marriott in Ireland, Lewin in London, now and forever Erich Krieger. Lying very much at ease, he was dressed in the uniform of an officer in a German cavalry regiment. His jacket was showing signs of hard use, but his boots were immaculate. Had one of the launch crew attended to them? Luke wondered. Or had he polished them himself?

Joe said, "Might be the time to get away, when they're lining up for their evening meal."

They crawled along until they were around the corner, where they found a flight of steps cut into the chalk. At the bottom they moved forward, exercising extreme caution. It was as well that they did so. Standing in front of what was clearly the exit from the cavern were two men, on guard, alert to their responsibilities, with a relief guard of four others lying beside them.

They retreated, up the stairs and back the way they had come. When they had put a safe distance between themselves and the sentries, they sat down to think things over.

"I don't mind betting," said Joe, "that if we'd been here last week we'd have got away as easy as kiss your hand. It's that turd Forgan what's got them on their toes."

"They're on their toes at the moment," agreed Luke. "They may not keep it up all night. Give them an hour or two and we'll try again."

They tried at eleven o'clock, at midnight, and at two o'clock. On this occasion all they witnessed was a smart and soldierlike changing of the guard.

"Nothing for it," said Joe. "We've got to find another way out. Must be a few round about."

They were back under the shaft. Luke found that he was shivering. It was not only the cold, not excessive for an autumn evening, it was the silence and the blackness that his flashlight barely penetrated.

Months ago, when he had first been shown the tiny office Kell had allotted to him, he had said, in a moment of flippancy, that if he suffered from claustrophobia he would soon be mad or dead. Was it possible that he did, in fact, suffer from that particular form of hysteria? It was not only the closeness of the walls that pressed in on them, it also was consciousness of the dead weight of the earth above them. There was plenty of fresh air at that spot, but he felt that he would be stifled once he moved away from this last glimpse of the sky, into the endless catacomb ahead.

"Come on," said Joe. "Whadder we hanging about for? Shan't find a way out sitting here."

"I was just thinking," said Luke.

"Then here's something to think about. When Pepin was looking for that arms dump, which he'd been told was above the main cavern—about the same height as the ledge we was on, but on the other side—he reckoned it would be on the left of where he started from and up, but no much up. So when there was two ways to choose from, he took the one on the left. And wherever he could, he went up, not down, if you follow me."

"Yes. I follow that. In our case, as we've got to make up the depth of that hole, we choose anything that goes up, and the steeper the better. And if we keep going left we ought, sooner or later, to reach the edge of the whole system. It must stop short of the river."

He wondered how much of this was designed to dispel the maggot of fear that was sending shudders through him.

One thought was uppermost in his mind.

As they went, he *must* memorize the route, so that if they reached a point where they could go no farther, they would at least be able to make their way back to the cavern and comparative safety. Behind him, Joe was hugging the right-hand wall. He wondered if he, too, was getting anxious about the return journey.

After leaving the passage they were in and crossing the first cave they came to, they took the second turn to the left. Then crossed another open space and this time took the first left. Forward, until they were forced to go right by a dead end. Then fork left, into a third cave, out of that by the first—no, second left. The first one had been downhill, so they had ignored it. Then a long, straight stretch and a further left turn.

Was it his imagination, or was the air growing so thick that it was becoming difficult to breathe?

While he was worrying about this, he found that he had forgotten the early moves. When leaving the first cave, had it been the second or the third turning? Oh, God! The whole sequence was slipping away. When he stopped, panic-stricken, Joe bumped into him.

"Wassup now?"

Luke said, "I'm sorry. It's just that—in case we had to go back—I was trying to remember the turns."

Joe said, "I wondered what you was muttering to yourself about. I should've told you not to bother. Pepin told me what *he* did. I thought we'd do the same."

He dipped his hand into the right-hand pocket of his jacket and brought out a fat reel of black thread. "Borrowed it from Pepin's old lady. Tied the end to a stone and wedged it into the wall at the place we came down."

"And you've been unrolling it ever since?"

"Right. The end goes through a hole in my pocket. What I did do, I kept next to the right-hand wall so the thread'd lie alongside the bottom of it. Easy to find then."

"Joe," said Luke, "you're wonderful."

"Pepin's idea, really."

"How much do you think you've got left on the reel?"

"Difficult to say. Hundred feet, maybe more."

"We'll go on as far as the cotton lasts. Then we'll make our minds up. If the worst comes to the worst we can at least go back."

To be able to go back. The relief was overpowering.

"Okay," said Joe. "Push on. Before the rats start eating the thread."

Even this gruesome idea did not damp Luke's spirits. He led the way forward and turned left into a passage that ran very steeply up. Suddenly the air seemed much cooler. As he went around a right-hand bend he saw a pinpoint of light above their heads. A flashlight? A candle?

When he stopped, Joe pushed past to look. He said, "Whadder you know? The goddess of love awaiting her two sooters."

The unwinking light was looking down on them through a small hole high up in the chalk wall. It was certainly a planet. Which one, Luke neither knew nor cared.

He said, "We've both got our knives. We'll soon have that hole wide enough to wriggle through."

It took them three long hours.

To start with, they tried standing, in turn, on each other's shoulders, but this arrangement was uncomfortable for the one below and insecure for the one above. Abandoning the idea, they set to work to cut a step halfway up the wall. One stood on it; the other supported him.

It would have been much easier if they had been dealing with rocks and loose earth, but this was solid chalk. Luke's knife was the first to break. After that he went more carefully, using the stump of the blade. Joe, equally careful, made faster progress, cursing steadily as chips of chalk fell down the back of his neck.

Just after Joe had broken his knife as well, Luke said, "I think I could do it." He replaced Joe on the step, grabbed the edge of the enlarged hole, and heaved himself up and out.

Then he stretched down both hands to Joe and pulled him up.

They found that they had come out on the fringe of the forest. Ahead of them the ground sloped down toward the river, hidden by a belt of trees.

And men were advancing among the trees.

They were soldiers, spread out in line. As they came nearer, he recognized the green insignia of the Rifle Brigade. He also recognized the young officer who was directing operations. What was his name? Barnes—no, Baines. He had met him, once or twice, in London.

He came up to Luke, peered at him in some astonishment, and said, "Don't I know you? Pagan, in the Intelligence Police? You seem to have had a rough night."

Luke became aware, for the first time, of the state of his clothes. He was covered with chalk dust and earth. His hair was full of it, and it spread down the front of his jacket like a white apron. His last spasmodic effort had cost him two buttons. Joe seemed to have come out with less disrepair.

"I don't want to hold you up," said Luke, "but if you could put me in the picture, I think I might be in a position to help you."

"I was going to ask *you* to put *me* in the picture," said Captain Baines. "Things have been happening so fast since we landed at Boulogne yesterday that we're all feeling dazed. First we were loaded onto a train for Amiens. Next stop the front line, we all thought. No. We were shifted onto a train for Étaples. Seems that some sort of emergency had blown up. A report had been received from the Intelligence Police. And it must have been some report! Went up like a hot-air balloon. Colonel Knox-Johnson to Brigadier General Macdonough to General Wilson, which explains why he picked on us, the Rifle Brigade being his old outfit. Apparently the Germans were threatening Etaples. It didn't seem possible. However, not to bother. You're in the army. Don't ask questions. Same sort of confusion when we got to Étaples. An irregular force, they called it. Down in the forest. Had to be dealt with. Hardly time for breakfast and off we go."

"You won't have a lot of trouble," said Luke. He sounded

happy, but secretly he was appalled at the wheels his report had set turning. "It's a handful of scallywags."

He explained who they were and where they were. Captain Baines seemed to be in no hurry. He had sat down to listen to Luke, and his men were lying comfortably on their backs. A sergeant walked across and said, "Permission to smoke, sir?"

"I think not," said Baines. "Too much dry stuff about. Some ass'll be sure to set fire to it." And to Luke, "It looks like a pincer movement's called for. Half the men back by the way you came up. I take it they just have to follow the cotton."

"I'll go with 'em," said Joe. "Pepin's mum told me not to leave her cotton lying about. She wants it back."

Luke said, "All right. Then you take the other half of your men to a place I'll show you. It gives a good view of the village, and you'll be able to see where you want to assign them. How long will you be?"

"Allow an hour."

"Is that enough? It seemed to take us a lot longer."

"Call it ninety minutes. Should be more'n enough."

"Sounds like a piece of cake," said Baines. He conferred with a Lieutenant Willoughby, who looked even younger than he. "Zero hour, eight-thirty. I'll give you a blast on my whistle, which you probably won't hear. But when you start shooting we'll hear you all right. Aim for their legs. One volley should do the trick."

Lieutenant Willoughby, who seemed to be a calm character said, "Eight-thirty. Aim for their legs. Understood."

"Then we'd better synchronize our watches."

* * *

Luke was back in the badger's hole they had discovered the day before. He was by himself. Captain Baines, with sixty of his riflemen, had crawled forward in the unobtrusive way that their predecessors had been taught by Sir John Moore and had practiced to the discomfort of the French in the Peninsular War. They formed a cordon around the back of Ezé village, facing toward the scrub and bushes that must hide the entrance to the cavern.

He had been observing their maneuvers for half an hour with admiration and with one eye on his watch.

Forty minutes to go.

He wondered how the other sixty men were getting along—stumbling, in the dark, along the difficult, twisting, underground route. There were points in the three open caves where a step off the direct path could lead to trouble. But with Joe as a guide, surely . . .

A rustling noise made him look up.

Joe was hoisting himself forward on hands and knees. As he came up Luke, who had been working out times and distances, said, "How the devil did you get here? You ought to be not much more than halfway along that underground passage."

"That's where I oughter be," said Joe complacently. "But I'm not, am I? Instead, I'm here, so's to watch the curtain go up."

"You mean you've left Willoughby's men to find their own way?"

"I don't mean nothing of the sort. He's got a bit of sense, that boy. He said to me, why go through the back door when the front door's open? Just you show me that hole you fell down. I'll rustle up a bit of rope. When I left them he'd already got about half his men down."

"We ought to have thought of that ourselves," said Luke.

After that there was nothing to do but observe the hands of his watch and fret at the slowness with which they moved. He was desperately unhappy about his report. Had he really painted the situation in unnecessarily black colors? Because if he had, it was he, and not the general, who had played Erich Krieger's game for him, by taking badly needed troops from the line of battle.

True, Krieger was going to pay for it. By dressing himself in uniform during this last appearance he might escape being shot as a spy, but there were earlier episodes that were not going to be tolerantly regarded by a court-martial. To have laid such a man by the heels was a partial victory at least.

"Zero hour," said Joe.

Captain Baines stood up, and the shrill blast of his whistle was echoed by the muffled sound of rifle fire.

"One volley, I made it," said Luke.

"More'n enough for that poxy crowd," said Joe. "They don't fancy long odds."

Figures were already beginning to appear, stumbling through the bushes. None of them showed any sign of wanting to fight. In one case a man was hobbling, and two men were half-carrying a third.

Luke counted them as they came.

"Forty-three, forty-four, forty-five. Now, surely . . ."

But the next to appear were riflemen, rounding up the stragglers.

"What the hell," said Luke and broke off.

From a cleft a quarter of a mile beyond the village a motorboat had appeared. Without any difficulty, without even using his glasses, Luke could distinguish the five figures in the boat: the three-man crew, B.S.M. Forgan, and their old enemy. He was wearing—a final flourish—his cavalry schapska helmet. From the top of it the plume of a white aigrette fluttered triumphantly in the breeze.

Luke watched him with gall and bitterness. Not a hope in hell of catching him. He could show his heels to any fishing boat. Soon he would be in Spain. Soon after that, if the Spanish ran true to form, back in Germany.

"And God rot him," said Luke, "with all the honors of war."

He said this aloud.

Joe, lying beside him, rolled over and said, "Wait for it."

"Wait for what?"

"Just wait."

As he spoke he saw the launch split from inside by a shocking explosion, hurling scattered pieces into the air. Then, as the sound reached them, the launch started to go down into a whirlpool of foam. For a moment, the two halves appeared together, upright, like the separate fingers of a hand, and sank slowly. As the disturbed water settled down, all that remained was a white aigrette feather, tossed around by the subsiding waves.

Luke let out the breath he had been holding and croaked, "How did that happen?"

"That was Pepin," said Joe. "Diddun I tell you he diddun like the Germans? Shot his father, diddun they? So when he was fetching that pistol for his uncle, he helped himself to a box of cordite. He knew all about cordite, on account of helping his father in the mine. Safe stuff, his father always told him. So long as you don't upset it."

"Upset it," said Luke weakly.

"Two things what upset it most are heat and vibration. So what he planned to do if and when he found the boat was hide the cordite away under the engine. You thought that would do the trick, diddun you?"

This was to Pepin, who had materialized behind them in his usual silent way. He was grinning so broadly that Luke wondered what would happen if the two ends of his mouth met behind his head.

"I dun for the focking boggers," he said.

"You see," said Joe proudly, "almost bilingual."